DEPUTY BRAND GETS HER MAN

THE TEXAS BRAND: GENERATIONS
BOOK THREE

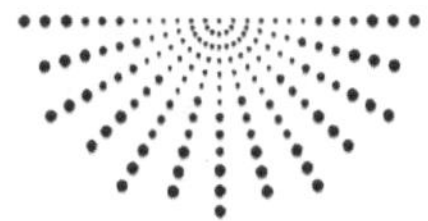

MAGGIE SHAYNE

OLIVERHEBERBOOKS

suspense and laugh-out-loud one-liners from Rachel, this book will have readers engrossed until the very end." ~**RT Book Reviews** on Deadly Obsession

"This is page-turning, non-stop suspense at its finest. Shayne brings the characters to life for her readers, who will not be disappointed with this fabulously entertaining story." ~**RT Book Reviews** on Innocent Prey

"One of the strongest, most original voices in romance fiction today." ~*New York Times* bestselling author **Anne Stuart**

"Maggie Shayne is a wonderful storyteller. Creepy, chilling, and compelling, her entries into the world of the occult are simply spellbinding!" ~**Heather Graham**, *New York Times* bestselling author

"A moving mix of high suspense and romance, this haunting Halloween thriller will propel readers to bolt their doors at night." ~**Publishers Weekly** on Gingerbread Man.

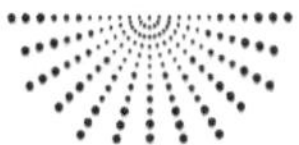

When Willow bellied up to an open spot at the curved hardwood bar early on a Thursday evening, Cat Shaw was handling the beer taps, two teenagers were waiting tables, and the guys she was looking for were nowhere in sight.

He was, though. Gringo Sombrero. His eyes had been on her since she'd walked into Two Lilies Honky Tonk. She'd felt him tracking her as she'd wound amid tables full of folks enjoying the food. He'd ditched the big sombrero he used to hide behind but not the bushy blond beard. She supposed she ought to try to think of him by his given name, since he was family, though not by blood. He was her adopted cousin Ethan's half-brother. And he still came in some afternoons to sit at his favorite table and people-watch.

He acknowledged her with a nod, and she replied with a smaller one and looked away wondering why her stomach was all churned up.

"What can I get 'cha, Deputy?" Cat asked. A purple paisley scarf tried but failed to tame her sable and gray curls. Behind her, a wall-sized mirror backed shelves full of liquor.

"Sweet tea'll do me, Cat. I'm on duty. You seen the Barker Boys around?"

"*Those* three." She rolled her eyes. "Ethan's…discouraged 'em from bringin' their business here."

"Yeah. He's out of town for the night, though," Willow said. "Had a gig in San Antone. I figured they might get brave."

"Not so far." She delivered a tall dewy glass of sweet tea on ice with a lemon wedge, and spoke softly, leaning in. "What've the Quinn County Creeps done now?"

"You know I can't tell you that." The three were jumping from one crime to another—vandalism, theft, random beatings. Always three guys, and one of them considerably larger than the other two, but that was it. She needed more.

"Fine, don't tell me," Cat said. "I'll wait for the grapevine. Should light up any time now." She turned her wrist as if checking a watch she wasn't wearing, then winked and headed for another patron.

Willow turned on her barstool, glass in hand just as Stu Barker's rusty yellow pickup truck, jacked up with extra-big tires, rolled in. It stopped in the strip of pavement right next to the "No stopping. Park in Rear" sign, on top of the painted arrow pointing the opposite way. Stu shut the rumbling vehicle off and got out. His two brothers got out, too—the wiry one from the passenger door, and the big one jumped down from the bed.

The front of Two Lilies was all glass, and there were outdoor tables on the patio beyond, but the glass partition was closed at the moment.

Willow set her iced tea down, slid off her stool, headed out through the single glass door as they approached, and pulled it closed behind her.

"Hey, boys, why don't you sit out here with me for a minute? I got some questions for you."

"Nobody's mannin' the bar out here," Stu said. He'd have

argued no matter what she'd opened with, though. His chin was jutting, jaw set. He'd come here looking for trouble.

"I'll buy," she said. She held up three fingers, not even looking behind her. "Cat'll bring 'em. That's a nice spot, right there. Corner table in the shade."

The two lesser Barkers looked to their leader, Stu. Tank was a big, mean bull, pawing the dirt and blowing, waiting for the chute to open. Tuck, his twin, was more like a scrawny terrier with patches of exposed skin—he was twitchy and nervous. There was not a complete set of brain cells between them.

Stu rolled his eyes but slogged to the table in the shade.

Before all three asses had made chair-contact, Cat was coming out with the beers and Willow's sweet tea. No tray, just hands. She was a pro.

"Anything else for you fellas?" she asked.

They grumbled non-answers. Cat scurried away with a quick, worried look at Willow. Will gave her a subtle "it's fine" nod.

"So," Willow said, after they'd each taken a pull from their foamy mugs, "three fellas dressed up like cops and robbed a man at gunpoint. Masked, but they match your descriptions."

"Wasn't us," said Stu.

"Yeah. We was with Dad last night," said Tank.

"How'd you know it was last night?" Willow asked.

Stu kicked Tank under the table, then said, "Because you're questioning us today."

"You guys order some cop uniforms off the Amazon, did you?" Willow watched them and wished she could use their faces as evidence in court.

"Maybe you've got 'em out in the truck right now?" she asked, glancing at the yellow pickup.

Stu said, "You ain't gettin' in mah truck without a search warrant, *lady deputy*."

He made it an insult. She pressed her lips and nodded. "It's illegally parked, I think," and she got to her feet and started toward the truck. "It's blockin' the driveway. I oughtta move it. Prevent an accident."

Stu jumped up too. He put himself directly in front of her and bent so close to her face she could smell his beer breath. "I don't think you want to do that."

"Oh, you're readin' me wrong, then, because I very much want to do that."

He drew back a fist to punch her. She never knew whether he'd have actually done it, though, because a different fist hit him in the face. It had come from behind her, like a piston driving directly over her left shoulder and crunching Stu's nose.

Gringo. Jeremiah. He put his hands on her shoulders, moving her gently to the right as Tank and Tuck surged his way like Dumb and Dumber. He put Tank to his knees with a shot to the front of his neck, but Tuck punched the Gringo right in his bearded chin, snapping his head back. Willow stepped in front of him and kneed Tuck Barker in the balls. He doubled over and fell to his knees.

"Assaulting an officer."

"He hit first," Stu muttered.

She put her hand on her sidearm but didn't pull it. The message was clear. The three goons got up and ambled toward their truck, yelling all the way.

"You assaulted us!" Stu accused.

"You drew back to hit me," Willow said. "I got witnesses. Don't come back here, boys. You're banned for life. And if it's you pulling all the bull around Mad Bull's Bend, you'll do time for it. I'll see to that."

Stu and Tuck got into the truck and slammed the doors. Tank climbed into the back causing the bed to sink six inches. They sped around the building, through the parking lot in back and out the other side—the one with the IN arrow, then roared down the highway belching black exhaust.

She'd kept her eyes on them the whole time.

"You should've arrested him," the Gringo said.

"If you'd've let him hit me, I *could've* arrested him," she said, finally turning to face Jeremiah. "And then I could've got a warrant and then got the goods on all three of 'em. You see how that works?" She raised her brows, because there was blood dripping from his bushy beard. "Where's that comin' from?"

He looked down, shrugged. "Chin, maybe?"

"Jeez Louise. Come on, come with me." She didn't take his arm or anything, just led the way. She grabbed some paper napkins from a dispenser on one of the tables, handed them back to him and kept going, inside, around the muttering patrons who hadn't expected a floor show with their meals.

As she passed the bar, Cat handed over the first aid kit, a large white tackle box with a red cross painted on it. One tableful of folks applauded as she passed. She didn't know if it was for her or the Gringo.

The stairs were just this side of the archway to the dance floor and stage, and she headed up them and into the private bathroom Ethan had built for Lily as a wedding present. It was dusky rose with creamy trim and even a corner shower with glass doors. There was a big counter with a basin on one end, and the mirror behind it was lined in lights. She put him in the chair, in front of the counter's lighted end.

Then she turned to look at his face and sighed. "Lord, why haven't you shaved that brush lot off?"

"Why? Would you like me better if I did?"

"Possibly, but either way, I could at least assess the damage." She started opening drawers. Lily kept the place stocked with all the usual bathroom supplies. But there were no electric trimmers she could locate. She did find scissors though, pulled them out, and came toward him. "What do you say?" she asked, opening and closing the blades like the jaws of a shark.

"I'm at your mercy, Deputy." He opened his arms to his sides, closed his eyes and waited.

Willow didn't know why she did it. She could've just handed him the scissors and wished him luck. But instead, she moved right up close to him, put her hand on his forehead, and pushed his head back. Then she held the soft beard between her fingers so it wouldn't pull too much, and she cut. And cut. And cut. The scissors were fine and sharp and they did a good job. She slid her palm over his cheek, then snipped. She cradled his jaw, then snipped. She inched her way across his upper lip, snipping with care, revealing his face more and more.

Then she stood back, staring at him. The blood was coming from a gash in his chin, but hadn't stained his neck or even his shirt, thanks to the beard. She gave him a wet cloth to hold there.

"There's a shaver in the cabinet under the sink, there," he said, dabbing the cut, and pulling the cloth away repeatedly. Every time he did, new blood welled. "Ethan and Lily threaten me with it every time they see me."

She got the electric shaver out while he dug around in the first aid kit. He plucked out a couple of butterfly bandages and a tube of antibiotic ointment.

"Band-Aids won't stick to whiskers," she said. "Besides, I think you need a couple stitches, there."

"I'll pinch it together if you'll shave around it," he said, and he took the cloth away. Blood welled and he pinched the cut together, wincing a little.

She plugged in the shaver and moved it carefully around his fingers on his chin. She knew it was hurting. "Looks deep."

"He was wearing a ring."

"Not by accident, I bet." She finished and set the shaver down. "Thanks, Gringo. That could've been my face."

"*De nada.*"

"But don't let it happen again."

He looked confused as he cleaned the wound with alcohol wipes and dabbed on ointment, leaning over the counter closer to the mirror, his head tipped up to focus on his chin. Then he applied the butterflies like it wasn't his first time and covered them with a bigger adhesive strip.

"There." He sat back.

"Yeah, not quite." She nodded at the mirror. He looked again.

He had uneven stubble everywhere except his chin.

"I see what you mean," he said, and then he reached for the razor, leaned over the sink, and resumed shaving.

When he finished, he turned to face her, running a hand down his cheek and grinning. When a dimple appeared, she could've sworn she heard the sound of a bullet ricocheting off stone inside her head.

Ohmygod that jawline, and that cleft in his poor, wounded chin.

"That feels good," he said, smoothing his cheek. "Glad you made me do that."

"Yeah, well…" She looked around for something to use to defend herself against the onslaught of whatever this was. She was a little bit light-headed, a little bit giddy, and a whole lot turned on—had been, right along, but she knew better.

She wanted to be sheriff of Quinn County one day. She couldn't be playing around with an ex-con who was the sole heir to a dead crime boss's ill-gotten wealth.

Up to now, she'd been keeping her distance from Jeremiah Thorne. But she'd felt something ever since she'd hit him with her pickup. And whatever it was, it had just taken a turn for the worse.

Looking around the small room as if for rescue, she spotted the tall skinny closet where the towels were stacked, opened it, and took the broom and dustpan from their hooks. She handed them to Jeremiah. "You'd best clean up all this hair or Lily'll have our hides for bar rags."

Then she left him there. But that face—sans beard—and its knowing expression were burned into her mind. That slight smile, and the twinkle of mischief in eyes so blue they sizzled…

She never should have made him shave.

Jeremiah watched Willow Brand walk out of the bathroom. She even looked good in her uniform pants, the least flattering pants ever invented.

If he'd known how much she would like him shaved, he'd have been bare-faced this whole time. She was something, Willow Brand. Her mother was full Comanche, her father, half. Her skin was dark, like her eyes and her hair.

It was good that she liked him. He could use that. He needed her help, and it would be best if giving it was her idea.

He cleaned up the mess of his whiskers on the floor and in the sink and left the place looking as good as he'd found it. When he headed down to pay his tab, Willow was already gone.

He frowned because there was a kid sitting on a barstool. He had dark curly hair and looked to be ten or so.

Jeremiah sidled up to the bar between the kid's stool and the one beside it, and signaled Cat. She held up a finger.

"I didn't know I had to wave," the kid said.

He had a spray of freckles across his nose. "Oh, yeah," Jeremiah said. "Otherwise she might never spot you. You must be new here."

"I never came in before. But at school everyone says the tacos are the best."

"They are, I can vouch for that."

"I made some money doing odd jobs after school. So I thought I'd surprise Grandma by bringing home tacos for all of us." He looked toward Cat, then back at Jeremiah.

"I bet that'll make your grandma very happy. You're a good kid."

"It's to thank her. She's letting me get a puppy!"

Cat finally arrived. Jeremiah said, "You go first, young—what's your name?"

"Frankie Miller." He thrust out a hand.

"Jeremiah," he said, shaking that scrawny little hand. It felt like it'd break if he squeezed it too hard. "Go ahead, Frankie. Place your order."

"I need enough tacos for me, Grandma, Grandpa, Sadie and Sally." He put his little hand into his jeans pocket and pulled out three crumpled singles and a fistful of change.

Cat sneaked a sad look Jeremiah's way. He shook his head and pointed to his chest, mouthing, "I got it." Then aloud, "Wait a minute, wait a minute. Isn't today's special first-timers eat free?"

"Right! Cat said. "You can pocket that cash, kid, you lucked out today. I'll go put that order in."

"I'm ready to cash out when you come back, Cat," Jeremiah said. Then he turned around and leaned back against the bar, watching the people come and go.

So far, coming here to the town of Quinn in Quinn County, Texas had panned out better than he could've hoped. He'd found his brother from another mother, Ethan, who'd accepted him unquestioningly. Insane. The guy was hitting it big in country music. He ought to be more careful. He hadn't even run a background check on him, far as he knew, just took everything Jeremiah said at face value.

He'd told the truth. Not all of it, but he hadn't pretended to be anything other than what he was. An ex-con raised by crooks. Ethan seemed to like him for some reason.

Beside him, the kid had turned his stool around and was leaning back against the bar, just like Jeremiah was.

His lips pulled at the corners. "So you live with your grandma? Huh?"

"Yeah. My mom died and my dad's in jail."

That poked him in the heart. He'd could've said the very same thing at Frankie's age.

"You guys live here in the Bend?" Jeremiah asked.

"Nah, back in Quinn." The kid spun the stool around again when Cat returned with two large bags of tacos and fixings and handed them over. He smiled, slid off his stool, and all but ran for the door, yelling, "Nice to meet 'cha, Jeremiah," like an afterthought just before he went out. He got into a car with an old fellow behind the wheel Jeremiah guessed must be his grandfather.

Since nothing more interesting than what had already occurred was likely to happen at Two Lilies that night, Jeremiah paid for his drinks and the kid's tacos, and drove his Jeep back to Quinn, where he was shacking up at the bunkhouse on the Texas Brand. His newfound brother's adopted family were kind, welcoming, and trusting. If he were anyone else, he could've robbed them blind. And if *they* were anyone else, he might have.

But they were his brother's family. If they had their way, they'd be his family, too. He didn't want a family, though. He'd never really had one, never really wanted one. It wasn't like he'd spent nights lying awake in his room in his father's mansion, staring at the ceiling through tears, aching for a normal life, for his mom to be alive and beautiful and happy, not broken, devastated, and lost like she'd been when she'd left him there and driven away into oblivion.

It wasn't like that at all.

Willow Brand liked him. Maybe she wanted him, too. Sure seemed that way before she'd left the bathroom. The way she'd run her hands over his face while trimming his beard. The way she'd run her eyes over it afterward. The totally turned on and slightly panicked look in them.

Hell, it had turned him on, too. Nothing wrong with that, as long as he got what he needed from her.

His old man had hidden eight pounds of solid gold somewhere in Quinn, Texas before he'd gone to prison for the rest of his days. He'd mentioned it a few times, written about it in the diary he'd kept his first year in prison. It had been sent along with the old man's other possessions to Jeremiah, the listed next of kin, when he'd died. But there'd been zero elaboration. No details.

At today's prices, eight pounds of gold would be worth way over half a million dollars. And Jeremiah was damn well going to find it.

The smoking hot Willow Brand just might have the connections to help him.

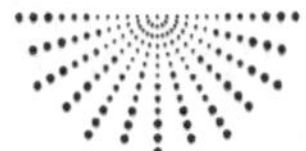

CHAPTER TWO

Willow had a flat tire and she was not in a good mood. She'd had her ass grabbed twice tonight, and she'd been called Pocohontas by a rhinestone cowboy from Jersey. Being in uniform, she couldn't even throw a drink in his face about it.

"It's because of what happened with the Barker boys the other day, that's what," she muttered, although that theory made very little sense. "I looked like a helpless female, bein' saved by a gallant white boy. Everybody saw it. It's prob'ly all over town."

She opened the hatch of her black and white Quinn County Sheriff's Department SUV and rolled the spare tire out onto the pavement. It bounced as she rolled it around to the side and then went back for the jack whose handle doubled as a lug-wrench, and quickly bent to loosen the nuts. She had to stomp on the handle to loosen the most stubborn one.

Headlights picked her out on the roadside. They weren't the first, just the first to slow down and pull over.

Since civilization was ten miles away in either direction, she unhooked the strap on her gun belt, and rose with the jack-handle. Then she saw that it was Jeremiah Thorne's russet orange

Jeep. He'd pulled over behind her, and left his four-ways on, like a law-abiding citizen would do.

She refocused on her work, not trusting herself with a word, a smile, or a welcome. By the time he came up to her, she was jacking the car up off the ground.

"Hey, Willow. Can I give you a hand with that?"

Without even looking at him, she said, "You put one hand on this jack and I'll beat you with the handle, you hear?"

He must've been surprised, since he took a step backwards. "I do something to make you mad, Deputy Brand?"

She stopped jacking, wiggled the tire off, and leaned it against the car. Then she picked up the spare and fit it over the bolts, figuring it was good that her hands were busy. "You need to understand somethin', Jeremiah Thorne. I didn't need rescuin' at Two Lilies the other evenin'. I don't need a man to defend me, or to protect me, or to change my goldang tires, and if I did, then I got a whole family of 'em to choose from. But I *don't*."

"I would've stopped to help anybody I saw along the roadside with a flat in the middle of the night," he said.

She put on all five nuts, finger-tightening them in opposing pairs. "I didn't get the chance to explain this to you before…actually, it didn't occur to me right away."

"Because I was so good looking under my beard?"

She shot him a look, not smiling at his humor. He was, though.

"Never do that again," she said. "Never interfere when I'm on the job. You understand? Dumb question. You couldn't possibly understand, being male. But you don't *need* to understand."

He was quiet for a moment, then said, "Be easier if I did, though."

She finished tightening the lug nuts, then lowered the jack, picked it up, and threw it into the back of the SUV followed by the flat tire. There was a place for them in the floor, but she didn't put them in it, just closed the hatch and headed for the driver's door.

"Maybe you could explain it to me, so I can understand it better?" the Gringo said.

Whirling to face him, she said, "All you need to understand is this, and it's real simple. If I need your help, I'll ask for it. And if I *don't* ask for it—"

"I keep my help to myself. I got you. And uh, I apologize."

His eyes were innocent and wounded. They got to her and she felt like an ass. She'd opened her door, but she didn't get in. Instead, she attempted to explain herself.

"I just responded to a call. A local said kids were harassing her milk cow. When I got there, she wouldn't even talk to me. Said to send back a real cop."

"Real, meaning…?"

"Maybe male," she said. "Maybe white. Maybe both, I don't know."

He nodded slowly. "Me stepping in makes you the weak female." He lowered his head until his chin touched his chest. "I should've realized. People around here can still be a little…"

"Yeah." She closed the pickup door without getting in. "Sorry I yelled. You were only tryin' to help. You're a nice guy and I bit your head off for it."

"Not really. I lied when I said I would've stopped for anyone. I only stopped 'cause it was you."

"'Cause we're family, sort've?" she asked and then cursed herself for asking.

"Nope. Nothing to do with that." His eyes had hold of hers, and she didn't look away. He smiled a little, and those dimples appeared again. "Would you have dinner with me?"

Willow lost her air, so she couldn't answer. Her brain said no a hundred times over. She opened her mouth to say it out aloud, but the word that escaped, was, "Yes."

He smiled and she swore those Hemsworth-blue eyes twinkled. "How about tonight?"

She frowned at him. "You crazy? It's midnight."

"So you're saying you already ate?"

She lowered her eyes. This was a *really bad* idea. And then she made it worse. "I've got half a lasagna in the fridge. Aunt Chelsea has a thing about feedin' people."

"Tell me about it. I have most of her plasticware in the bunkhouse fridge. There's enough for a feast."

Willow took a deep breath. It would be a chance to get to know him a little better, one-on-one, and to figure out whether he took after his criminal father or noble brother. How better than over a meal? Alone. In the middle of the night.

This was a really bad idea.

"So, what'll it be? Your place or mine?" he asked, with a wink that said he was kidding, and a glint in his eyes that said not really.

"Mine," Willow said. "And for food and conversation only, you understand?"

"Scout's honor," he said, but he did the salute so wrong she knew he'd never been a scout.

"You can't bring your car. Folks'll talk."

"Whatever you say, Deputy."

Jeremiah couldn't believe his luck. He'd fantasized about things like this. He did not dare believe that fate was finally throwing him a bone, but it sure seemed like things were going his way.

Willow had him follow her to a spot where folks pulled off to go fishing. He parked there, then rode the rest of the way to Sky Dancer Ranch with her. It was within walking distance, he noted.

When he first got into her SUV, she was stiff and nervous. He figured it was natural. She was a woman behind that badge, and she was alone at night with an ex-con. He tried to think of a way to ease her mind and couldn't come up with any. Then they were on her family's place and he didn't have to think. Words came naturally.

"This ranch is incredible." Even in the dark, the rolling meadows and white fences stood against the horizon. He'd seen it by day only once or twice, and only in passing. He'd never come all the way down the driveway into its heart. The house was modest but modern, with plenty of big windows and porches.

She took the driveway's left fork, though, away from the main house, out past a copse of scraggly loblolly pines, to a small white cottage with a picket fence all the way around it. There were flower boxes full of gold and orange, and a tangled flowerbed in front that looked like it needed weeding. A row of sunflowers, their yellow heads drooping, stood guard along the white fence in front, and stepping stones led to the front door.

"Here we are," she said.

"It's like something out of the Shire."

"You're *a Lord of the Rings* fan?"

He shrugged one shoulder, averted his eyes. "I've seen it." *Multiple times.*

"Huh."

He didn't like the sound of that, so he nodded at the pretty cottage's weed patch border, the only unkempt spot in sight. "What's up with that? You need a hand clearing it out?"

"No! That's my herb garden. I'm lettin' some of 'em go to seed. They need to thicken up."

"Herb garden."

She nodded and led the way across her grassless lawn to the raised bed in front of the house. "There's rosemary, nearest the door for the scent." She ran her hand across the small shrub's needled branches, then held her palm up. "Smell."

He leaned close and sniffed and the scent lit up pleasure centers in his brain. Being that close to her lit up more, though.

"And there's white sage, beside it. Desert thyme, basil, oregano, parsley… The chili pepper patch is around back."

"You must do a lot of cooking."

"Some."

They moved across a small porch with bundles of herbs hanging upside down, then through her front door.

"No grand tour needed," she said, flipping on lights as she walked inside. "Living room and eat-in kitchen here. Bedroom and bathroom over there. And if you don't mind, I need to change."

"Take your time," he said. "You want me to heat up the lasagna?"

She looked back at him just a beat too long, like she was deciding whether she wanted him rummaging around in her kitchen. "That'd be great, thanks. It's in the—"

"I'll figure it out."

She vanished into a room in back. He took off his shoes and headed into her kitchen, flipped on the lights. It was golden yellow with white cabinets and woodwork, and there were plants in every window, some hanging, others resting on the sills. The fridge was a simple white model, no extras. The lasagna was easy to recognize. "Aunt" Chelsea's plasticware was familiar to him.

He had to get a place of his own before that woman fed him into obesity.

He removed the square dish, loosened its lid, and stuck it into the microwave to reheat. The place was so small, he could hear the shower running.

Okay, maybe she wasn't uncomfortable being alone with an ex-con after all. And why should she be? She was a cop and she had a gun.

Cops are always the enemy.

The words floated through his brain in the voice of his father.

It had been a phrase he'd repeated often—like he was making sure he'd never forget it.

Jeremiah opened cabinets until he found plates, drawers until he found forks, and he set the table. When the microwave beeped, he scooped the sizzling, bubbling food onto the plates.

Willow emerged. She wore a sweatshirt over baggy, drawstring pants, and was rubbing her long, dark hair with a towel.

"That had to be the world's fastest shower."

"I just needed to wash the day off," she said. "But I didn't want to keep you waitin'."

"Perfect timing." He pulled out one of the little padded chairs for her with an exaggerated sweep of his arm and she sat down. Then he went around the table and sat down. They dug in, and he shook his head after the first bite. "Your aunt can cook like nobody's business."

"She's had to change it up, though, since Uncle Garrett's heart attack. It's been a struggle for her."

"I thought his heart attack was from the smoke inhalation," he said. He'd been there, he and Ethan. They'd carried Garrett and Lily out of the flames.

"It was, but it turns out he has quite a bit of plaque in his arteries, and that really only comes from what you eat, so she's recreatin' every recipe healthier. Which is hard with lasagna."

"This is delicious, though. You telling me this is healthy?"

"Healthi-*er*. Meat-free, whole grain pasta, and cashew cheese."

"Ah."

They ate in silence. He liked the quiet. He'd never enjoyed folks who felt the need to fill every silence with idle chatter. The quiet gave his eyes time to really look at her. There was something enticing about the hollow beneath her ear, and for a while he got stuck there, and then his gaze slid lower to her neck where it curved into shoulder. His heart beat faster.

She caught him looking, and blushed a little. "So what's goin' on with you?" she asked. "That inheritance from your father still held up in probate?"

"Anything the state can link to one of his crimes is forfeit," he said. "I was lucky to get the Jeep. But I made a lot when I worked for my father and spent very little."

"Especially not while you were in prison."

He lowered his head. "I was paid really well for that, too." Why had he said that? It wasn't her business where his money came from.

"Paid? For doing time?"

He nodded and chanced a look her way again. "The guy who did the assault was indispensable to my old man's organization. Running things from prison meant he needed guys he could rely on, on the outside. So…I got paid to take the fall."

Her brown eyes were bigger and browner than ever. "A year of your life…"

"I was promised it wouldn't exceed a month." He shrugged. "After a year, I realized I was on my own. Dad wasn't even tryin' to get me out. So I offered up everything I knew on the old prick, and they turned me loose."

"And he died in prison and left everything to Ethan," she said. "I'm really sorry your father was such a jerk to you."

He shrugged. "Ethan didn't want it, so it's coming to me anyway. And I'm all right either way. Eager to buy a place of my own, get out of that bunkhouse."

"Yeah? Where you plannin' to buy? Here in Quinn County?"

"I don't know yet."

She frowned at him, so he went on.

"This was the last place my old man spent time before he went to prison," he said. "I was just a kid, not even in kindergarten yet when he was locked up. I was hoping being out here, I could… understand him better." He ran a hand across his chin, where there was stubble.

"I get that," she said. "I don't really know much about that time, bein' that I wasn't born yet. But I could ask Uncle Garrett about it, if you want."

"I should man up and ask him myself," he said. "It's just awkward, bein' that he's the one who arrested him."

She nodded. "I get it. And I really don't mind. Just know my uncle ain't one to blame the son for the sins of the father. Hell, he adopted your brother."

Willow pushed away from the table and took her empty plate to the sink. "Should I look around for some dessert?"

"I'd settle for a nightcap," he said.

He took his plate over there, too. She was rinsing hers under the faucet, stacking it in the drainer. Then she walked away and he heard her pouring while he rinsed his.

She handed him a glass with three fingers of whiskey in it, crossing back into the living room, but not sitting back down. She was standing near the front door, his signal that it was time to drink up and leave.

He walked over there and stood facing her, then slugged the whiskey back, swallowing it in a single gulp. She did likewise. He set his empty glass on the stand beside the door, where she'd dropped her keys. Then he took her glass from her and set it there, too. And then, moving real slow, he put his hands on her upper arms, tipped his head down, and kissed her. She didn't turn away; he'd given her plenty of time. She watched his mouth as he lowered it to hers, then her brown eyes fell closed just before touchdown.

He kissed like a man who loved kissing, drinking her in. She didn't know why she kissed him back, or when her arms had twisted around his neck, or how their bodies had mashed up against each other like they were trying to meld. He was running his hands around her back and shoulders, and her butt like he was committing her to memory. And she was riding his thigh like it was her horse. The signals her body was sending drowned out the desperate shouts from her brain.

He's an ex-con.

The way he moves his lips over mine, with just enough suction.

He nipped a little, and her lady parts tingled. She threaded her fingers up into his hair and nipped back, and he turned her, and they bumped against the wall.

Knock-knock-knock. "Willow?"

The sound of her mother's voice and the knowledge that she'd open the door in the next heartbeat was the douse of ice water Willow needed. She pulled away only slightly and Jeremiah's arms fell to his sides.

They each took a step apart from each other, but their eyes clung. Willow was breathing like an Olympic gymnast after a dismount.

The front door opened.

Willow's mom looked at her, and the slightest frown bent her eyebrows, and then she saw Jeremiah, and they rose up high.

"I had a flat on the way home," Willow said. "Jeremiah stopped to help me change the tire, and I offered to share Aunt Chelsea's lasagna with him to thank him." She was talking way too fast, she realized too late.

Her mother listened with care and didn't interject, just tilted her head a little further at the less-than-honest parts. Like she knew.

"Well, actually, he offered to help, and I yelled at him for it. The lasagna's more a peace offering."

"Huh," her mom said, then she glanced Jeremiah's way.

He smiled at her, and Willow saw the moment those dimples made impact. Her mother actually blinked.

Then she looked down at the bundle in her arms and shrugging, returned her attention to her daughter. "I saw your lights on and I was too excited to wait. I got this today—for the cradle."

Willow took the bundle unfolded it. It was a hand-quilted cradle liner with blue lions, pink bears, green elephants, and yellow donkeys.

"It's for Lily and Ethan," Taylor said, "for the baby. Garrett's going to re-finish your cradle. But don't worry. He won't change it too much, and your name will remain carved into the headboard."

Taylor's eyes shifted to Jeremiah's as she explained. "The cradles are heirlooms, made for us by a Comanche shaman who fills them with blessings."

"*Cradle*, she means." Willow put emphasis on the singular. "We only have the one."

"Right. Gosh, I need to remember to get it out of the attic for Garrett before we leave. He's eager to work on it."

"You're going away?" Jeremiah asked.

"Our biggest trip of the year. Three horse shows in the same weekend, and we'll hit 'em all," she said. "We leave next week." Then she lowered her head. "I should've waited until morning to show you this, though. Really didn't mean to interrupt. Good-night, sweetheart." Then to Jeremiah, "Goodnight."

Then she ducked right out the door, pulling it closed behind her. Willow watched her walk back along the flagstone path, into the driveway, and all the way beyond the reach of her porch light, out of sight.

Willow turned to face Jeremiah, met his eyes, and swore she could hear sizzling. "You need to be out the door in the next two minutes, or she'll think we're in here having sex."

"What if we were?" he asked, and he held her eyes with his, not letting go.

"We're not." She reached past him without touching, despite the butterflies in her stomach and elsewhere, and opened the door.

"But what about all that kissing—"

"Yeah, um, I'm not lookin' for…I mean, I'm not fixin' to get mixed up with a man right now."

"No?"

"No," she said. "I want to be sheriff one day, and that's gonna take a lot of work, a lot of focus."

"I get it." He lowered his head. "Okay then, I apologize if I—"

"Don't apologize. I was as into it as you were." Their eyes locked tighter. *Sssssss.* "But still…it was a momentary lapse. It's just not the right time for me."

"Right. I just…I really hate to leave."

She really hated to let him, but she opened the door wider and stood there. He moved right up close, stood in front of her, and pushed it halfway closed again. Then he leaned in slow and she met him halfway. They kissed in slow motion, and a quicksand pit opened up in her middle.

After a long, long moment, he pulled away, opened the door wider again, and stepped through. "Night, Willow."

"Night, Gringo."

She closed the door, then moved to the window to watch as he walked back along the curving driveway to where it rejoined the main one, veering right, toward the road. She watched until his shape was swallowed up by the darkness. Then she locked up, turned off the lights, and went to the kitchen to wash Aunt Chelsea's lasagna dish.

Willow was in the Quinn County Sheriff's office at seven a.m. She'd dropped the flat tire off at the motor pool with a note to repair or replace. Until then, she was driving around on the spare. Her shift didn't start until three, but she was on a mission, one in which she was completely immersed when Uncle Garrett came in bearing two things he was forbidden, donuts and coffee.

"Don't give me that look, Will," he said. "Mine's decaf. And I'm only havin' one donut. The suddenly crucial question is, which one?"

She didn't bother to hide what was on her computer screen. She was running a background check on Jeremiah. He'd already seen it, and she wasn't one to sneak around anyway.

"Jeremiah do something to make you think he's worthy of investigation?"

"Yep."

"You fixin' to tell me what it was?"

"Nope."

"Is this background check legal?"

"It's…a gray area," she said as if with great authority.

He reached past her and tapped the x to close out the program, but Willow had seen enough. Jeremiah Thorne had been a criminal every day up until the day he'd arrived in Quinn County.

"You find what you needed?" Garrett asked.

"I found some things. Don't exactly know what I need. When his father came to Quinn way back then, Jeremiah was a toddler, livin' with his mother. A year later, he was livin' in his father's mansion, even though the old man was in prison. Somehow he got custody."

Garrett lowered his head, shaking it slow. "I didn't know any of that. Who raised him, then? I didn't think de Lorean had a wife or—"

"I don't know. The records don't say."

"Sounds like he had it rough in the lap of luxury. No wonder he ended up in prison."

"He told me his father paid him to take the fall for his right-hand man. Said he couldn't run his organization from behind bars if his best guy got locked up, too." She was watching Uncle Garrett's face as she spoke. "That sound plausible to you?"

"Keep talkin'. I'll let you know."

She nodded, then pushed off with her feet to roll her chair toward the donuts. "He says he got very well paid to plead guilty. His old man promised he'd get off with little or no time, got him a good lawyer, too, but he got sentenced to five years. His father stopped payin' the lawyer and the boss he was doin' time for stopped takin' his calls."

Nodding slowly, Uncle Garrett said, "That would explain why he turned on his father."

She nodded. "He gave evidence on the organization that the DA didn't already have, and they let him out. Then his old man died in prison and left Jeremiah completely out of his will as one final smackdown."

"He left everything to Ethan," Uncle Garrett said. "But Ethan didn't want it." He shook his head slow. "That man messed his boys up about as much as a man could. Too bad Jeremiah's mamma didn't know about our doorstep."

Yeah, Willow thought, but then he'd be her cousin as much as Ethan was, and that would make things *weird.*

"And we know the rest," she said.

"Yep. He came here, found his brother, and carried my back-side out of a burnin' buildin'," Garrett said.

She sighed, lowering her head. "He's not like our Bubba, though, raised here, by good people. Jeremiah was raised in a snake pit by God only knows who."

Her uncle was watching her closely. "I'll ask you again, has he done somethin' to make you suspicious of him, Will?"

She pressed her lips to remove the memory of Jeremiah's kisses. "Naw, not a damn thing. He's lookin' for...I don't know, closure I think. Wants to know about his father's time in Quinn."

Garrett's face turned a little darker. "I can tell him all about that." Then he frowned. "But he might not be ready to hear me share recollections about the time I put his old man away for the rest of his life."

Willow helped herself to a donut, eliminating one of Uncle Garrett's options. He quickly took a glazed with no filling, and bit into it like he'd found nirvana.

When he'd finished chewing and taken a swig of decaf, Uncle Garrett said, "Actually, I put everything on paper at the time. Everything about the investigation, including all the things I learned afterward. The computers were new to the department and I hated 'em."

"You're joshin' me."

"They're in my personal files, in the office. I didn't want 'em where anyone could get at 'em. Ethan's past is his own business, you know?"

"Is that legal?" she asked, flipping his earlier question back on him.

He caught it and grinned at her. "It's…a gray area. I'll get you the files."

CHAPTER THREE

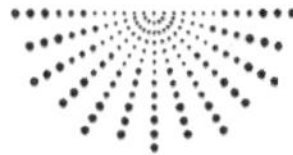

That weekend, Willow and her mom walked down to the stream that bordered the meadow where the mares grazed on Saturday mornings. This morning was no different. Well, slightly different. As always, Taylor brought a thermal coffee container and a pair of mugs. Ceramic, because coffee didn't taste the same in anything else. As always, Willow brought the snacks—a pair of cinnamon buns she'd picked up in town for just this occasion. And as always, the air was warm with a dry breeze, and the stream was cool and babbling, and the mares grazed, barely noticing them, peace emanating from their very pores.

But one thing was different. Her mom knew about the lava bubbling just beneath the surface between her and the Gringo. And Willow wasn't ready to discuss it. She didn't even know what to make of it.

Her mom had chosen a spot, sat down on a boulder, and was pouring coffee from the Thermos. She filled the first mug and handed it to Willow, who took it and remained standing, despite a nearby fallen log.

"Do you miss teaching, Mom?" she asked after taking a sip,

just to start the conversation off on a safe topic. Her mom's recent retirement from the university seemed like a good one.

"Not a bit," Taylor returned. "Guest-lecturing a couple times a month is plenty for me. But I do miss the digs." She pushed off her fawn-colored Stetson and let it hang down her back.

Willow noticed more silver in her long, dark hair than had been there in the spring. "I bet you do."

"There are still opportunities, though. I might go on one next May. Rumor has it this Native site might be a thousand years old."

"That's exciting!"

"It is," she said, and the sparkle in her eyes proved it. And then she sipped from her mug, and went quiet.

Willow did the same. A lot of the time they spent down here, they spent in silence, just being together and being with the land. The sounds of birdsong were nature's symphony, and they were backed up by the water laughing and tumbling over stones and splashing back on itself. The air tasted like peppery sagebrush and sunshine.

Relaxing a little, Willow sat down on the log and sipped her coffee.

"So," Taylor said at length. "Jeremiah Thorne, huh?"

Willow choked and coffee came out her nose. She coughed, swallowed then asked, "What about him?" She hadn't looked at her mother.

"That's what I'm asking you," her mom said.

Willow set her mug of Joe on a flat fungus the size of a plate, growing off the side of a tree nearby. "What is this here, a shelf fungus?"

"A change-of-subject fungus, no doubt," her mom replied. "Do you like him?"

She shrugged. "What's not to like?"

"Must be something, or you wouldn't be so unsettled about it."

"I don't love that he's an ex-con who did a year for assault." She shrugged. "But he says he didn't do it."

"Do you believe him?"

Willow took a deep breath. "Yeah, I do. That's the problem. Why would I believe him when he's saying the same thing every man convicted of anything in the history of the law says?" She shrugged. "I'm not sure I'm objective."

"That *must* mean you like him."

"Oh, I like him all right." Willow's head was down, but she lifted her gaze to see her mom's mischievous grin. "Did you know there were dimples hidin' under all those whiskers?"

"I did not," her mother said, and she laughed softly.

But it died when hoofbeats approached, and three familiar forms came nearer, broad shouldered and topped in cowboy hats. Willow's father and his big brother in every sense of the word, Uncle Garrett, rode side by side, but it was the guy bringing up the rear who held her attention. Jeremiah, riding like he was used to it. He was wearing the sombrero, and for some reason she thought it was hot. Why would she think that?

Uncle Garrett's star was pinned to his chest, so he was on duty, and Willow's dad didn't look too happy. Neither did Jeremiah.

Taylor rose up, coffee mug in her hands, and called out, "What's wrong?" Because it was obvious something was.

Uncle Garrett looked at Willow's father. "You tell her, Wes."

Her dad shook his head, "Uh-uh, this is your deal, not mine." That with an apologetic look at Jeremiah.

"What's your deal, Uncle Garrett?" Willow noted the looks exchanged between her mom and dad. Those two could communicate without a word. Sometimes it seemed as if they had telepathy or something. Creepy.

She looked at Jeremiah, wishing he'd say something. He held her eyes, gave her a very slight flash of dimple that told her everything was okay.

"Well, I don't mean to offend you in any way, now, Willow," Uncle Garrett began.

"Sounds like you're about to, though." She got up, too, lifted her chin, looked her uncle in the eye, and waited to be offended.

"Jeremiah, here, says he was with you last night, around midnight. Is that true?"

Taylor stepped in front of her daughter. "Garrett Ethan Brand, how dare you ask your niece—my daughter—something like that?"

"I *told* you," Wes muttered, picking up his hat to run his other hand over his hair, then lowering it again.

Willow moved up beside her mom and squared up to her uncle, much as she could with him being atop a horse. "Yep, you were right. You offended me."

Her mother's hand curled over her shoulder. "We were *both* with Jeremiah around that time," Taylor said. "I was eager to show Willow the cradle liner I had made for Ethan and Lily's shower. I saw her lights on, so I knew she was up and I walked out to the cottage." She looked at Willow, her brown eyes urging her to go ahead and tell the rest.

Willow sighed, looked at Jeremiah again, realized he'd probably been told to keep quiet until she'd provided him an alibi, for *what*, she couldn't imagine.

He looked right back at her. The amount of pissed off she was at her uncle was uncomfortable and unfamiliar. Uncle Garrett looked crestfallen. He was not being a jerk on purpose, and he was not enjoying it.

And yet she was mad. "Fine, you want details? I got details. I had a flat on the way home from work. Jeremiah saw me changin' the tire and stopped to help. I invited him home for leftover lasagna as a thank you."

"I saw him when he left, too," Taylor put in.

Willow narrowed her eyes. "I *knew* you were secretly watchin'."

Taylor shrugged. "If you knew, then it wasn't a secret." Then she returned her attention to her brother-in-law, the sheriff. "Jeremiah left about fifteen minutes after I did. Walked past the fork in the driveway. I was still on the front porch."

"Walked?" Garrett asked, shifting his gaze to Willow. "Why was he walkin'?"

Willow glanced at Jeremiah again, but he gave a subtle shake of his head and she knew for sure he'd been told to keep quiet. She didn't like that notion one bit. Was her uncle trying to catch her in a lie? Trying to catch Jeremiah in one, more likely, but still...

"I didn't want my *very curious mamma* makin' somethin' out of his visit, so I asked him to park at the pull-off and ride the rest of the way with me. He obliged, like any gentleman would. We went to the cottage and ate leftover lasagna from Aunt Chelsea. Mom came out not long after we got there, and Gringo left a few minutes after she did. End of story."

"All good, all good," Uncle Garrett said in the tone he'd use on a spooked horse. "I just need the timing of all that, as close as you can—"

"From the time he came upon me with the flat, he was with me about an hour and twenty minutes," Willow said. "It was around midnight when he pulled over behind me on the road, and about one-twenty when he left my place. Tack on ten minutes for the walk back to his car. Now, will you *please* tell me what this is all about?"

Garrett nodded. "Somebody threw a brick through the window at the pharmacy last night. It hit that old wall clock that's been hangin' there since I was knee-high to a grasshopper. Right in the face. A cryin' shame is what it is. But at least we know exactly what time it happened, 'cause that clock stopped dead. Seventeen minutes after midnight." He gave a slow shake of his head, then nodded at Jeremiah. "You're off the hook, son, as I knew you would be."

"Why was he on the hook to begin with, Uncle Garrett?" Willow asked. The edge in her tone surprised her. From the quick quirk of his eyebrows, she thought it surprised Jeremiah, too.

He spoke while Uncle Garrett was still wiping the wounded look off his face. "An anonymous caller said they saw me do it," Jeremiah told her.

Willow tilted her head to one side, then turned to her uncle again. "What was taken from the drug store? Cash, or opioids?"

"Neither," Garrett said. "Looks like pure vandalism."

She met Jeremiah's eyes and saw a reflection of her own doubts about that.

"Well," Taylor said, "would you gentlemen care for a mid-mornin' snack? We have fresh apple pie and more coffee at the house."

"I have to get back to work," Garrett said. "Willow, Jeremiah, I apologize for all this. Willow, I really had to ask—"

"You were just doing your job, Sheriff," Jeremiah said. But he'd been calling him Garrett up until then.

Uncle Garrett felt that formality as it was intended, then wheeled his horse and rode back alone.

"I'd best go with him," Willow's dad said. "Somethin's...off."

"Somethings been off ever since the fire," Taylor said. "Go on, take care of your brother."

Wes and his horse galloped off after Garrett.

"I'm fixin' to walk the stream a bit further before I head back," Taylor said to Willow. "You should ride back with Jeremiah."

"Mom, I don't—"

"Don't back talk your mamma." Taylor handed the thermos and empty mugs to Willow. "Take those, will you? I'll pick 'em up later." And then she was waving, turning, and walking away along the bank of the creek where it cut the meadow in two. She vanished into some trees, leaving Willow all alone with Jeremiah

Thorne, the Gringo, her adopted cousin's half-brother. Lord, the Brand family tree was more like a briar-patch tangle.

He took his foot out of the stirrup, and reached down for her. She grabbed his forearm and the reins, put her foot in the stirrup, and swung her leg forward and over the mare's neck, so she mounted in front of him.

"Did they even introduce you?" she asked, patting the horse's neck. "This is Starlight. She's a three-year-old rescue. You could count her ribs when they brought her to us."

"I didn't know you took on rescues here," he said.

"More and more," she replied. "I don't think it's responsible or ethical to breed animals into existence when there are so many alive being abused. I've been arguin' since I was ten that if you do one, you're obligated to do something about the other. Well, my folks never could win an argument with me, so that year they took in a rescue just to shut me up. It went so well, they took in a few more the followin' year, and a few more the year after that. Now a quarter of the herd are rescues. We heal 'em, rehab 'em, train 'em, and then re-home 'em someplace where they'll be cared for proper."

She squeezed with her heels and clicked her tongue, and Starlight started off at a bone-jarring trot.

Jeremiah was behind her in the saddle, right up tight. And the bouncing motion of the horse…

She eased the mare into an easy walk, but that was almost worse, that slow, rhythmic rocking. Her breath stuttered out of her and she relaxed back against Jeremiah's chest without even meaning to.

"I'm sorry about all that," he said. His voice was deep, and she felt it resonating inside his chest, because her back was resting there. "I'd have never used you as an alibi like that, but I figured your mom already knew, so—"

"I'd have told them if you hadn't, whether my mother had

seen us or not," she said. "It stinks, you having to account for yourself like that just because you're an ex-con."

"You don't believe Garrett about the anonymous tip?" he asked, and he sounded surprised.

She twisted in the saddle to look back at him. "Oh, I totally believe him. He wouldn't lie about somethin' like that. Besides, he likes you."

"Then it wasn't because I'm an ex-con," he said.

She shrugged. "The anonymous tip might've been. Somebody in town might be jumpin' to conclusions, judgin' you, maybe even to the point it fools their own eyes."

"Or they just don't like me and are setting me up."

She looked back again, frowning this time. "Nobody in Quinn would do that. You're Ethan's brother."

He shrugged. "Maybe to some, that loose link to the exalted Brand clan doesn't outweigh prison time."

"I don't think most folks in town know you did a year at Huntsville, Jeremiah."

He was quiet for a beat too long. Then he said, "You checked up on me."

She realized she'd given it away. He'd never told her which prison. "Yeah, I did. I admit it."

He sighed. She felt the wind exit his chest. Then he said, "You could've just asked me whatever you wanted to know."

"And you would've told me the truth?"

"Maybe. Maybe not, but that would be up to me, wouldn't it?"

She didn't like that answer. It wasn't the one she wanted. "I'm sorry I went behind your back. But I'm going to make it up to you."

He bent his head a little, so he spoke close to her ear. "I'd really like that—"

"That's not what I meant."

Then he nibbled her ear.

The jolt of sensation arrowed from where his teeth nipped,

straight to her core. She kicked the mare's sides and launched her into a full-on gallop toward home. It had been reflexive, like he'd hit her in the knee with a hammer.

He held on tight, and *that* felt great. When they arrived at the stables, she slid off the mare's back before he could. He dismounted right after.

Able, their stable foreman took the reins from her. "I'll rub her down, Miz Willow. You've got comp'ny." And then he nodded toward Jeremiah, touching his hat brim. "Mr. Thorne."

The Gringo nodded back.

"Thanks, Able. Mom's thermos and coffee mugs are in the saddle bag. Will you set 'em aside someplace safe for her? Come with me, Jeremiah."

His eyebrows shot up as she led the way from the stable back up the long twisting, forked driveway toward her little cottage on the ranch.

Every part of Jeremiah from his follicles to his toenails lit up when she said she had something for him and led him back to her cabin. Her long, energetic strides told him she was in a hurry. He hadn't expected her to be so obvious about it in front of the hired man, though. He was still a pace behind her, and he didn't rush to catch up, first because he enjoyed watching the swing of her hips in those jeans, but only for a second. It was the wind whipping her hair to one side that was more interesting. She almost always had it up for work. He didn't think he'd fully appreciated how long it was until just then.

She glanced back at him. "Are you lookin' at my butt?"

"I was. Then I got tangled up in your hair."

"Well, don't get too tangled. I told you, this ain't about that." They followed the flagstones to the front steps.

"It ain't about your hair?"

"Or my butt," she said, swinging open her door and walking inside. "C'mon in."

He followed her in, pulled the door closed behind him. It looked the same as it had before. Neat and tidy, small and compact. Her sofa was a loveseat, with a matching chair and a rocker.

"Have a seat," she said, with a nod at the overstuffed chair. She kept walking, though, straight through to her bedroom. He knew it was her bedroom because she left the door open when she went through. He could see part of her unmade bed, and something lacy hanging from the nightstand. She took a cardboard box off that same stand, causing the lacy thing to fall to the floor. It was a bra. His throat went dry.

She came out, pulling the bedroom door closed behind her, brought the file box to the mini-couch where he was already sitting, having ignored her suggestion of the chair, and dropped it on the table.

"What's this?" He knew exactly what it was. He just hadn't expected to get it this fast or this easily.

"This is everything Uncle Garrett has about the last time your father was in Quinn."

"Wow, I can't believe..." He opened the topmost folder and glanced through a few of its pages. "How did you get it?"

She didn't answer right away so he glanced up. She was frowning at him.

"I asked him, how do you think?"

"And he just...gave it to you?"

She nodded. He was already letting the boxful of information pull him in. There'd been some cattle rustling, apparently. Tearing himself away, closing the folder for good measure, he focused on his benefactor. She was watching him, her eyes sharp, like she was watching for something, or trying to see inside him.

"I appreciate this, Willow. And don't worry, I won't let on that you showed it to me."

She tipped her head to one side. "He knows it was for you," she said.

"You told him?"

"Why wouldn't I?" Her eyebrows came together just a little bit, forming a crease at the top of her nose.

It was the first time she'd looked at him as if not completely impressed. Had he blown it? "People aren't as...open where I come from," he said.

"Prison, you mean."

Ouch. Was she reminding him or herself? "Even before. I was raised by...employees. There was a live-in nanny, teachers, and household staff. Every one of them worked for my old man before and after me. You know?"

"They were criminals?" Her voice had gone soft.

He nodded, but he was itching to get into those files. And yet, he couldn't afford to be rude to Willow. And he didn't want to be. He told himself it was because he might need her help again before this was over, so it was best to keep this fire kindled. But deep down, he knew that wasn't the reason.

He pushed the file box aside. "I don't like talkin' about those times."

"I don't suppose I blame you." She frowned at him. "But I have to shower up and get into the office. I have paperwork before my shift tonight."

And all of the sudden, he wasn't in such a hurry to get away from her. The file box would keep. "You haven't had lunch," he said. "Tell you what. I'll head into town and order sandwiches to go at the WTD. We'll have time to eat together if I go right now."

She tipped her head sideways, glanced at the file box again, then nodded. "Sure. Thanks. Lunch at the West Texas Diner would be great, actually, I'll have a—"

"I know what you like," he said. "And how you like it."

She raised her eyebrows at him and he winked. But he left it at that and rose to his feet. "I'll get us a picnic table by the creek, okay?"

"Okay," she said.

Then she walked into her bedroom again.

Man, this was going better than he had ever expected. He grabbed the box and hurried out the door. His Jeep was at the head of the driveway, off to one side, since he'd followed Garrett there to prove his alibi.

It bothered him that someone had named him as the vandal who'd busted out the drug store window. He assumed it must've been someone who resembled him. Still, calling it in anonymously seemed odd. It had really bothered the clan patriarch to question him, though, he could tell.

That Garrett Brand was strange. Sometimes it seemed as if his decent, upright citizen persona was real. But he couldn't've been a lawman for twenty-some odd years if it was, could he?

He'd been raised to believe lawmen were as corrupt as anyone, that people were the same on either side of the badge. It was just that the ones behind it got away with shit the ones in front of it didn't.

He could not wait to delve into the files. He wanted every detail he could get about his father's time in Quinn, everywhere he'd gone, everywhere he'd stayed, everyone he'd met. Somewhere in the files was a clue to a half million bucks, tax-free. Whatever was going on with his old man's will wouldn't matter if he found the gold.

He sped to the diner, a small square building with a flat roof higher in the front than in the back. There were seven picnic tables outside, four of them a few yards away, near where Burr Creek thundered through one of its narrow, rapid passages.

He parked the Jeep, and slid his police band radio out of its slot in the dash to stick it in the glove compartment. He kept the thing out of habit. Knowing what the cops were up to at all times could save a criminal's freedom or even his life. The radio was a tough habit to break, but he didn't think the deputy or her family would understand that, so he tucked it out of sight whenever they were around.

He locked the glove compartment, then walked up to the window with a file box tucked under this arm. He ordered Willow's grilled tomato sandwich with pickle on the side, extra potato chips, and a Diet Coke. For himself, he ordered a burger and fries, then asked the teenage boy manning the window if he'd have someone bring the food down to his picnic table when it was ready, and whether he could borrow a pen.

Then he headed around behind the building and across its grassy lawn to one of the tables near the stream, sat down, and began flipping through the topmost folder. He was going to read every word of it and study every smudge on every page, but first he'd skim through it to see what jumped out at him.

He used the pen to underline anything that looked promising. Red ink. He hadn't realized when the kid had handed him the pen. Oh, well.

He heard someone coming and looked up, but it wasn't Willow. A noisy family, two little girls who must've been twins, three or four years old, and a slightly older boy carrying a long, leggy pup who couldn't stop licking his face. Hey, wait, that was the kid he'd met at Two Lilies getting tacos to surprise his grandma. Frankie. That must be the pup the kid had been so excited about.

He waved, and Frankie recognized him, grinned, and waved back.

The smaller kids converged on a table way too close to his, with a couple who must be their grandparents. The man used a walker, the woman a cane, and neither moved very fast.

He glanced out at the parking lot, but there was no sign of Willow yet. The teenager came down with their meals in baskets, set them on the table, and headed back. Jeremiah returned his attention to the folder.

De Lorean spent time at the Bluebonnet Inn, 27 Brackle Rd. I spoke to the owner, Sara Lopez. She claimed she barely spoke to de Lorean during his time there. He mainly just slept there and didn't interact with her or her teenage daughter, Juanita. She seemed upset when I told her he was a criminal on his way to prison for murdering the mother of his baby son, among other things.

Jeremiah underlined that section and kept reading, but the kids were so noisy it was tough to concentrate. And then one of the twins, yelled, "Doggy SWIM!" and Jeremiah looked up just in time to see one of the little girls hurl the gangly pup into the fast-running creek.

He swore in a way that was not appropriate around kids, lunged off his bench, and ran to the water's edge. The pup was caught in the current, dunking and emerging while speeding downstream.

CHAPTER FOUR

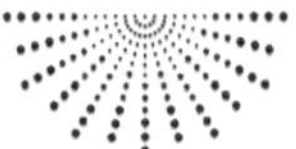

illow was just getting out of her SUV, when she saw the Gringo running along the creek shore like his life depended on it, and before she knew it, he was in the water, and she couldn't see him anymore.

She ran across the lawn, saw an old couple pointing and a young boy shouting, and two little girls looking like they were in big trouble. Jeremiah's file box was on the picnic table, one file folder open, and sheets were blowing all over the place. Before she could even figure out what the heck was going on, Jeremiah came trudging up the bank, soaked to the skin, holding his arm funny. Maybe he'd injured it.

Since he was apparently in no danger, though, she started gathering up the pages from the grass, noticing several of them had passages underlined in red. As she gathered, she skimmed those passages, wondering what he'd found that so interested him. Witness interviews. Mainly, the witnesses' names were underlined. And not all of them. In each statement one or two lines were also marked. "Suspect ate there four times and witness waited on him each time," in one. "Suspect spent time at the Bluebonnet Inn," with the owner's name in another. "Suspect purchased ammo from witness's gun shop," in a third.

She gathered the last few sheets and was tucking them back into the folder as Jeremiah walked back, so her back was to him, until she heard the odd little whimpering sound, and turned, puzzled.

The Gringo held a sopping wet puppy cradled in one arm against his chest. And the look in his eyes as he stroked the shivering little thing was the most honest expression she'd ever seen him wear. It struck her like a clapper strikes a bell.

The little boy, maybe ten or eleven, blew past Willow so fast he almost knocked her over. "You saved him! Man, you saved him! Thanks, Jeremiah!"

He scrambled the puppy from Jeremiah's arms into his, and it licked his face happily.

The couple made it to them then, moving much slower than the little boy had. The two little girls walked along beside them, heads down.One of them looked up at Willow and she thought if her eyes got any bigger she'd fall in.

"Are you gonna arrest us?" she asked, reminding Willow that she was in uniform.

"For throwin' the puppy in the water?" added the other.

"We thought he'd *like* swimmin'," said the first.

"*We* like swimmin'," explained the second.

"How'd you like it if some little heathen threw *you* in the creek?" asked the long-suffering big brother, hugging his dog.

The pup was light brown, with a black face. His legs were too long, and his head and feet were too big for his body.

Willow glanced at the grandparents, and at the girls, and then she crouched down low to put herself at eye-level with them. "Cruelty to animals is against the law. But I don't think you meant to be cruel, did you?"

They shook their heads.

"From now on, you treat that puppy just like you would a

little newborn baby, cause that's what he is, really. And part of your job from now on is to protect him and watch out for him. And when he grows up, he'll protect and watch over you. You think you can you do that?"

"Yes, Ma'am," they said in unison.

"You promise?"

"Yes, Ma'am!"

"Well, all right then. I'll let you off with a warnin' this time, long as you keep that promise."

They turned and ran back to their own picnic table, followed by their brother, carrying his wet pup. Of them all, the puppy seemed the least upset by events.

The grandparents thanked Jeremiah profusely, then went limping back and ordered the kids to pack up their toys and get back in the car. They were taking their meal to go. They'd clearly had enough.

Willow faced Jeremiah, and he said, "Why are you smiling?"

"I didn't know I was." But she must be. She was suffused in what felt like warm syrup from her head to her toes, and she wasn't even sure why. Her throat was tight, and her eyes were suspiciously warm.

She nodded at the food. "You want to eat soakin' wet, or…"

He peeled off his T-shirt, and she stopped smiling, and that warm syrup heated to a low simmer as she gawked at his chest and shoulders, and when he turned to drape the T-shirt over a nearby tree limb, his back.

Suddenly aware she hadn't done so in too long, Willow took a breath, and it might've been noisy.

"You okay, Willow?"

"Good. Good." *His eyes are up there.* She lifted her gaze. He was sitting down, wet jeans and all, and reaching for his meal.

So she sat down across from him and reached for hers. It was perfect, exactly what she always got there.

"It's a little creepy you knowin' my order by heart, you know that, Gringo?"

He looked across at her. "I can see that. It isn't that I stalked you. I just heard you order it when we were with the whole gang a few weeks ago, and it stuck in my mind."

She remembered. It had been hot, and the entire tribe of cousins, adopted cousins, and cousins-in-law had come for ice cream one Sunday.

"You got some kind of super-powered memory, do you?" It was so distracting, talking to him naked from the waist up. She took a long pull from her straw, then focused on her sandwich.

"Just where you're concerned," he said.

She stopped chewing, then finished and drank to wash it down. "Why?"

"Why what?" He'd downed half his burger already.

"Why just where I'm concerned?"

He shrugged and kept on eating. Between bites, he said, "I don't really know. Something about you makes me...pay attention. That's all. I swear I'm not creepy."

She laughed and then when she caught hold of herself again, she said, "You jumped in a creek to save a puppy, Gringo. You're the furthest thing from creepy."

"What was I gonna do? It's a puppy."

She laughed again. Then she nodded at his file folder. "You're already finding things of interest, I see."

His smile died as his eyes shifted from hers to the folder and back again.

"The pages were blowin' all over. I noticed the red underlines when I picked 'em up. Lucky I came along when I did, or the whole thing would've been gone." Not really. It wasn't like she'd have loaned Uncle Garrett's only copies out without backing them up. She'd made copies.

He said, "Just...people he interacted with. I thought I might talk to some of them. What? You're making a face."

"I'm just wonderin' what you hope to get out of that." Then she shrugged. "But it's none of my business."

"I don't really know what I hope to get out of it, either. I'm just…following my gut. I want to talk to who he talked to. I want to stand where he stood, see what he saw, much as I can."

She gazed at him and her heart hurt for him. She could not imagine having the upbringing he'd had. Plenty of money, from the sounds of things. But not one bit of love.

"I can help," she said. "We can retrace your dad's steps through Quinn together, if you want. You know, when I'm not on duty."

"You'd do that for me?"

"Sure, I would. You're family." She tapped the file folder. "I gotta go. You figure out where you want to start and we can reconvene tomorrow. All right?"

"Sounds good," he said.

She got up, gathered her rubbish and took it to the trash bin on the way back to her car. She'd read his background check three times before Uncle Garrett had interrupted her, but she didn't think she'd really known anything real about Jeremiah until she'd seen the look in his eyes with that puppy.

A doubting little voice inside whispered that Jeremiah wasn't like the people she knew, that he'd been raised by criminals, and that he withheld information as if he had something to hide. He assumed others did the same. He was neither trusting nor trustworthy, her little voice said.

But she knew a gangly pup who thought otherwise.

Jeremiah didn't particularly want a peace officer following him around Quinn while he hunted for a half-million in gold that, for all he knew, might be stolen. If it wasn't stolen, it was at least what the cops would call ill-gotten, which meant they'd confiscate it, which meant he'd be in trouble. There were issues holding up the execution of his father's will, and his existing funds wouldn't last forever.

He pulled over onto the side of the road in front of the address in the police file labeled The Bluebonnet Country Inn. Only it wasn't blue and it wasn't an inn. It was a white two-story Georgian with flower boxes, a pristine sidewalk, and a Cat Shaw Realty sign on the lawn. Cat's headshot smiled at them from the lawn sign, right over her phone number.

Willow pulled up facing him in her personal pickup, not her Sheriff's Department SUV. She got out and so did he, and she came walking toward him all long and lean in jeans and boots and a T shirt with a plaid flannel one over it, unbuttoned. She wore a white cowboy hat that contrasted with her jet hair.

They met at the paved driveway's mouth, where stone pillars held a black iron gate that stood wide open. He tore his eyes off her to take a look at the place itself. Where would you bury gold around here?

"I don't see an inn sign," he said.

"Yeah," Willow said. "I never heard of the Bluebonnet Inn, and I've lived here my whole life."

They walked up the driveway to the place. There were no curtains in any of its tall windows, but there was a car in the driveway. Wait, he knew that car.

"Isn't that Cat's car?" Willow asked like she'd recognized it at the same instant. She didn't wait for an answer, just marched up to the door, knocked twice and then opened it and leaned inside. "Cat, you in here?"

"Depends on who's askin'!" The voice floated down from the second story, and soon her footsteps followed. Cat's brown & silver curls were covered in a purple paisley bandana, and she was brushing her hands together. "Oh, hey Willow," she said, then with a very curious look, "and Jeremiah!"

"Ma'am," he said, and would've touched his brim, if he'd been wearing a hat, but he wasn't quite as cowboy as his newfound little brother.

"What brings you out here?" she asked, looking from one of them to the other. Another woman came down behind her, white hair with black strands, brown skin and brown eyes.

Jeremiah said, "Willow's helping me retrace my father's steps when he was here. He was…Vincent de Lorean.

"Ohhh," Cat said. "I wasn't here then. Juanita was though, weren't you?" she asked, turning to the woman behind her. Then she said, "Oh, Juanita, I'm sorry, this is Deputy Willow Brand and Jeremiah Thorne. You know, he's Ethan Brand's brother."

"Oh," she said, nodding at them.

"Juanita's the owner. She inherited it from her mom, who passed recently."

"I'm so sorry," Willow said.

"*Gracias*. I appreciate that."

"So then, you've decided to sell?" Willow asked.

"Yes. I have a little place out past Mad Bull's Bend, closer to my daughter and her husband. This is way more house than I need at my age."

"That seems like a wise decision," Willow said. "Sheriff Brand's file said Vincent de Lorean stayed at this address, but he called it the Bluebonnet Inn."

"That's right," Juanita said. "It was once when I was young. When my mother got older, she retired here. She didn't want to leave. And she never had to."

Cat nodded, and said, "Oh, it was so pretty when I first moved down here. All the trim was blue, and there were blue shutters and blue flower boxes full of bluebonnets and violets and blue-bells and something yellow, as I recall. Just so pretty."

They were standing in the foyer and it was so empty their voices echoed. Jeremiah raised his head again. He was eager to get to the meat of the conversation. So he waited for a lull in the chitchat, then asked, "Juanita, do you remember any details about when de Lorean stayed here?"

Juanita nodded. "I only remember because I was so shocked to learn one of our guests had murdered someone. I remember when the sheriff came to tell Mamma and me, and he asked me the same things you're asking me now. But the man only came here to sleep. He didn't take his meals here, even though they were included. I barely exchanged two words with him the whole time." She was looking all around the foyer as she spoke, first at the chandelier high above, then the staircase, then the floor.

"What happened to his things?" Jeremiah asked.

She met his eyes then. "He'd taken everything with him and checked out before he was arrested," Juanita said. "Sheriff Brand went through his room, but it was as clean as it had been when he'd arrived."

Jeremiah lowered his head.

"I'm sorry to disappoint you," she said. "I wish there was more I could tell you."

Willow said, "That's okay. I appreciate you talkin' to us." Then she turned as if to leave.

That didn't suit Jeremiah's goals. "Do you think I could take a look around?" he asked.

"Well, it's not ready to show yet," Cat said. "But I've got no objections to an early tour. If it's all right with Juanita."

Willow was frowning at him, curious, but she didn't say anything. And so Cat led them through the place's ground floor, while Juanita trailed behind. He got the feeling she was not enthusiastic about the tour and eager for them to finish their business and get on their way.

They went through the formal dining room, professional kitchen, and personal living space on the ground floor, and then one guest room after another upstairs, ten of them total, each with its own attached bath. The colors were boring and beige with carpet above and hardwood below.

"The place is like a blank slate," Cat said, trying to spin the boring into a positive. "A person could do anything they wanted."

"Is there much property with it?" Jeremiah asked.

"Decent sized back yard and garden area. Come on, it's this way." She led them into the kitchen again and out a back door. The lawn was mostly bare, with a few patches of scraggly weeds. The garden was an untended and overgrown square of brambles with a dry fountain in the middle made of three saucer-shaped tiers, the smallest at the top, and a small, dry basin at the bottom full of weeds and debris. Vines were trying to reclaim its concrete.

He walked away from Cat and Willow while they were chatting about Lily's pregnancy and the shower being planned. Cat was dating Lily's dad, so it was all in the family.

The "lawn" was in plain sight, but the garden had a few areas that would be hidden from the perspective of the house, even from some of the upper windows. He moved around, keeping an eye-line back toward the house until he was all the way around to the back side of the fountain. From there, no window was visible. There was a narrow strip of ground going back three or four yards where you could conceivably dig a hole and bury something without being seen. Eight pounds of gold wouldn't take up much space.

Yeah, he was going to have to come back here, preferably with a metal detector. He didn't think his father would have hidden it inside the house, not for long-term safekeeping. People knocked out walls and remodeled all the time.

He'd have buried it somewhere, for sure. He'd heard the old man say a hundred times, "the safest place to hide loot is in the ground." It was his second favorite refrain, right after, "the law is always the enemy."

The ladies would be getting curious if he lingered much longer, so he continued around the fountain, pretending to inspect the concrete. "I don't see any cracks. You could probably get this thing going again without too much trouble," he said, like he knew a damn thing about fountains.

"Possibly," Cat said. "Ethan has a guy. He did that water feature at the honky tonk."

"I'll get you the number when I see him later, if you want," Jeremiah said.

"Thanks for the info, Cat," Willow said. Then to him, "Ready?"

"Yeah. Thanks, Cat. Nice meeting you, Juanita." He had to get a metal detector pronto. And not locally. Probably best to drive down to El Paso.

He fell into step with Willow and they walked back up the driveway toward their respective vehicles. She said, "Well? Did that tell you anything you wanted to know?"

"No," he said. It had come out involuntarily, and it was true, and now he had to explain himself. He said, "I'm not sure I believed her." That too, was the truth.

"What made you feel that way?" she asked.

He shrugged, and then continued with the honesty bit, because it seemed to be working. She was getting drawn in. "Whenever she was talking about my father, she looked everywhere except at any of us." And he knew just by Willow's expression that she'd noticed it, too. "Maybe we ought to know a little bit more about her."

"Well, I can't run a background check on her just because you think she's lying," she said.

"I wasn't asking you to."

"I feel like you kinda were."

He had been. She didn't miss a thing. "I didn't mean for you to feel that way, Willow. Seriously. I didn't, I was just thinking out loud."

She nodded slow, her eyes on his. "What were you lookin' for out back? You weren't inspectin' the fountain, that's for dang sure."

He'd planned ahead for this, at least, and the lines he'd come up with spilled as smoothly as water had once flowed from that water feature. "I wondered if there was a bench and if maybe he sat on it and planned all the crap he pulled in Quinn. And I wondered if any of the older guys I worked with were out there planning it with him." He shrugged. "Stuff like that."

She met his eyes. He gazed right back, not even blinking. He was very good at lying to someone's face. However, it had never given him such a sick feeling before. He almost had to lower his gaze from hers. It felt like he couldn't hold the lie when her intense brown gaze was probing his eyes.

Then she blinked, and he was saved. He turned away and sighed, a little light-headed. What the hell was that about?

They were standing beside their respective cars on the roadside, neither in a hurry to leave. It was a warm day, but not hot. Autumn was full on, and while it didn't cool much, the days got shorter, the nights downright chilly.

She said, "Can I ask a rude question?"

"Sure, ask away."

"You said there was a snag with your inheritance. What if it doesn't come through? Will you be okay, financially?"

He frowned at her a little. "I'm supposed to have a call with the lawyer tonight. Should find out what's up then."

"Yeah, but…are you worried?"

"A little. I'm not exactly a skilled laborer. What I have won't last forever." Unless he found the gold. "I kind of need the inheritance."

"Or a job," she said, eyebrows high, challenging him.

He shrugged. "Ethan keeps trying to hire me on at the honky tonk. Needs security, he says. Not sure I'm cut out to be a bouncer."

"What are you cut out to be?"

"Independently wealthy."

She rolled her eyes. He didn't think she'd liked his response at all. And he needed her to like him. And maybe not just because he might need her help to find his treasure. Maybe not just because of that at all. So he said, "Nothing I'm ready to talk about it. Is that okay with you?"

"Well, of course it's okay with me. It's your thing, you don't have to tell me ever. Unless you want to."

He nodded. She looked like she was waiting for something, but he'd been about as honest as he could for about as long as he could. It felt off. Wrong. Vulnerable, like he was showing his belly, and he needed her to stop looking at him the way she was.

"What are you doin' after your shift?" he asked.

"Gettin' a shower, and a meal, and hittin' the hay."

"You want some company?"

"For which?" She shot him a mischievous grin.

"Well, we can start with the meal, and see where it leads."

She lowered her eyes, but raised them again, seemed to square her shoulders, and said, "I'm not ready for it to lead anywhere, Jeremiah."

She was serious. He felt a crushing sense of disappointment.

And yet he heard himself saying, "I hear you. Listen, I know you don't want the family gossip to get hold of us having another midnight meal together. You want to come to my place?"

"Your place is the bunkhouse."

"I can meet you somewhere so you don't have to bring your car. Nobody would come knocking at midnight, short of an emergency. And it can just be food, nothing else."

She looked at him in a way that made him feel transparent. She said, "I'll see how I feel after my shift. I might be too tired. I'll text you, all right?"

"All right, yeah. Sure."

She opened her pickup door.

He put his hand on the roof, and looked around just in case, and then leaned in for a kiss, and she kissed him back, but very softly. It was almost a sad little kiss. What the hell?

He said, "Thanks for the help today."

"Any time," she said with a smile that didn't reach her liquid brown eyes.

He'd screwed up, somewhere along the line, he'd screwed up, and knowing that was like drinking battery acid. He wanted to fix it, but he wasn't sure where he'd gone off track.

He headed for his Jeep, digging the keys out of his pocket as Willow drove away. She didn't even look back.

Jeremiah Thorne was looking for something and lying about it. Moreover, Willow thought he might be using her to help him find it. *That* burned.

She changed into her uniform in the gas station restroom while Willie gassed up her Department SUV. Willie was a long-faced young man who slouched when he walked, and kept his head and his gaze lowered. He was shy and would back away if you got too close to him. He'd been that way since high school.

She'd have used the nicer restroom, the private one upstairs at Two Lilies, but she'd wanted—no *needed*—to get away from the Gringo. When he was close, all she could think about was getting closer. Even when they were just sitting in the truck together, she kept wishing he'd slide over or put his hand over hers on the shift-knob.

She couldn't go to the bunkhouse tonight, she thought, heading back across the gas station pavement toward her truck at Pump Three. Other vehicles were pulling in, pulling out, and sitting still in all directions and heat rose in invisible ribbons from the blacktop. She couldn't be all alone with Jeremiah Thorne in the bunkhouse, a place where nobody was going to walk in and interrupt them. She'd been alone with him in her own cottage, and even now, she was unsure how far that would've gone if her mom hadn't come along.

Jeez, what would Ethan say if she had sex with his brother?

Honk! Honk!

She all but jumped clean out of her skin, then saw the big red pickup and recognized the very cousin she'd been thinking of. He pulled up beside her, "Hey cuz. You seen Jeremiah today?"

"*What?* Why?"

Her reaction had been abrupt and strange, she realized, so she quickly said, "You scared the daylights out of me. Gimme a second."

"Sorry. You seemed deep in thought. Everything all right?"

At that moment, the radio in her car crackled. The windows were up, so she couldn't make out the words. "Last I saw the Gringo was when I dropped him off at Two Lilies. Don't know where he was goin' from there."

She started for her car.

Ethan and his big truck rolled along with her. "Why'd *you* drop him off at Two Lilies?"

Shoot, she'd said too much. "'Cause that's where he left his Jeep."

"So you two were together this morning?"

"I'm helpin' him trace his father's…your father's…de Lorean's time in Quinn. You know, that time he came looking for you, crossed the elder Brands, and wound up in prison."

"Why the hell would he want to do that?"

She shook her head, shrugged. "Closure?" She didn't tell him she thought his brother was looking for something. Ethan was a little sensitive about anyone judging Jeremiah based on his criminal parentage, for obvious reasons. Ethan didn't like folks judging his brother due to his time in prison, either.

Was she doing that? Was she being all suspicious of Jeremiah's motives because of what she knew? That he was an ex-con, raised in a criminal organization and groomed to work within it.

The radio crackled again.

"I gotta go, Ethan. We should do something soon. I miss you."

"Bunkhouse bonfire?" he asked.

"We have a guest in the bunkhouse," she reminded him.

"Leave that to me. You're working nights though. When do you have off?"

"Day after tomorrow."

"Day after tomorrow. It's on. You can bring uh…never mind, you're off the hook. You can pitch in a twenty and call it good."

"Look at you, all organizin' a bonfire," she said.

"Yeah, Drew taught me. Sort of."

Another crackle. She said, "See you Saturday night," and walked to her car, pulled open the door, keyed the mike. "Car three to dispatch. Repeat the last call."

"It's a break-in, Will. Out on the Bend Road. 2105. You're the closest at hand."

She started her engine, flipped on lights and siren, and peeled out of the gas station. "Any injuries?"

"None reported. Nobody home at the time."

Willow tried to put Jeremiah out of her mind and shift into cop mode as she drove. She was still unsuccessful as she turned onto Big Bend Lane, where large, beautiful homes with land-scaped lawns that used too much water sat like the crowned jewels of the county. 2105's paved driveway curved upward toward an asymmetrical house that seemed entirely wood and glass. But one of the wall-sized window panes in front was smashed. It lay in a large pile of shards on the floor inside and in the raised flower bed outside. The raised bed was bordered by red landscaping bricks.

She stopped a few yards shy of the glass out of caution, then got out of her car and took a look around from the outside. While she stood there looking, she realized someone was looking back from the other side of the dark hole that used to be a window.

"Oh, thank goodness," said a short, lean young woman, maybe a few years younger than Willow. Her dark hair was twisted up behind her head, and she wore round tortoiseshell glasses over big brown eyes. Her capri jeans had flowers embroidered at the bottoms of each short leg. "Do you see this mess? Who would do something like this?"

Willow shrugged, taking it in as she did. "No idea. You?"

"None," she said. "Come on in, the door's…" she nodded left.

The main entrance was a green door with stained sidelights at the top of four half-circle concrete steps. There were rearing horses on either side of its stoop.

The door opened and she was greeted by the small, pretty woman. Behind her, a man, 6'1", fit, blond hair, blue eyes, beach boy vibe that seemed out of place so near the desert.

"I'm Deputy Brand," Willow said.

"Richard Montrose," he said, leaning past the woman. "My wife, Elena."

"Deputy," she said.

"Sorry we're meeting under these circumstances." Willow followed them inside, where they took her to the broken window right there in the foyer, which had three of them lining it floor-to-ceiling. A brick lay on the floor's plush carpet, right in front of a fireplace. It matched the bricks in the flower bed in front. She pulled a large zipper bag from a pocket and picked up the brick with it.

"Can you tell me what happened?"

"Well, I was out," Elena said. "Lunch with the girls at Two Lilies. Can I get you a drink? Ice water?"

"No, thank you. Mr. Montrose, same question?"

"I was at work when it happened," Richard said.

"And where's that?" Willow asked.

"El Paso, I'm an attorney," he said. "Michner and Reed."

The way he said it made Willow think she should've heard of them.

He said, "I got home first and found it like this. Elena got here a few minutes later."

Willow nodded, looking around the room. Nothing was out of place, other than the glass, but the pieces were as they had fallen, she thought. There were no crushed places where someone might've walked over them to enter the home. "Was anything missing?"

"Nothing that I could see," Elena said. "And Richard didn't notice anything either."

She nodded, noticing an Apple laptop on a coffee table, and an iPad lying on a stand in the foyer. "Huh. And the front door was still locked?"

"Yeah," Richard said. "Just like we left it."

"And you didn't notice anyone in the area, anyone unusual?"

"Not a thing," Elena said.

"Well…" said her husband.

Willow and Elena both looked his way.

"I can't be sure it meant anything, but I did see a vehicle coming down the road just as I was coming up. Doesn't mean it was coming from *here*, of course, but there's not a lot of traffic up here during the day."

"Can you describe it?" Willow pulled out her phone to key it in.

He nodded. "Jeep, one of sporty ones. Copper-colored."

Willow stopped tapping keys and tried to keep the frown off her face as Richard Montrose described Jeremiah's Jeep. "I don't suppose you got a plate number?"

"'Fraid not."

"Exactly what time was that?" she asked.

He looked at his watch, and it was a helluva watch. Big, gold, and expensive. "About ninety minutes ago," he said.

"Are you sure on that?"

"I get home at the same time every ladies' lunch day," Elena said. "Three-fifteen."

"And I got out of the office early, so I was here at three," Richard said.

"Okay. All right." Jeremiah was with her at that time. Not that she thought he'd be apt to throw a brick through the window of a stranger's home to begin with. But something was tickling the back of her neck like a spider's leg.

"All right, I guess call your homeowner's insurance. I'm fixin' to talk with your neighbors, see whether anyone saw anything. I'll keep you posted. You give us a call if there's any more trouble."

"That's it?" Elena asked. "There's nothing more you can do? I don't feel safe. Especially not knowing why someone did this."

Willow felt for her. "Maybe get yourselves one of those doorbell cams, like most of your neighbors have. Get some plastic to staple up to protect your house until you can get the window replaced."

Elena closed her dark eyes, nodded, opened them again. Richard's phone rang, and he looked at it and said, "I have to take this. Excuse me."

Elena rolled her eyes, but then walked Willow to the door.

"Be thinking about anyone who might be angry with you," Willow told her. "This seems like busting the window was the entire goal. Could've been a random vandal like neighborhood kids on a dare, or someone who's good and teed off at one or both of you. I think if you give that some thought, the answer might come to you."

"Okay," she said. But her eyes clung, and Willow thought she needed something more.

"I don't think this is anyone who wants to hurt you," she said. "They'd do more than break a window, you know? But if you don't feel safe, maybe stay at a hotel or a friend's place for a few nights. If we're lucky, I'll catch this person in the meantime."

She nodded rapidly, sighing in relief. Maybe she'd just needed validation that it wasn't overreacting to stay elsewhere overnight. "That's what I'll do. Yeah, I'll pack a bag right now and go to Mom's." She turned to go back into the house, but then stopped, and slowly faced Willow again. Willow noticed her fists clenched at her sides. "Do you…could you stay until I get out of here? It'll only take me a few minutes to pack a bag."

"Okay. Sure. I'll just sit here in the car, okay? Unless you want me to come back in?"

"The car's fine." She spun on her heel and went back inside.

So Willow got into her SUV, cranked up the AC, and made some notes for her report. Someone rapped her window out of nowhere, startling her. She looked around fast, but no one was there, just a walking stick with a brass handle. It drew back to rap again, but she said, "Stop!" and put the window down, noticing the silver-haired head at the very bottom.

The head moved backward a step, so Willow could see the small woman to whom it belonged. She was about 4'10" and her back curved over her walking stick.

"I seen him," she said. "I seen him good." She tapped the binoculars that hung around her neck.

"Did you recognize him?"

"Nope. Don't reco'nize much of anybody. I'm not from here. Abby Sinclair."

"Deputy Brand," Willow said. "So you're not a local?"

"Stayin' with my daughter for a week." She nodded toward another large house visible from the driveway, further up, across the street. "But I seen him, I'll tell you what."

Willow tipped her head sideways and considered her options. She needed a win, as she was far from impressing anyone at the QSD, other than her uncles, who were impressed by her just for existing.

What the hay? She had nothing to lose. "Could you describe him to a sketch artist for me?"

"To. A. Tee," she said, and she snapped her thumb to her fore-finger on each word like Baby Shark.

"Can I get your number?"

"Oh, honey, I don't swing that way," she said, and then she laughed and slapped her thigh. Then she started reciting her digits so suddenly that Willow barely had time to key them in.

CHAPTER FIVE

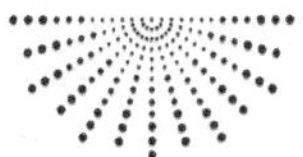

"So we're getting' a sketch artist in from El Paso first thing tomorrow mornin'," Willow said.

Jeremiah couldn't take his eyes off her. She was sitting outside in one of the lawn chairs he'd found around the place. She had her long legs stretched out in front of her, and her head tipped back, so she could stargaze, he figured.

He'd made them sandwiches, toasting the bread and heaping on grilled veggies straight from the small fire he'd started in the firepit. They were damn good sandwiches, if he said so himself.

She hadn't stopped talking about the case since she'd arrived, overnight bag in hand so she could make use of the bunkhouse shower while he finished cooking. She'd never worked with a police sketch artist before and was excited about it.

"You really like being a cop, don't you?" he asked when she stopped for a breath.

"I really do," she said. "I'd like it more if I were better at it, though."

"You don't think you're good at it?"

She glanced his way and rolled her eyes. "I can't even get the goods on the Barker boys, and everybody knows they're guilty as sin."

"Well," he said, "maybe when you catch this window-breaker, you'll feel better about that."

"Maybe." She took another bite of her sandwich. He'd quartered them once off the fire, because he'd used huge slabs of sourdough to make them. She was working on her third portion, but slowing down.

After she swallowed, she said, "This is the best sandwich I've ever had. You oughtta tell the cook over at Two Lilies how you make 'em"

It was an odd request. "Don't you want me to tell *you* how to make them?"

"Oh, I wasn't put on the planet to cook," she said.

"Really?"

"What? Why do you sound surprised?"

He shrugged. "The whole herb garden thing."

"Oh. Yeah, those are for medicine, not cooking."

"Medicine. Like ginger-tea-for-a-cold medicine?"

"Not exactly." She pulled a small drawstring pouch from a jacket pocket then slid it right back in. He'd caught a glimpse of intricate beadwork along the upper third of the pouch. "*Medicine*," she said. Then she handed him her plate, a half-sandwich still on it. "I'm fixin' to wrap that up and take it home."

"I'm flattered. And prepared." He got up and went to take a square container with a tight-fitting lid off a flat rock nearby. "It's one of your aunt Chelsea's," he said. "I figure it's okay to re-lend, long as I keep it in the family."

"I'll make sure she gets it back." She sat up in her chair to take the container and he brushed his fingers over her hand when she did. He saw the way her breath hitched, and it felt good clear to his toes.

She opened the container put the remaining half-sandwich inside and snapped on the lid.

He almost held his breath, then wondering whether she'd get up and leave, and for a moment, it seemed like that's what she was about to do. But then she set the container on the ground beside her chair, took a long sip from her long-necked brown bottle, and leaned back in her chair once again, tipping her head back. Stargazing.

He returned to his own chair strategically placed beside hers before she'd arrived, grabbing another beer on the way, and took a similar position. "It's beautiful out here," he said.

"It's different than where you're from," she replied. "In a lot of ways." Then she sat up and looked at him. "I'm gonna ask you something, and if you don't want to discuss it, that's fine. I'm just…curious about you."

He sat up too, and set his beer aside. "All right."

"Will you tell me what happened to your mamma?"

He wondered if it was a test. It seemed likely, the way she was watching his face, awaiting his answer. He'd been questioned by enough cops to know the look of someone watching for a lie. But it was colored by something else. Something soft, something real. And maybe hopeful. His answer was going to prove something to her.

"I don't…talk about my mother," he said. "Usually."

"I'm sorry. Forget I asked."

"She was great. She was, you know, everything. I guess moms always are, to a little kid. I was with her 'til I was four, I think. She was beautiful. She had wavy blonde hair. She would sing and dance me around on her feet. And it was just the two of us. And then one day, she drove me to my father's mansion, told me she loved me and would miss me and to be a good boy, and she drove away."

He had howled, he remembered it. Standing on the front step wailing and trying to run after the car, as strong hands grabbed hold and brought him inside.

"Where did she go?" she asked, and her voice was more breath than substance.

"To the highest point she could find and right on over," he said. Willow gasped and pressed a hand to her chest. "'Course, I didn't know that 'til later," Jeremiah went on. "He'd somehow got custody of me despite being in prison. I had a nanny, Marianne, until I was ten, then she left and was replaced by Reggie. Reggie was fun, kind of an Alfred to my Batman…you know?"

"I don't. I haven't seen a single Batman movie."

"Oh, you need educating." He smiled but if it looked as fake as it felt, it wouldn't fool her.

"That was it, then?"

"Well, we had a cook, had an excellent chef for a while, and there was always an assistant cook, a couple of maids, a driver, a gardener. My tutor for many years was a stern old goat called Mr. Ford." Saying the name brought the man's face to mind, long and narrow with a goatee that made it even longer. "I never believed that was his real name. He was smart as hell, but cold as ice. Never expressed an emotion. For about six months in ninth grade, I seriously thought he might be a cyborg."

"Jeremiah, that sounds like a terrible childhood."

"Yes, it was. I was a poor little rich boy. And that is the first time I've ever told the whole truth to a peace officer, Deputy Brand. First time I've talked about my mother to anyone, too."

He watched her face, wondering what she'd make of that. Her lips pulled into a slow smile and she got out of her chair and came closer.

"Thank you," she said. "I'm honored."

"You believe me, then?" he asked, rising from his chair as well. They were standing very close.

"Why wouldn't I believe you?"

He shrugged "People don't believe ex-cons."

"I do. I could tell you were being honest…about all that." She pressed her palms to his chest, then slid them up a little higher, to his collar bones.

"How can you tell?"

"Cops have ways."

He wanted to ask what they were, those ways, so he could use them himself. Instead, he said, "Will you be honest with me back?"

"Maybe." Her fingers slid around his neck and interlocked behind it.

"What changed your mind about coming over here tonight?"

She gazed into his eyes. "I was drivin'. I was sleepy. A song came on the radio and the truck just sort of turned on its own."

"Huh," he said. "What song?"

She held his gaze a little harder. "*Desperado*. Ronstadt's version." She paused, lowered her eyes momentarily, visibly deciding to say a little more. "I think you're a good person, Jeremiah Thorne. Don't you prove me wrong, you hear?"

Then she pressed her lips to his, and he was gone. He wrapped his arms all the way around her waist, picked her right up off her feet, then carried her into the bunkhouse, kissing her all the way.

Willow's voice of reason was drowned out by the demands of her body. She wanted this man, had wanted him since she'd laid eyes on him, even when he'd been hiding behind a full beard and sombrero.

He kicked the bunkhouse door closed behind them. Willow shucked her blouse as he shuffle-walked her back to the bunks, fully supported by his arms around her, guided by his thighs pushing hers. When her legs hit the back-most bunk, she bent her knees and sat on its edge.

He followed her down, pressing her back. She put her hands on his shoulders and applied the smallest amount of pressure.

He stopped, braced above her on straight arms, blinking down at her in the near darkness of the bunkhouse.

"That little drawer." She nodded toward the back wall, at the little drawer he'd barely noticed, that was built into it.

He opened it, and rifled through the packets in there. "Nice."

"Never let it be said the Texas Brand Bunkhouse isn't fully equipped."

He closed the drawer, and pulled something from his jeans pocket. "But I, too, am fully equipped."

"Get that much action, do you?"

He lowered his head. "I bought these the day after we kissed. When your mom interrupted and—"

"I remember."

"I had no reason to carry 'em around before that."

"Noted," she said. It was sexy, how nervous he'd become.

His body still above hers, he lowered his gaze to her chest, where she wore a lacy white bra, then he was touching her, his eyes on hers as often as they were on her breasts. He reached behind her to unhook the bra, took it off, gazed at her and exhaled.

Then he bent to use his mouth, and she lost her mind.

She pushed off his shirt, unbuttoning it partly, then wrestling it over his head, and then his jeans while he was undoing hers, and their hips were arching against each other, pressing their hands in between.

Naked, he cupped and fondled her in a way that sent delicious sensations from her core to her extremities. And then it happened, he slid inside her, and held her so closely there wasn't room for air in between. He moved slowly, and he kept kissing her, then looking at her, and stroking her hair back from her forehead, and then kissing her again.

Those lingering looks between the kisses, those eyes tracing her face as if he had reached all the way into her heart and soul. His vivid blue eyes were still fixed on hers when she shattered. She kept her eyes open and let him see.

Something startled Willow awake. She was in a familiar bunk in the familiar bunkhouse where she'd fallen asleep in the arms of Jeremiah Thorne, an ex-con who was lying to her about…something. Maybe lying was too strong a word. He was keeping something from her.

She'd known that already, and she'd slept with him anyway, like a self-sabotaging rookie. Oh, but how could she do otherwise? If she could've made a different choice tonight, she would've.

She was alone in the bunk, so she sat up slow. The bunkhouse wasn't pitch dark, because there was a near-full moon beaming through the windows along the length of the long, narrow building. There wasn't a lot of room to hold things of a personal nature in a bunkhouse, though. If you had a bottom bunk, you could make use of the underneath. Most of the hands who'd stayed brought a footlocker along to hold their stuff.

She needed clothes.

She got out of the bunk, onto her knees, quiet as she could be, and moved from one wad of clothing to the next, gathering up her things. None of the Gringo's clothing was on the floor.

So he's up and dressed. Great detective work, Sherlock.

Her phone was still in her jeans pocket, thank goodness. Battery life 7%, so she wasn't going to use the flashlight feature. But she got upright, all the same.

Where the hay was Jeremiah?

She could see, sort of, and she knew the bunkhouse well.

The four bunk beds were in the back of the building along the left and rear walls. Two small bathrooms were across from the bunks on the right wall. Each had just enough room for a shower, toilet, and sink. She went to each, and found their doors slightly open, the rooms empty.

Then she crept forward, past the bathrooms, past the large closet. One narrow section of it was devoted to bedding. The shelves were always stacked with bedding bundles, wrapped together in blue ribbon—Chelsea's special touch.

The place felt empty.

She walked by the side door, just past the closet on the left, into the kitchen that took up the entire front. The kitchen was empty. She was out of bunkhouse to search. Jeremiah must have left.

She went back to the bunk, confident in her movements, and into the bathroom where she gathered up her discarded uniform, put it into her backpack, slung its strap over one shoulder, and headed for the front door again. Only, this time as she passed the side door, movement caught her eye, and she stopped in her tracks, turning fully that way.

Jeremiah was out there, bathed in moonlight, standing with his back to the bunkhouse, near the still-smoldering fire pit. She hadn't told him there was going to be a bunkhouse bonfire yet. She probably should ask, rather than inform, since this was his temporary home.

Last night had been something. Seeing him out there reignited everything she'd started to feel for him. Tingles swam laps along her spine and her stomach knotted up in that peculiarly sexual way. He wore a light blue, short-sleeved button down, unbuttoned. She moved closer to the door, watching him through its glass. It was darker inside than out, so he probably couldn't see her there. She wished he'd turn around so she could admire his chest.

Then he did, pivoting forty-five degrees so the moonlight

bathed his chest and so did her eyes, until she noticed he was talking on his phone.

That little kernel of information had been obvious from the first glimpse of him but hadn't made its way to the thinking part of her brain until her hormone flood had subsided enough for it to take a gasping breath of awareness.

Who was he talking to at two in the morning?

She bit her lip and her hand was shaking when she took hold of the doorknob, twisted it, and finally opened the door just the slightest bit. She leaned close, putting her left ear to the opening.

His deep voice sent chills right down her spine.

"It might be buried out there at the inn. I picked up a metal detector this morning. I'm goin' back there soon as Willow's busy on her shift."

He sighed heavily. Then he said, "About her…I don't know. I don't feel good, deceiving her like this. She's…kind of amazing. Deserves better."

He heaved a sigh, then tapped the phone without saying goodbye and returned it to his pocket.

Willow hurried to the kitchen to look like she was busy doing something besides listening in. Impulsively, she grabbed the coffee carafe off the counter and set it under the kitchen tap. Then she opened a cabinet to pull out a filter and a bag of ground roast. She'd filled both basket and carafe and was putting them into place by the time he came back inside.

He saw her there and smiled with sleepy eyes. "Hey. You're up."

"Yeah." Her voice sounded tight to her own ears. She wondered if he'd noticed.

"And making coffee at two a.m.?"

Right. It was still the middle of the night. She pasted on a smile before turning to face him. "It's a gift. In the morning, all you'll have to do is push the button. You're welcome."

"Oh. You're leaving?"

The disappointment in his voice seemed genuine. But then again, he was good at deception, right? She'd been smart to think this was a bad idea and stupid to ignore that feeling.

"I should get home. The bad thing about sharin' a driveway with your parents is they know every time you leave, and every time you return."

He moved a step closer and reached out, smoothing her hair behind her ear, caressing her cheek in the process. Her body responded with tingles and delicious chills and a deep longing.

"It was amazing," he said.

"I agree." It wasn't a lie, not that she owed him the truth when he'd been lying to her.

His fingers trailed up and down her nape. "I…want to…you know, see you."

Sure he did.

But why? What the hell was he up to? And how was she fixing to find out if she gave him the brush-off now?

Actually, hanging out with him would make it easier to learn the truth. But she didn't know if she had it in her.

She took a deep breath and said, "I don't know yet. This is… unexpected. And I'm a little…"

"Disoriented? Confused? Scared?" he asked, then said, "So am I."

But his earlier words replayed in her head. *I don't feel good, deceiving her like this.*

If he felt bad, then maybe he had a conscience, some sort of moral compass that applied to people, not just puppies. Maybe she could get him to tell her the truth. Maybe she could find out for herself.

"You seem pretty sure of yourself to me."

"You're not what I expected, Willow. I was unprepared for you." He bit his lip and stopped talking.

"Whatever that means." She heaved a sigh and pressed a palm to his cheek, a gesture so impulsive she couldn't prevent it. It happened before she knew it. And she whispered, "Say more," and she latched onto his blue eyes with hers and willed him to spill his guts.

"I…I'm not sure of myself. Most of the time, I'm not even sure who I am. I was being groomed to take over for my old man, my education customized around it. And first time I got sent out with the guys to bust some loser's kneecaps…" He didn't finish. Instead, he repeated. "I don't know who I am."

"I do," she said.

His brows rose. He was so good looking she wanted to kiss him, even after what she'd heard. "Tell me, then. Who am I?"

"Whoever you decide to be. You're the one in charge of that, you know." She searched his eyes and decided she had to get a look at that phone and find out who he'd called tonight, who he'd told that he was deceiving her. And yes, she'd feel guilty for snooping on him but she'd heard him admit he was deceiving her, so the way she saw things, it was justified.

He was hunting for something. Something physical. Something that might be buried behind the former boarding house. And he was going back there after she started her shift tomorrow night.

Well, she'd be ready.

He leaned in for a kiss, and she pretended not to notice as she swayed out of reach and changed the subject. "By the way, the gang wants to hold a bunkhouse bonfire tomorrow night. It's my night off. But I said I'd ask if it was okay with you."

They were still standing very close to each other. Her hands were at her sides, but his were on her hips.

"It's your bunkhouse," he said. "I'm squatting here. But sure, it sounds like fun. What should I do?"

"Everybody contributes something. Beer or pizza or chips and dip. Ethan's organizin' it, so talk to him."

He moved a little closer. "I don't want you to leave, Willow."

She lowered her head so he wouldn't see how damn good

those words felt to her, even while she reminded herself they were as likely a lie as the truth. She had no business feeling so dang excited about the two of them, while also feeling terrified. Her feelings were coming on like a landslide.

"It's better if I go," she said. "Trust me, once the family gets hold of this…whatever this is, they'll be plannin' our nuptials and namin' our firstborn, and *nobody* wants that."

He sighed but didn't argue. "You're probably right. Okay, then, get some sleep," he said. "I'll see you tomorrow." And instead of leaning down as if to kiss her, he waited for her to lean up.

"You too," she said, and then she mustered every nanogram of will she had, and turned and walked away from him, out the door into the cool perfection of a West Texas night. Bugs were whirring and chirruping and in the distance, and a coyote howled a long, warbling love song.

Maybe she'd made a huge mistake giving in to her baser urges and sleeping with Gringo Sombrero. But that didn't matter. What was done, was done.

Her mission now was to find out what the hell he was up to.

What was he looking for in Quinn?

CHAPTER SIX

"I still don't get why you don't just ask him," Drew said. She was standing by the dry fountain behind the former Bluebonnet Inn.

Willow was on a stepladder near the back door where a security camera was mounted. "Because he'd be as likely to lie as tell the truth," she replied. "And I don't trust myself not to believe him purely because I want to."

The cameras had been installed on the vacant house many years back, after some kids started using the backyard garden as a party spot. Drew had downloaded an app. Willow got the password from Juanita, and now they would be able to monitor anything within range.

Drew held her phone, and called. "A little to the left."

Willow moved the camera.

"No my left," Drew said.

Willow moved it again.

"Right there, perfect." As Drew said it, she moved around the fountain, watching herself on her phone. "Yep, best view of the spot Jeremiah seemed most interested in, and most of the backyard, too. Tighten that thumbscrew so it stays that way."

Willow was already tightening it.

"I hope it's as good a view after dark," Drew said. "He's not gonna dig up private property in broad daylight, after all."

"Probably not."

Drew stood there, arms crossed, tipping her head (and ponytail) left and right, still watching her phone as she moved around the backyard. "It's an out-of-date system. No battery backup, it's hardwired right into the house. I wish we had better equipment."

"Doesn't your mom have better equipment?" Willow asked. Penny Brand was a PI, after all. She'd assisted the women of Quinn County in a *pile* of divorces.

"She has it all right. Has it locked up. Orrin and I get the cast-offs, which are no better than what's here, so..." She shrugged. "And during the bonfire, I'll get a look at his phone. But you'll have to distract him. Think you can manage that?"

Willow averted her face, turning to walk back toward the house, but not inside. They had no key, and she didn't want to tell her secret to more people than necessary, so she hadn't consulted Cat.

They went through the garden gate, which was white-painted wrought iron, in need of a fresh coat, some straightening, and some squeaky hinge oil. They'd parked in the driveway, rather than out by the road where their vehicles would more likely be seen.

Drew drove a little EV. She was the most modern-minded member of the whole clan, and maybe the most strongly opinionated. She was also the youngest cousin, so the rest of them tended to look out for her.

Aunt Penny, Drew's mom, a PI and lifelong sleuth, and had planned to name her baby girl Nancy, after Nancy Drew. According to family lore, the baby girl had wailed every time her mamma'd called her Nancy, until one day, before leaving the hospital, her daddy had called her Drew. The baby smiled and she'd been Drew ever since.

Her young cousin followed her to her pickup. She had taken Willow's phone, and was tapping its screen. When she handed it back to her, she showed her a new icon on the screen. "Here's the app. All you have to do is tap it, and then tap its camera icon to bring up the live feed. I've already put in the password, which we will delete as soon as we finish. Got it?"

"Got it."

"Good. It'll backup the recordings to my secure cloud until we tell it to stop."

"You have a secure cloud?"

"And a VPN," Drew said with pride. "Well, Mom does."

Willow didn't know for sure what a VPN was. She opened her pickup door, but Drew didn't move toward her own small, white vehicle. She looked like she had something else to say, so Will faced her again, and asked, "Whatever it is, spill it. I have an appointment with a sketch artist at nine."

"You'd think Uncle Garrett would put a day shift deputy on that," Drew said.

"He offered. I said no. It's my case."

"Anything I can do to help?" the eager amateur detective asked.

"Not yet, but I'm not too proud to tell you if I need something."

Drew smiled, a bright summer-girl smile amid her butter-scotch blonde waves and Texas tan. There was something about brown-eyed blondes, wasn't there?

But then her face went serious again. "Have you talked to Ethan about spying on his brother like this?"

"No." Willow took a breath, preparing to justify herself when she knew damn well she couldn't. "Look, it's between me and Jeremiah. I heard him say he was deceivin' me, and that he was here lookin' for somethin'. Not his long-lost brother like he told us all, but somethin' his criminal father left here for safekeepin'. Somethin' physical that could be buried."

"And why do you have anything to do with any of this, cuz? What do you care if he's deceivin' you?"

She shifted her eyes to her steering wheel. "I'm a deputy sheriff. If he's deceivin' me, it might be because he's doing somethin' criminal."

She looked back at Drew to see if she'd bought it.

Drew's eyes and mouth were both open too wide. She closed her mouth, then said, "You had sex with him."

"I did not!"

"Ohmygosh, you *so* had sex with him. You're blushing! Willow, you have to tell me everything. Better yet, wait, I'll get Maria and Lily and we'll—"

"I don't want anyone to know!" she blurted.

Drew bit back the rest of her suggestion. Then she pursed her lips, and gave a slow nod. "Okay. I won't breathe a word. Promise."

"Okay."

"As long as you tell me everything."

Willow looked at her watch, then shook her head. "I have to meet the sketch artist."

"Can I come along? I've never seen a sketch artist in action before."

Willow realized Drew had her over a barrel. Not that she'd use what she knew against her. Probably. "Okay fine, you can come with me and watch the sketch artist."

Jeremiah went back to bed after Willow left him in the middle of the night. He woke up late the next morning, hugging his twisted up blanket and muttering Willow's name, listening to his heart pound unnaturally in his chest in a way that had to mean something was wrong with it.

Then he realized the pounding wasn't his heart, but somebody knocking on the bunkhouse door. Or maybe a combination of both.

Groaning, he rolled out of the bed, shuffled to the front door, and pulled it open to find his younger-but-bigger brother Ethan on the other side. He probably should've noted the look on his face before he pulled the door open.

Ethan's big fists gripped him by the front of his T-shirt. "I saw my cousin Willow sneakin' outta here like a thief, long about two a.m. What the hay is goin' on?"

"Don't you think you should ask me first and beat me up after I've answered?"

"That's why I didn't punch you in the face when you opened the door."

Jeremiah pulled himself free and smoothed his rumpled T-shirt. He felt at an extreme disadvantage in his shorts, and he was afraid his brother would kill him if he admitted to defiling his beloved cousin.

God, she'd been something, though. He couldn't get her out of his mind, that crazy long hair, that satin skin, the sounds she made, the taste of her kisses…

"Well?" Ethan demanded.

"Willow's helping me retrace our old man's steps while he was in Quinn, before he was arrested."

"At that time of the mornin', all alone out here?"

"She works the night shift, brother. Stopped by when she got off." And man did she ever get off—three times by his count. "She fell asleep while we were talking, and I didn't have the heart to wake her. Hell, Ethan, it's a bunkhouse. Everybody crashes out here when they feel like it."

Ethan lowered his head, and maybe his temper cooled a little bit.

Jeremiah said, "You want to come in? Talk for a minute?"

His oversized brother looked past him toward the kitchen counter. "You got coffee?"

Jeremiah turned to the coffee pot, then he remembered what Willow had done for him that morning and hit the button. The brew started brewing. When he turned again, his cousin scowled at him. He realized he was wearing a goofy smile and promptly wiped it off, cleared his throat, and changed the subject.

"I had emails waitin' after Will left," Jeremiah said to change the subject. "Lawyer says somebody's contesting our father's will. I might never see a nickel, the way things are going."

"He said that, did he?"

"No, I added that last part. He says I oughtta wind up with at least half. They're liquidating everything."

"Cuttin' you a check when it's settled?"

"Not even a check. Electronic deposit soon as the judge rules. Gavel comes down, money comes in. Whatever's left of it." He grabbed a pair of mugs from the cabinet above the pot. He'd been in the bunkhouse long enough that he knew where everything was. And he knew the trick of swapping the carafe for a mug, then swapping that mug for another mug until both were full. He expertly shifted the pot back into place, and handed a mug to his brother.

Ethan took it, took a sip, nodded in approval. "Good coffee."

"Thanks." He'd have to ask Willow for tips.

"So do you know who it is?" Ethan asked. "The person contesting the will?"

"No, they're anonymous for the moment, but it'll have to come out, he says. I'm not ashamed to tell you, brother, the investments I've been living off have taken a hit this year." He'd be all right, though, once he found the gold.

Ethan had a way of listening that made you feel like he cared about every word you uttered. "Come be a bouncer at Two Lilies," he added at length. "We'd be proud to have you. And I'll tell you, we're fixin to need more help once the baby comes."

"I'm considering it," he said. But not until he finished his mission.

"Why do you want to retrace de Lorean's steps in Quinn?" Ethan asked as if he'd read his mind.

Jeremiah sipped his coffee to avoid meeting his brother's eyes. It was getting harder to lie to peoples' faces since he'd come here, and he was damned if he knew why.

"I don't expect you to understand. You barely knew our father. You were still a baby when your mother left you on the doorstep of the Texas Brand. But I did, even though he was in prison, he was my dad. I visited every weekend, and for a long time I thought he…"

"Loved you," Ethan said. "That-son-of-a—"

"This is the last place he was free," Jeremiah said. "He never made bail. He was convicted fast, sentenced faster, and he died in prison. I just…I want to walk his steps in those last few days. I want to see if I can figure out who he was, at the end."

Ethan nodded slow, and there was a long stretch before he spoke. He said, "You want to find something that redeems him in your eyes? For pushing your mother to suicide and killing mine with his bare hands?"

"There is no redemption for that. Not for what he did to our mothers."

Again, his brother nodded. "What, then?"

Jeremiah replied without any forethought at all. "I want to find some trace of decency in him. I think that's what it is. I want to find one good thing. I think I need to." It amazed him to realize it was the truth. He hadn't even realized it himself until Ethan had asked.

"You know why you want to find it?"

"No. I got no idea."

"I think I do," Ethan said. "But I think you have to find out for yourself."

His brother nodded slow. "Well, if I never do, enlighten me at some point, huh?"

"Deal." Ethan sipped his coffee.

"I have one more thing, Ethan. But first, I need your word as a Brand that you won't punch me in the face. All right?"

The big guy set his mug down slow and said, "All right," in a slow, *what-the-hell-is-this-now* kind of a way.

"I want to say that…if there *was* anything between Willow and me—not that there is. Things couldn't be more innocent here—but if there was, it would be between her and me, don't you think? Her being a grown woman and a deputy sheriff and all? She might not appreciate you, getting—"

If you disrespect my cousin, Jeremiah, I'll have somethin' to say about it, and I don't much care if she appreciates it or not. You watch your step with her. She's a sister to me."

He hadn't grabbed him again, but he might as well have. Jeremiah was shaken, not because he was afraid. He was smaller, quicker, meaner, and had more experience fighting. He was pretty sure he could take Ethan if he had to. His brother's size would slow him down as much as his inherent kindness and empathy.

But he didn't want to fight his brother. Ethan was all the family he had in the entire damn world, and suddenly, that meant something to him. It hadn't before.

It was probably good to be aware that his brother wouldn't be on his side if it came down to a choice between him, his blood, and the Brands, his adopted clan.

Finding Ethan had briefly made him feel a little less alone in the world. But that feeling's dark opposite had crept over him again when he'd seen the warning in his brother's eyes.

Yeah. He was on his own. Just like always. He should've known better than to think otherwise.

"Hello again Miz Sinclair," Willow said, entering the interrogation room where the Montroses' elder neighbor was waiting. Drew came in close on her heels.

When she'd first arrived, Willow had handed her cousin a blazer from her locker and told her to transform her ponytail into a bun. She'd done one better, with a sleek French twist, and from somewhere in her backpack, she'd pulled a pair of silver wire-rimmed glasses with lenses Willow thought were clear glass. She looked downright professional by the time she walked into the room behind Willow.

"This is Drew Brand, and she's assisting me today. Drew, meet Abby Sinclair."

Drew smiled warmly. "Abby, can I get you anything? I'm sure there's coffee somewhere."

"Sure, if you want to kill me," Abby said sternly.

Drew went blank and shot a *did-I-blow it-already?* look Willow's way. Then the old lady slapped her thigh and laughed hard, and slapped it again, and then stopped laughing, took a breath, and said, "Lord, I love messin' with the young'uns."

Drew closed her eyes, shook her head. "You really got me, ma'am," she said. And then she pulled out one of the two chairs across from Abby and sat down.

"Our sketch artist should be arriving any minute now, and then we can—"

The door opened behind them. A young man with sable curls, rectangular eyeglasses, and an oversized case in one hand looked around the room, then addressed Willow. "I'm Joshua Stone, lookin' for Deputy Brand?"

"You found her," Willow said. "This here's our witness Abby Sinclair, and my uh—"

"Drew," Drew said. She'd risen from her chair and turned, and was holding out a hand, even though the young man's were already full.

"Oh, uh…" He handed his coffee to Willow without looking at her, wiped his palm on his pleated khaki pants, then closed it around Drew's. "Nice to meet you. Drew, is it?"

"Named after Nancy."

His smile was involuntary and wide. "That's cute. You're a deputy, too, or…?" As he asked, his gaze moved down, no doubt noting she wasn't in uniform.

"PI," she said. Then, "Almost."

He laughed when she added the almost, and she laughed because he had, and dipped her chin low, a pretty pink blush creeping up into her cheeks.

Willow cleared her throat, turning both heads, holding up the coffee that wasn't hers.

"Oh, gosh, sorry." Joshua took his cup back, laid his case on the table and sat down in the chair beside Drew's, which was, after all, the only one available.

On the other side of the table, Abby was grinning from one of them to the other, a twinkle in her eyes.

"All right, Abby, if you can describe the person you saw, Joshua will try to sketch it out. And I've got some paperwork so… Drew will text me when you're done."

Everyone nodded, so she left the room. She didn't want to influence the artist or the witness with so much as a crook of her eyebrow. Not when she so hoped the drawing would show one of the Barker boys. Who the hell else in town would throw a brick through a gigantic window just for the hell of it?

But she was eager, and needed a distraction, so she spent time catching up on paperwork she'd been neglecting until eventually her phone pinged.

Drew: Ready

She headed back to the room, just as Abby Sinclair came out of it. And when she met Willow in the hallway, she elbowed her, tilted her head toward the two still in there, and wiggled her eyebrows up and down.

"Thanks for coming in, Miz Sinclair."

"He did a good job. Seems like a nice young man. Drew's your sister?"

"Cousin," Willow admitted.

Abby nodded knowingly.

"Do you need a ride, or—"

"Drove myself here, can drive myself back They ain't come for my keys yet." And with that, she continued walking in her slightly bent stance, across the station and out through its pebbled glass doors.

Willow watched her out, then went into the interrogation room, where Drew and Joshua were leaning over his notepad, which was on the table. They rose when she came in, and parted to let her see.

She looked at the face and sighed in disappointment. "That's the homeowner," she said.

"No, no," Drew all but whined. "She'd *know* the homeowner, wouldn't she? She's a neighbor."

"Nope. Just in town visitin' her daughter," Willow said. "Man, I was so sure… But no, that's Richard Montrose. I talked to him and his wife the day it happened."

"Dang." Drew seemed more disappointed than Willow was.

The young sketch artist was silent, waiting for someone to tell him he could go. Willow noticed the guy hanging there in limbo, and got over her own let-down. "That's a dang good likeness, though. I knew who it was at a glance. Nice job."

"Thanks."

"Why haven't I seen you around here before?" she asked, her gaze shifting briefly to Drew, who was hanging on every word.

"I'm new. Finishin' up my masters in art. This is a side-gig."

"It's a side-gig at which you excel," Willow said. "This department will be callin' you again. That is, if you're gonna be around."

He nodded, smiling and trying not to look at Drew and looking at her anyway. "Yeah, for a while."

"Good. Stop at the desk, they'll pay you."

He nodded, turned toward the door, and Drew looked a little bit flustered, so Will said, "Show him where it is, Drew."

Nodding fast, Drew walked the young artist out, and when she beamed her killer smile at him, Willow was surprised the guy didn't fall over in a dead faint.

Jeremiah was in town, at the WTD, a roadside diner out-of-towners called retro and locals knew had been that way the whole time. It was shaped like a silver bullet, with three neon tubes—red, green, and yellow—above the front. One neon tube was intact. The other two had sections that flickered and buzzed.

According to Garrett Brand's scrupulous notes in the police file, Vincent de Lorean had a few of his meals there. It was a hole-in-the-wall place, if ever there'd been one. It sat alongside the state highway without any kind of warning, as out of place as a bird in a fish tank, about halfway between the Texas Brand and Quinn proper.

Jeremiah picked up his phone, opened his journal, and tapped *new entry*. "Background info. Willow says the WTD's owner refused to sell when the highway came through and has managed to keep the deed against all the state's efforts. After a while, the powers that be just gave up. So here it sits, right where it's been since the highway was a dirt road." He tapped the app to stop recording and pulled in.

It was lunch time, so he figured he'd grab a sandwich or

something and ask if anyone there might remember his old man from that long ago. But when he went inside, he lost track of his plan, because there was that same family. The kid, Frank, along with his grandparents and the two rowdy little girls.

He glanced outside as he slid onto a stool at the counter, and spotted their car, now that he was looking. It was running, and he wondered why for a moment, then saw the pup. He was standing on his hind legs looking back at him. Then he realized the car was running for a reason—air conditioning for the dog. He looked bigger. A *lot* bigger. That wasn't possible, was it?

Frankie was too busy to even look at him, though. He was bent over a notebook, writing. Homework in August? He didn't think school had even started back up yet.

The little girls didn't seem to recognize him, and the grandparents were too involved in their meals to pay him any mind. There were three other groups of folks in the diner, so he didn't stand out much, nor did he want to. He scanned the place but didn't see any problems. A couple at one table seemed happy and hungry, two older guys sat at another, one with a nasty scar, and a group of seven elderly women were gathered around two tables that had been pushed together. The ladies caught his eye because they all had snow white hair, but their skin tones were every shade of the spectrum, all of them chattering and laughing.

"What can I get 'cha?" asked a young Native man of maybe nineteen. He wore a long, striped polo shirt under a white apron and he stood behind the counter.

"Just a coffee for now." He didn't want to hang around long enough for Frankie's family to recognize him and start a whole thing. He glanced their way as he thought it, and caught Frankie looking at him. He nodded, sent a half smile over, but Jeremiah thought his eyes looked sad. Then he bent to his notebook again.

The server, who's name tag said Charlie, flipped over a coffee cup in front of him, and filled it. It was one of those heavy ceramic cups you only see in diners, off white with a green stipe around the top. The coffee tasted better out of them, for some reason. "Listen, Charlie, I'm trying to find info on my old man. He used to come here a long time ago. Is there anyone—?"

"You want to talk to Marv," Charlie said. "Hang here a sec." He replaced the carafe on its burner, and pushed a swinging door into the kitchen in the rear. After a moment, he returned followed by a woman whose straight posture and strong stride didn't match up with her map-lined face. When she smiled her eyes disappeared amid the wrinkles.

"You're Marv?" he asked, not hiding his surprise.

"Short for Marvella. And you are... Oh, I know who you are. You're Ethan Brand's long-lost brother, Jeremiah Brand."

"Thorne," he said. And at her confused frown, "Jeremiah Thorne is the name my mother gave me."

"Right. Well, what can I do for you, Jeremiah Thorne?"

"Well, first, I wanted to say Willow—uh, that is, Deputy Brand —told me your history here, how you fought the state and won. I respect that."

She waved a dismissive hand. "That was mostly my folks. I was just a young thing."

"Still. I'm here because my father ate here frequently when he was in town, almost thirty years ago."

"And you think I might remember him?" she asked. "From thirty years ago?"

"Twenty-seven to be exact."

"Twenty-seven?" She rolled her eyes at him, shaking her head as she walked the length of the counter to the cooler and helped herself to a bottle of Coke. She was twisting off the cap, still grinning at him when she apparently finished doing math in her head, and piecing together the rumors she'd heard. "Wait, that was when that criminal was here, looking for young Bubba Brand—Ethan, now, I suppose. De Lorean. I'll never forget it. He was in here every day for..." her eyes widened. She took a long pull from her bottle, then slammed it down onto the counter. "That's who your father is?"

"Was," he said. "He died in prison."

"I'd heard that, too." She lowered her head, shaking it slowly. "You and Bubba Brand, you got some baggage. I hope you're sharin' that load. Seems a lot."

"Not so much," he muttered, but she didn't hear. Louder, he said, "Can you tell me what you remember about him?"

She reached her hands over the counter. "Well, what can I say? I was waitin' tables, then, me and three other girls. Business was really hopping. It was our heyday. Mr. De Lorean didn't seem like a criminal to me. He was handsome, charmin', funny, a big tipper, an even bigger flirter. I was half in love with him by the time he stopped showing up, and so were the other gals. We could hardly believe it when we heard what he'd done." She gazed at Jeremiah, and tilted her head. "You have his bone structure. You're *very* handsome."

"Thank you, ma'am. That's…um, do you remember anything else?"

"Only…well, I mean, I don't know her but…he came in here for dinner one night with that pretty young thing from the inn. What was it, the Bluebell, the Blueberry—"

"The Bluebonnet?"

She snapped her fingers and pointed at him. "That's it."

"Do you mean Juanita Lopez?" he asked. "Wasn't she still in high school?"

"Oh, you already know then. I think Juanita was as smitten as the rest of us. Sure looked that way to me."

The bell on the diner door jangled and he turned to see young Frankie coming inside. He hadn't been aware the kid had gone out. But he returned to his table, head down, and stared at his food, which had to be cold by then. The rest of the family was finished.

Jeremiah sipped his coffee. Marvella said, "I'll rack my brain to try and remember any other details," she said. "He drove a fancy black car. I always wondered how it always seemed so shiny when every other vehicle wore a layer of dust. But aside from that..." She shrugged.

"Thanks," he said. "I'll leave my phone number, if that's okay."

"I never say no when I handsome young man offers me his number."

He left a generous tip, because he wasn't about to be shown up by his father and he headed to the Jeep.

He was nearly back to Quinn when a shuffling, snuffling sound from the back seat startled him so much he almost went off the road. And then he did, pulling onto the shoulder and stopping the car.

Twisting around, he looked behind him.

There on the floor, next to a shredded paper bowl that had, no doubt, held food, was Frankie Miller's puppy. And there on the seat, was a little dog bed, a chew toy, and a sheet of paper torn from a notebook.

Dear Jeremiah,

My grandparents say Beans has to go. They're too old to deal with a dog like him and my sisters are always hurting him. Not on purpose. They just get excited, you know? Grandpa was going to take him to the pound, but when I saw you in the diner, I knew just what to do.

You are a good person. I know that because you saved Beans once. Now I need you to save him again. Please don't let me down.

Maybe you can let me know how he's doing. Maybe I can even visit him some time. My address and our phone number are below.

Thank you,

Frankie Miller

Jeremiah reached down to the floor and picked up the pup, who was all head and paws and long skinny legs. He had a brindle pattern coming in, brown with black and gray, an entirely black face, and huge puppy brown eyes, currently looking up at him.

"Beans, huh?"

The pup farted aloud.

"Ah, I see." He leaned back to roll the window down a bit.

The puppy leaned up and licked his face.

CHAPTER SEVEN

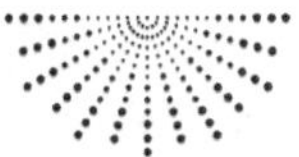

illow and Drew were sharing a basket of french fries from the local dive bar. Willow was in uniform, and feeling guilty as hell for spying on Jeremiah. Of course, she wouldn't be spying on him unless he went back to the Bluebonnet Inn looking for his treasure. In which case, he deserved spying on.

Right?

"Too bad about the sketch this morning." Drew dragged a fry through a puddle of ketchup on the way to her mouth. "You uh… worked with that sketch artist before?"

"Joshua Stone, you mean?"

"Oh, was that his name? I didn't remember."

"You're not s'posed to be interested in men at the moment, according to what you've been saying for the past—"

"Yeah, well, you're not s'posed to be spyin' on your boyfriend, so—"

"He's not my boyfriend."

'Cause you slept with him just the one time." Sarcasm dripped like ice cream in the Sonoran.

Willow shifted her gaze left, shrugged one shoulder, and said, "So far."

Drew burst out laughing and Willow grabbed a French fry. The pile was dwindling. Her text beeped. She looked at it and muttered, "Speak of the devil," and showed Drew the phone.

Hot Gringo: I have a problem.

"You have him listed as *Hot Gringo* in your contacts?"

"His ringtone's that gunfighter riff. You know the one I mean? Wait, I know." She texted Jeremiah, "Call me."

A second later, he did, and her phone played the opening guitar riff of the *Gunfighter Ballad, Melody of the Old West*.

Willow was grinning, but Drew gaped at her, so she stopped grinning and asked, "*What?*"

"You…made him a custom ringtone. On your phone. And named him Hot Gringo."

"And?" Willow asked, awaiting a reply that made sense while the guitar continued playing on her phone.

"Well, go on, answer it, I don't need to hear the whole dang song."

Willow answered the call, irritated that Drew was reading so much into things. She needn't worry, Willow was a grown-arse woman and knew what she was doing.

"Hey," she said toward the phone. "Drew and I are sittin' at The Waterin' Hole. I figured it was easier to talk than text. What's up?"

"I'm not far away. Can I show you?"

Drew widened her eyes. "You should know you're on speaker, there mister *'can I show you?'*" she said, dropping her voice way down low when quoting him.

"I didn't mean…I'm almost there. Meet me in the parkin' lot?"

"I gotta get to work pretty quick anyway," Willow said. "See you soon." She disconnected, then put cash on the table for the fries and the sweet teas they'd drank. Grabbing one last fry, she pushed back her chair. Drew came with her.

"You didn't have to buy," Drew said.

"Well, for now, I'm employed and you're not, Nancy Drew."

She made a face and shuddered. "I'm so glad they didn't name me Nancy."

"Try bein' Deputy Willow," she replied. "Criminals shudder at the name. But only cause they're gigglin'."

Drew laughed, lowering her head to hide it and failing. "Back on topic, Mom pays me and Orrin to help out, and we learn the biz while we're at it. It's a good deal."

Will looked at her. "I should be payin' you, too. But if I did, it would be official, and I can't officially hire you, because then there's a paper trail, and it's not like I'm really investigatin' him anyway—"

"You don't have to pay me," she said. "For *this*, I mean. If I help with real cases, then, yeah. I'll accept a fee. This here is…sister to sister, even though we're only cousins."

"We're way more than cousins." Willow slid a hand over Drew's, then ruined the sappy moment by adding, "*Nancy.*"

They were outside in the parking lot. It was warm, but the days were marginally cooler as September edged in. Jeremiah's copper colored Jeep had just rolled to a stop in a spot a few yards away, so they sauntered over there. And then he opened the driver's door, and—

"Oh my Lord, a puppy!" Drew squeaked as the puppy leaped out and raced toward her. She scooped the little guy right up. His long legs kept sliding down her. He was almost too much for her to hold.

"Is that the one you saved from the river?" Willow asked.

"He *saved* a *puppy*? From the *river*?"

Drew was gone. Charmed by the enemy and his cute companion. Willow was going to need another ally. She faced Jeremiah again. He was standing, and he handed her a sheet of paper with Frankie's note on it.

She read it and her eyes burned. "That's so sad."

"I know. But what can I do?"

"Well, for starters, you have to make sure the kid sees him every weekend, at the bare minimum."

"But—"

"What's his name?" Drew asked.

"Beans."

"Oh, Beanie, Beanie, Beanie," she sang. "What a good boy you are. Yes, you are, Beans, you're a good, good boy!" The pup wriggled with so much joy, Willow didn't know how Drew didn't drop him.

"I didn't plan to...you know, keep him," Jeremiah said.

Drew, Willow, and Beans all looked at him in horror, then Willow showed Drew the note, so she could get the full impact, then held Jeremiah's eyes while she read it, and crossed her arms over her chest.

He said, "Well, I mean, I don't even have a place of my own yet, and when I do—"

"Nobody's fixin' to worry about a dog in the bunkhouse," Willow replied.

"Beans wouldn't even be the first," Drew added, and the dog started wriggling again, so she took him back to the Jeep, and set him on the driver's seat. She closed the door, to keep him in. A parking lot with rigs rolling in and out was no place for a fearless puppy.

He sat behind the wheel as if he were planning to drive, and she loved on him through the rolled down window.

"Are you sure that's the same dog?" Willow asked. "He seems a lot bigger."

"Well, it's been almost a week."

She tilted her head at him. "That's not very long."

"You have to keep him," Drew called back from the Jeep a few yards away. "That little boy's countin' on you. He trusted you with him. You can't betray that."

"I can't?" He looked at Willow.

She shook her head side to side and wondered why he was asking her.

But he sighed as if she had determined his fate. "Well, I guess—"

"Yay!" Drew raised both fists, then quickly resumed petting the pup through window. "Everyone can meet him at the bonfire tomorrow night." Her phone signaled. Drew pulled it out and said, "I need to take this," and wandered a few cars away for privacy.

Willow wondered if it was a certain art major and part-time sketch artist.

Jeremiah said, "So you've seen how my day went. How was yours?"

"Got all pumped up about an eyewitness who saw someone at that house that was vandalized, but it turns out she only saw the owner."

"That's too bad. You seem...bothered by it."

"I called in a sketch artist. That's department resources I spent, and it amounted to nothing. I think I might be the worst cop on the planet."

"You're not. You're a good cop. I found a lead because of you today," he said.

She raised her head and her eyebrows. "You did?"

"Yep. I was at the WTD. My old man ate there frequently according to your uncle's notes, which you kindly got for me. And I talked to the owner, Marvella."

She smiled and said, "Marv's a character, isn't she?" And he nodded, smiling. "Did she remember him?"

"She remembered him bringing Juanita Lopez with him to eat one time. She thought there was something going on between them."

"Juanita was still a teenager," she said. "Was she sure?"

He shrugged. "She seemed pretty sure."

Willow frowned. "Juanita told us she barely exchanged two sentences with him."

"Yeah, she did."

"That's curious."

"I thought so, too," he said. "Maybe we can look into her a little more deeply."

Was he pushing again for her to do a background check? "That would be illegal," she said softly. She stood there facing him, about two feet between them in the parking lot. A dust devil rose like a miniature twister between them. Her heart hurt.

"No," he said quickly. "But maybe you know of some way I could. You know, legally."

Seriously? Was she buying this? Had he really not meant what he'd obviously meant for the second time?

She started talking just to outshout the whirlwind in her mind. It felt like that dust devil had slid right inside her head and grown into a full-blown twister. "You could go to the county seat, run through all public records bearing her name," she said. "Maybe narrow it down by checking the year your father was here, maybe a year before and after. See if you find anything that links them."

"I can do that. Yeah, I can do that."

Her watch signaled her and she glanced down at it to see her alarm. "I gotta go, I'm on duty," she said. "Before I do, do you know if there's another Jeep like yours in town? That same rusty orange color?"

He frowned at her, and she could've sworn an invisible shield slammed down over his eyes, and a gulf opened between them. "Not that I know of. Why?"

"Ah, it's the only other clue to the vandalism. Homeowner said he saw a copper-colored Jeep near the scene."

His posture changed. He drew himself inward, his chin pulled back, and he even leaned away from her.

"So, I'm being accused again?"

"No! I know it wasn't you. I was with you at the time."

"Well, then what the hell is this?" He asked it in a voice that had gone louder.

Drew turned from the Jeep, where she'd returned to puppy-loving, her face an unspoken threat.

Willow held her palm downward to tell her to cool her jets. "What do you mean?" she asked softly. "I wasn't accusing you of anyth—"

"But somebody was. *Somebody* says they saw my Jeep at the scene of a crime. A few days ago *somebody* said they saw me smashing the drug store window. So what's going on?"

"You think it's connected?" Willow asked.

"I think somebody's messing with me."

"It could be a coincidence," she said.

"Or it could be I'm the only ex-con in town." He lowered his head, shaking it slow. "I guess that priceless Brand connection only goes so far."

This had really struck a nerve with him. She felt like she'd discovered his weak spot and regretted being the one to have jabbed it. "I'm real sorry about it, either way, Jeremiah," she said. "I'm fixin' to look into this. If somebody's messin' with you, they're about to regret it."

She couldn't name the emotions that crossed his face. His anger and defensiveness morphed into something else entirely. Surprise or awe. He was lookin' at her like he couldn't quite believe she was for real.

Well, he hadn't been raised to trust the law, she figured.

Her radio crackled again. "I gotta go." She headed toward her car.

He snapped out of his state, and came after her. "Wait! What do I do about the dog?"

"Just love on him and everything'll work out," she called over her shoulder. "Least that's what my dad always told me."

He came closer. She didn't want him to try to kiss her, well, she did. Dang, she *really* did, but not there in front of enough locals to make it common knowledge by sundown. And he had that look in his electric blue eyes.

"You'd best get that dog home," she said. It came out a little raspy. "He can't be cooped up for so long. He's a pup. There'll be accidents."

"Ahh…" He looked worriedly back at his Jeep where Drew and the pup were smooching. Willow got into her SUV.

"Okay, yeah, you're right," he said, facing her again as she closed the door. Which felt rude, so she put the window down and changed the subject.

"How's your credit score?"

"Danged if I know," he said. "Why?"

She shrugged. "You made a good point before about not having a place of your own. Maybe it's time to start lookin'." She reached for her radio mic to report in, giving him an apologetic wave.

He waved back and headed to his Jeep. Drew stepped out of the way, and Jeremiah got in, simultaneously moving the pup to the passenger side. Willow watched him back out into the road and drive away as Drew came across the lot toward her.

She leaned on the open window and said, "Girl, what are you doin'?"

"My best to keep my hands off him," Willow replied.

"Shouldn't be so hard. You heard him say he was deceivin' you."

"And yet I keep thinkin', what better way to find out *how* he's deceivin' me than gettin' a little closer? You know?"

"How do you get closer than sex?"

Willow shrugged. "More sex?"

"You be safe, you hear me? Until you know what he's lyin' about, make his condom wear a condom!"

Willow's shocked laugh sounded like a bark.

But then Drew stopped grinning. "Protect your heart, too, cuz," she said, her voice going softer, her face, serious. "At least you know he has ulterior motives goin' in."

Willow nodded. "Forewarned is forearmed," she said.

"Then again, how bad can he be?" Drew asked. "He *saved* a *puppy*."

"Yeah," Willow said. She looked down the road in the direction he'd gone and breathed the word again. "Yeah."

The pup was lying on the rug near the side door, snoring like a chainsaw. He was perpetually hungry, and hilariously clumsy, even tripping over his long ears sometimes. Smart, too. He'd learned multiple commands today with almost no effort at all.

It was midnight. Willow's shift was over.

He looked at his phone, tipped his head to one side. It hadn't been a very productive night. He'd taken the pup with him back to the former Bluebonnet Inn an hour ago and thrown the main power switch at the electric pole out front. Shut everything down including the old cameras he'd noticed there, if they were still working. He doubted they were, but still.

He'd spent forty-five minutes waving his metal detector, which he'd driven all the way to El Paso to buy, over every inch of that back yard. Aside from some odds and ends—a pair of eyeglass frames with no lenses, some barbed wire, and a handful of roofing nails—he'd found nothing.

He looked at his phone again. It was surprising to him how much he wanted to call Willow.

Then call her, he thought. It was no big deal. He was aching to get her back into his bed. And, yes, he liked her. She was easy to be with. And she'd listened to him today; she'd heard him when he'd said someone might be deliberately accusing him of petty crimes around town.

She was on her way home right now, and within a few minutes would be driving past the turnoff for the Texas Brand, and this very bunkhouse.

He tapped her face on his phone. He'd snapped a pic of her on her horse, Sundance, one day awhile back when they'd all gone riding. Bright smile, cowboy hat, long dark hair flying in the breeze—that was the photo on her contact entry in his phone.

She picked up on the first ring. "Why am I not surprised you're callin' at this particular time of the evenin'?"

"I don't know. Why are you not surprised?" he asked.

She hesitated for a moment before answering. "Because I'm drivin' home, and I'm *not* comin' over there."

"Are you sure?" he asked. "I'm better manscaped than I've ever been in my life."

She laughed softly. Then, "Takin' things for granted, aren't you?"

"Not even a little bit. I'm just…a hopeful guy."

"Right. That's one of the first things I noticed about you. Your optimism."

She laughed at her own joke.

He imagined he could feel her warm breath on his ear. He stayed quiet, so she'd talk some more.

"It's movin' a little fast for me, you know?"

He nodded, though she couldn't see. "'Specially now that I'm a suspect in two local crimes?"

"You aren't a suspect, Gringo. Something's goin' on. I should've seen it myself. Both those crimes were vandalism, just a smashed window, nothin' taken, in either case. I'm on it. I put in a request for the anonymous tip recording about the drugstore. I want to hear it. And I know it wasn't you. I don't want you to think that's got anything to do with…this."

"Okay," he said. And oddly, he believed her. "Could you…maybe tell me what's got you so hesitant, then?"

"Well…I mean, to be straight-up honest about it—"

"Please, yes, be straight-up honest about it."

"Fine. When we're together I can't keep my hands off you," she said.

He felt warmth bloom in the center of his chest, spreading outward. "I really like that about you."

"So maybe," she said, "we could just…talk for a while like this."

A shiver ran up his spine. She was too smart to fool in long conversations. If he had to lie to her about anything, she might see through him. But he couldn't say no, could he? Moreover, he didn't want to say no. "Where are you right now?"

"Drivin' about five miles outta the Bend. You're on my headset, cause I have the windows down."

"That long hair of yours must be whipping in the wind."

"As a matter of fact, it is."

He smiled, grabbed a beer from the fridge and went out the side door to a folding chair by the empty fire pit. The pup scrambled to his huge feet and came trundling along after him.

He could picture Willow plain as day, driving in the dark with her windows down. "You haven't passed the turnoff yet, then." He didn't have to tell her which turnoff he meant. His.

"It'll be a few minutes."

"Okay. So what should we talk about?"

"Hmm," she said. "Tell me something about you that I don't know. Like, uh, what do you want?"

"What do I want?" He took a swig from the beer can. The pup was wandering around, smelling everything he came to. "Right now, I want you to think about takin' that turnoff, showing up here, and crawling into my bed. My brain isn't functioning much beyond all that."

He heard her exhale, imagined her smiling and shaking her head. "What do you want *out of life?*" she asked.

"I just told you."

She laughed aloud that time. He did, too. The pup heard him laughing and came bounding over.

Then he got serious. Willow was trying to get to know him better. He wondered how much of himself he could reveal without scaring her away, and decided a layer of honesty might be a good start.

"I was raised by criminals. People who worked in my old man's organization to one degree or another. I was taught not to share anything with anybody for just about any reason. Being open is…hard for me."

"Honestly, *that* was pretty open. Full disclosure, I read your file."

"How could you not? You're a cop and we're…whatever we are."

"There was a photo of you at your mother's funeral," she said. "It must've been the worst day of your life."

"I never really believed it, you know? That she would have killed herself just as soon as she left me there. But I was a kid; what does a kid know?"

"Why didn't you believe it?"

"Because she told me she'd come back," he said. "She promised. I just kept expecting her to show up saying it was all a mistake."

"Hell," she said. "That must hurt so bad."

"Less when I'm with you. Shoot, I didn't mean to say that." He really hadn't. It had just come out. And it was true; there was something about being with Willow that soothed that wounded part of him. Was it just the presence of a woman in his life? Or was it this woman?

"Hell," she repeated. And then she said, "Hey, Gringo?"

"Yeah, Deputy?"

"I'm takin' the turnoff."

Minutes later, he met her at the door, pulled her right into his arms, and kissed her like he meant it. Beans jumped and barked and pawed at her legs.

"Hey, hey, dude, enough. Down," Jeremiah said, pumping his palm toward the floor.

The pup sat.

"Wait." He held up one finger.

Then he turned his attention back to Willow, "Where were we?"

"You taught him that already?"

"We've had most of the day together. I got him a vet's appointment tomorrow. And best of all, a long-lasting chewy treat for tonight." He kissed her again and the pup whined. Jeremiah grabbed the treat off the counter and tossed it toward Beans. Then he started undressing Willow.

First the shirt, button by button. He pushed it off her shoulders, down her arms, moving her legs with his as he did. He slid the bra straps down her shoulders, kissing her mouth, her neck, her face.

"Slow down, Gringo. I need a shower," she said.

"What a great idea. I'll help."

She peeled his T-shirt up as he shuffled them toward a bathroom. He let go of her long enough for her to pull it up over his head and arms, then resumed kissing her all the way into bathroom and up against the wall.

"The pup?" she asked.

"He's all right," he said, nodding toward the cute little guy, who was gnawing his large bone-shaped treat as if his life depended on it.

He took advantage of her turned head to kiss and nibble her neck.

He wanted her with his entire being, and the power of it shook him a little. He'd never felt anything this strong. He reached one arm sideways to adjust the shower knobs. She undid her pants and let them fall, and he shoved down his jeans and almost tripped into the shower. Their clothes got soaked. They kicked themselves free, and then it was hands and mouths and warm, slick skin, and her legs were around his waist, and the water was rushing over their entwined bodies.

He held onto her like he'd never let go. In that moment, he never wanted to.

For the second time, Willow crept out of the bunkhouse in the wee hours like a thief in the night while Jeremiah lay nude and deeply asleep. She didn't want to leave. She wanted to wrap herself in his arms and stay until morning, but that would risk being seen, and she wasn't ready for all that with the family. She didn't even know what she and Jeremiah were doing.

He hadn't opened up a bit about what he was lying to her about, and damn him for that, because it was starting to feel like things could be good between them.

Drew's little Beetle was parked by her cottage when Willow pulled in at last. She shut off her pickup and got out. The lights were on inside, gleaming through the little paned windows in front. Night bugs were chirping up a lullaby. There wasn't a hint of a breeze, and the night air was warm and dry.

She walked up the little stepping stone sidewalk to the front steps, which were stone and had moss growing in patches. The door was unlocked. She rarely locked up when she left. So she went on in.

Drew was asleep on the little sofa, curled up like a child. Her laptop was on the coffee table, open.

Frowning, Willow closed the front door. Then she knelt at the coffee table and turned the laptop around, jiggling it to life as she did.

There were several video clips on the screen.

"It's surveillance footage from the Bluebonnet house," Drew muttered. She scraped her hand across her face and sat up, blinking sleepily.

"What did we get? I haven't had time to look."

"Nothin'. Just scrub brush and wildlife."

"Really?"

"Really."

"Can you send me that footage?"

"Don't need to. It's on your phone, on the app we installed. Remember, I showed you?" She stretched and yawned.

Willow wondered why Drew had come all the way over here and waited up for her when she could've just sent a text. "Do you want to sleep over?"

"Nah, the folks'd worry. I just needed a quiet place to study where nobody could find me."

"Oh. Cool. Yeah, anytime Drew. My place is your place."

"I know," she said. "Thanks. But I'm headin' out now, cause I'm an early riser, and you need to spend the next several hours asleep." She looked at the clock on the wall as she said it, then lifted her eyebrows. "How was it? With the Gringo?"

Willow opened her arms and fell backwards onto her own sofa. "Unbelievable."

"Yeah?" Drew's smile was bright.

"Yeah. And that's all you're getting. Did you call the art major?"

"He called me," she said. "Asked me out. I told him I'd think about it, because I take these things much more carefully than my older and supposedly wiser cousin."

Willow rolled her eyes. "Go home and let me sleep."

"Night, Will."

"Night."

Drew scooped up her laptop and let herself out. She turned the lock before pulling the door closed behind her.

Willow went to her bedroom, peeled off her clothes and fell into her bed. But every time she started to drift off, she fell into Jeremiah's arms again, holding him, kissing him, moving with him. Eventually, she let the visions sweep her into dreams, and then she slept for a solid eight hours.

When she got up it was nearly noon, and nobody had bothered her. She made a single cup of coffee, stared into the fridge for a minute, and decided to have lunch at the WTD. She found the files Drew had sent on her phone and watched the video of the Bluebonnet Inn's back yard from the night before while she sipped.

The footage flickered. She frowned, stopped, went back, played it again, and watched closer. For sure, it flickered. She played it a third time, watching the counter instead of the footage this time. Sure as all get out, right at the flicker, the counter jumped ahead forty-four minutes! How the hay...?

He'd disabled the camera somehow! Or someone had. He hadn't dug anything up from what she could see on the live feed, the backyard looked undisturbed. But it was too big a coincidence that there was a forty-four-minute gap in the footage just when she'd expected Jeremiah to go out there on his treasure hunt.

He had to be the most frustrating, untrusting, sneaky-ass man on the planet.

She got dressed and walked right past her truck and on to the horses. It smelled so good in the cool of the stable. She went into the tack room to get her saddle and a bridle. The West Texas Diner was close enough to go by horse, and she didn't like going anywhere by vehicle if you could get there by horse. She had time, and Sundance needed the exercise.

She opened the back door of the barn and gave a whistle.

The horses turned her way, but only Sundance came

galloping at her, his mane nut-red in the sun. "What a beauty you are, Sundance. You're a good boy, yes, you are."

He nickered and nuzzled her face. She said, "Come on," and he followed her inside and stood like a perfect gentleman while she slid a blanket and saddle onto his back. She'd taken a halter instead of a bridle—no bit for her boy. He didn't need it.

In no time at all they were riding cross-country, a far shorter distance than going by road. She intended to ask Marvella about her memories of Juanita Lopez and the criminal de Lorean. People often remembered more in the hours and days after an interview, their memories having been stirred up.

God, it was good to think about something besides her and Jeremiah.

She tried not to let her thoughts slide back to the infuriating man and instead focused on the gentle rocking of the animal beneath her, and the breeze in her hair.

They arrived all too soon. She took the rope from her saddle and tied Sundance loosely to a shady spot behind the diner, where some tender looking grasses were growing. A kid came out the back door with a bucket of water, sloshing over both sides.

"That a clean bucket, son? It been washed since anybody drank from it?"

"Great grandma puts boilin' water in after a horse drinks," he said.

"Good man," she said as the boy set the bucket in front of the horse and patted her neck. He was maybe nine, red-headed and freckled in jeans and a T-shirt.

"Thanks, kid." She handed him a couple of singles for his trouble, and headed around front and inside.

The interior of the diner was long and narrow, with red vinyl stools lined up in front of a counter and booths along the front wall, with a narrow walking space in between. The kitchen was even narrower behind the counter, with an open pass-thru in between.

She'd no sooner ordered a full-on breakfast, which they served there all day, when a loud buzzing sound drew her gaze around just in time to glimpse one of those crotch-rocket motorcycles fly past, bike and rider entirely in black. In a heartbeat, the diner's front window exploded inward. People screamed and ducked and a brick landed on the floor.

Willow dove off her stool, running for the door, shouting, "Is everyone all right?" And as they nodded, she raced outside and around back to Sundance, untying his lead on the way. She jumped into the saddle, and squeezed his sides, "Let's go, boy! Giddyap!"

Sundance loved to *giddyap*.

He was fast, one of the fastest on the ranch. Could've been a racehorse, but Willow wouldn't have it. She steered Sundance off at a sharp bend, short-cutting cross country, catching up enough to see the biker. As she rode, she grabbed her phone and tapped the mic symbol to record a message to dispatch. "Unit three, I'm in pursuit of a motorcycle, no plates—"

She came to another big bend in the road, and again, steered Sundance off the road. They jumped a fence, all but flying. Willow couldn't help but thrill to the ride. The wind in her ears, her hair flying like Sundance's mane. They came to the end of the shortcut and onto the road again—and there was the bike right in front of them, skidding around to face them and revving, then shooting forward.

Sundance reared and tried to pivot at the same time, and then he went over backwards, right on top of her.

CHAPTER EIGHT

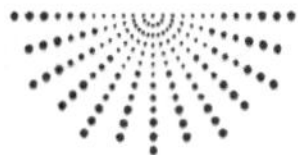

Jeremiah was on his way to the site of his father's showdown with the Brands, a canyon at the far western part of the ranch. His old man might have had time to hide something there when he'd been waiting to ambush Garrett Brand and his brothers and his kid sister, Jessi, who was scarier than all of 'em.

It had been a stupid mistake to take on a family like the Brands out of vengeance. But they had his son, and de Lorean wanted Ethan back. Jeremiah supposed that would've been enough to make his old man take stupid chances.

Imagine him murdering Ethan's mother and then thinking he ought to be the one to raise him. Hell, he almost wished *he'd* been rescued by a family like the Brands. Maybe he'd have turned out to be decent, like his brother.

He'd pulled the Jeep over alongside a stretch of pavement and looked at the map unfolded on the seat. He'd resorted to the map when the GPS had refused to locate the canyon. Thompson's Gorge, according to Garrett Brand's notes. It was apparently several miles west and there didn't appear to be a road that led out there. He had no idea if it was drivable. His Jeep was not an off-roading model. Mud-bogging had never appealed.

He looked off to the left, and saw badlands and desert, boulders and drifts, and he knew plain and simple his Jeep wasn't equal to the terrain. He was going to need an ATV.

The radio crackled, then he heard a dispatcher's voice. "A deputy on horseback is in pursuit of a suspect on a motorcycle who just vandalized the WTD. She's gone silent, we can't raise her.

A female deputy on horseback? Willow?

He jammed the Jeep into gear, pulled a U-turn in the road, stomped it, and didn't let off the gas until he got onto the state highway seventeen minutes later, he skidded to a halt on the shoulder amid three cop cars and an ambulance, dove out of his Jeep and ran.

He stopped when he caught sight of Willow, lying on her back on the ground. Her horse stood nearby. Someone came running up behind him. Ethan. His red pickup was sideways in the road behind him; its driver's door open wide. The EMTs closed ranks around her there on the ground, most of them kneeling, some standing.

Jeremiah couldn't see Willow. Ethan was swearing and pushing his way forward, so he stayed close, riding his brother's wake, but then Garrett stepped in front of them, hands to their shoulders. "You have to stay back, boys. Let 'em have some room."

"What happened?" Jeremiah croaked.

"Anonymous caller said the horse spooked, reared up so bad he flipped backwards and landed on top of her. Added 'it wasn't on purpose.'" He looked over where Sundance was standing. Another deputy had him by his halter. The horse kept picking up one foreleg.

Jeremiah edged past Garrett while the sheriff was focused on keeping his son out of the paramedics' way. A minute later, Ethan did, too. They strode up behind the EMTs where they could see

Willow. She had a neck brace on, and a backboard underneath her. They were fastening straps to hold her in place. Her eyes were closed and she wasn't moving.

Jeremiah swore under his breath, pushed a hand through his hair, front to back, and swore some more. He saw blood on the pavement and something dropped out of his stomach. He didn't realize he'd dropped with it, right to his damn knees.

They hefted the backboard and carried her toward the ambulance with its rear doors open, then placed the backboard and Willow onto a waiting gurney.

Jeremiah got up off his knees, followed them, and realized others were doing the same. Orrin and Drew had shown up, maybe getting the news the same way he had. With all their sleuthing, they probably had a police scanner.

A big black pickup with the Skydancer Ranch logo on the side sped toward them. It skidded to a halt in the road and Willow's parents, Wes and Taylor, got out and came running, leaving the truck's doors open behind them.

"Just give us enough room to work," said a young medic who was pulling Willow's eyelids up and shining a light into them.

Drew Brand shot him a look, and said, "It's you. You're an EMT, too?"

The young man glanced at her and recognition flashed in his eyes. They clearly knew each other. "Among other things," he said.

He put the light away and looked at the medic on the other side of Willow from him, who was removing a cuff from her arm. "One-fifteen over seventy-two."

The young medic said, "Her vitals are strong. Looks like she hit her head pretty good. We need to get her to El Paso. You can meet us there."

"Can I—" Jeremiah began, then stopped himself before he could complete the thought. *Can I ride with her?*

Everyone was looking at him oddly as they closed the doors.

He didn't bother trying to tack a lame ending onto the sentence. Let them make whatever they wanted out of it.

He strode back toward his Jeep.

His brother Ethan's hand fell heavy on his shoulder. He knew without looking who it was but stopped walking. Everyone else was heading for their vehicles, too. As they passed, Willow's father sent him a long, hard look. He was an impressive man with the sculpted face and piercing brown eyes of his Comanche ancestors and silver white hairs interspersing the black. Jeremiah felt as if Wes Brand moved past him in slow motion, that steely gaze penetrating his very soul. So he shifted his eyes away from it, and they fell on Willow's mom, an older version of her daughter. She gave him the very slightest nod. There was encouragement in her eyes. "See you at the hospital, Jeremiah," she said.

Her husband shot her a look, and she slid her hand into his and hurried toward their black stallion of a pickup truck.

Sheriff Garrett was leaning into his SUV, speaking into the radio mic. His brother-in-law and chief deputy, Lash, was leading the team around the bit of road where the accident had happened, directing the deputy who was taking photos of twisty skid marks on the pavement.

Orrin and Drew were heading his way, on their way to the little white EV they'd driven there.

Drew said, "You're coming to the hospital, right?"

Orrin sent his sister a frown.

Jeremiah just nodded, turned, and went to his Jeep. He got behind the wheel, and realized Beans was home alone. He'd intended to pick the pup up once he'd figured out how he was reaching the site.

He took out his phone, and called the landline number Frankie had given him. A woman answered, and he said, "Hey, Mrs. Miller? This is Jeremiah Thorne, I have the dog."

"It's Mrs. Delmar," she said. "What can I do for you, Mr. Thorne? We can't take Beans back, if that's what—"

"No, uh, I need a dog sitter for a few hours tonight. I thought if Frankie wanted to—"

"Oh, thank goodness. He's been heartbroken. Frankie! Frankie!"

Thundering footsteps and his grandmother's muffled voice preceded Frankie's excited, "Jeremiah? You need me to watch Beans?"

"Yeah. Listen, kid, can you get someone drive you over to the bunkhouse? I don't like you riding that far on your bike."

"Sure, Grandma will take me."

"The key's under the old milk can that sits by the bunkhouse door," Jeremiah said. "Have your grandmother help you unlock it, in case you have trouble. I'll run you home after I get back, but it might be late."

"That's okay, no school yet."

"I'll pay you for your time, kid. I appreciate it."

"You're welcome. Grandma's getting her keys. See you later, Jeremiah."

"See you later, Frankie."

As he disconnected, his heart was slightly lighter. He'd made Frankie happy. That was worth something. The kid and his dog were like a couple points of light along a dark stretch of highway.

He started up the Jeep and pointed it toward El Paso, got about ten miles, but then he couldn't keep going. Images of Willow lying so still, of the blood on the ground he was pretty sure had come from her head, wouldn't let up. What if he got there too late? What if she…?

Something welled up in his chest and his eyes were watering so much he couldn't see. He had to pull over. So he did, along the shoulder. Then he gripped the steering wheel in one hand and pressed his fingers to his eyes but even then he kept seeing the blood shining in her dark hair.

His stupid nose was running.

He opened the glove compartment, and his father's

journal fell out. The whole reason he'd come here was in that journal. Freaking stupid quest, stupid gold. He opened it to the page he'd marked, tore it out and crumbled it in his fist.

Knuckles rapped on his window, startling him bad. He shoved the crumpled page into his pocket and looked up.

His brother stood there with his angel-blonde bride Lily beside him. She was frowning so hard her eyebrows met.

Jeremiah put his window down. Ethan looked at him and his eyes widened a little bit. Then frowning again, he said, "So it's like that, is it?"

"I don't know what you're talking about, bro. I'm having an allergy attack." He glanced at Lily. "Don't suppose you have a Benadryl on you?"

"Fresh out," she said. And she tilted her head to one side and searched his eyes. "You okay?"

Of all the Brands, only Lily would ask a villain like him if he was okay. Then again, she was only a Brand by marriage.

His throat knotted up so hard he couldn't talk, so he nodded instead. Then he grabbed the water bottle in his console and took a drink. It was piss-warm. He said, "We should get going. Make sure she's okay."

"So why'd you stop then?" Lily asked.

"Told you. Allergy attack. I think it's easing up."

Lily's face was soft. "You can ride with us, get the Jeep later, if—"

"He's got it, hon," Ethan said, like he knew Jeremiah needed to be alone. "You've got it, yeah, bro?"

"Yeah, I got it. Thanks."

When Willow opened her eyes, her mom was sitting beside her

bed, holding her hand, gazing at her face and smiling. "There you are, my girl. There you are."

Tears pooled in her brown eyes and spilled over, down her cheeks.

She realized her dad had been standing with his back toward her, gazing out a window, but he turned fast when her mother spoke, and came to the other side of her bed, crouching low and clasping her free hand. "Willow," he said. "My Willow." His hand came to her face, but she pulled her eyes from his to look at her surroundings. Hospital room. What the hay had happened?

"It was him, wasn't it?" her dad asked in the low tones that were always a warning someone was in trouble, generally someone who'd wronged another Brand. It went deeper when the harmed party was his only child.

"What was who?" she croaked, then put a hand to her throat, pulling it free of her dad's to do so and noticing the IV lines piercing her forearm. "What happened?"

"What do you remember, Willow?" Taylor asked. She sent her husband a stern and quelling look, then offered Willow water from a cup with a bendy straw.

She drank, and when her mom pulled the cup away, she grabbed it from her, and drank again.

"Careful. Maybe get a nurse, hon?" she said to Wes.

"No, wait," Willow said. Her voice was still weird, weak and scratchy. "What did you mean, it was him?"

Her dad looked at her mom, and she nodded.

"You were on Sundance, in pursuit of a suspect on a motorcycle. Marks in the pavement suggest the biker spun around and went at you, scaring the horse into—"

"Is Sundance okay?"

"He's okay, baby," her mother said. "A little road rash, but he's fine."

She blinked, frowning away the clouds over her brain. "Yeah. The guy on the bike threw a brick through the window at the

WTD. I think it's the same person who threw a brick through the Montrose's window, and the pharmacy window.

Her dad's face froze for a moment, then softened into abject relief as he shifted his gaze to her mom's.

Her mom was smiling. "She's okay," she said. "She's okay."

He came around the bed and wrapped her in his arms, and they just clung for a moment. That was when Willow realized there'd been some question as to whether she *would be* okay. She looked around the room a little bit more, noticing things she hadn't. Cards and letters were tacked to the wall beyond the foot of her hospital bed, filling the cork board there. Right beside it was a white board with the name of her nurse and the date.

She blinked and looked again. "I've been here two days? Two days?"

"You've been unconscious, honey," her mother said. "Go get the doctor, Wes."

"Who caused the accident, baby?" her father asked. "Was it Jeremiah?"

"*Jeremiah*? Why on earth would you think—no. It wasn't him. Like I said, it was the motorcycle I was chasing. They spun around and charged us. I think it was deliberate."

Her father closed his eyes and sighed.

Her mother said, "I told you."

"Why would you think it was Jeremiah, Dad? It's not like you to judge someone for their past."

Shaking his head, her father muttered something about getting a doctor and left the room. So Willow turned to her mother. "Why did he think that?"

"Well…" Taylor titled her head, her eyes searching for words. "You've said his name. A couple of times."

"Jeremiah's name?"

"Not exactly. Gringo, is what you said." Then she repeated, "A couple of times."

"You said that twice. How many times, Mom?"

"Seven...when anyone was around to hear you." She smiled slowly. "I think there's a lot of good in him. He's been here about as much as he could be without bein' obvious." She shrugged. "It was obvious to me, anyway."

"What was obvious to you anyway?"

"He cares about you. In case you needed that verified, I can testify," she said, holding up her right hand. Then she leaned closer. "Chelsea said that Maria said that Ethan and Lily found him pulled off the road on their way to the hospital that day. He was leaned over the steering wheel, and it looked like he'd been cryin'. His eyes were all red, and puffy."

"Sounds more like he'd been drinkin'. Did they smell his breath for tequila?"

"*Willow...*" The tone had been ever so slightly scolding, but her mom didn't finish the thought. Instead she stroked her hair back off her face with her soft, cool, strong hand and said, "You don't need to think about any of that right now. All you need to focus on is recovering."

"Yeah." But she was focused on the Gringo, and given how the Brand family grapevine worked, she was sure everyone knew it.

Jeremiah waited until the last Brand had gone home, which they only did when forced by staff at the end of visiting hours.

But it was a small-town hospital with a skeleton staff, and it was easy to bribe a nurse to let him slip in late. She'd seen him with the family over the two days they'd been waiting for Willow to wake up. It had been a scary time. Nobody knew if she'd wake up at all, or how she'd be when she did.

So he stayed, and he charmed a nurse and brought her a signed copy of his brother's newest CD. And that's why he was by

Willow's bedside at ten-fifteen p.m. when she opened her beautiful eyes and looked into his.

Her smile was immediate and radiant, but she squelched it like pinching out a candle and shifted her gaze to the wall clock. "How did you get in?"

"Bribed a nurse. That's off the record, Deputy." He gazed at her face, into her eyes. They were clear, if tired. "You're okay, then?"

"Looks like. They been runnin' tests on me all day. If there was bad to find, they'd've found it. That's what I'm tellin' myself, anyway."

"I had to see you, Willow, and I figured you'd prefer I do it out of view of the whole dang clan."

"Yeah, well, they're already speculatin' about us. That cat might be well and truly out of the bag."

"How do you want to handle that?" he asked. He moved his chair closer to her bedside, then reached for her hand.

She looked at his but didn't take it. "I don't know. I've been in la-la land for two days. You gotta give me a minute."

He smiled at her. "I'm sorry."

"It's okay. We have to address it. Do we pretend nothin's goin' on between us or do we pretend we're in a relationship?"

"*Pretend* we're in a relationship?" He repeated her words like an idiot.

"Well, the third option is to admit we're having casual, meaningless sex and I'm not feelin' great about sharin' that with the fam, you know?"

She sat up in the bed, swung her legs out. "I want to get out of here. Right now, I want to go. Will you drive me home?"

"Do you think you should?"

"Yeah."

"How will we explain—"

"Oh, Mom and Dad are already onto us, believe me. Apparently, I said 'Gringo' a few times when I briefly surfaced."

He winced as she held a wadded paper towel to her arm and pulled out the IV. Blood welled, but she pressed it hard and held.

Then he blinked at her as her words made their way to his brain. "You called for me?"

She nodded and her eyes dared him to use that fact to contradict her "casual and meaningless" statement.

He didn't, but he thought it meant something. It meant something that he'd been sick at the thought of her being hurt, bereft at the thought of her dying. And he thought it meant something that she'd said his nickname from the borderline of coma.

But she was right. This was no time to talk about those things. He wasn't sure what they meant himself, and *he* hadn't spent the last forty-eight hours unconscious.

She'd said his name, though.

He stared at her, sitting there on the edge of her bed with her bronze legs sticking out from her hospital gown in ugly tan socks with rubber treads on her feet. She wasn't looking back. She pulled the paper towel away from her arm, and it didn't bleed again. "Look around for a band-aid, will you? And get me my clothes?"

He started to turn away just as she slid off the bed and onto the floor. Her knees gave out as soon as her butt rose from the bed. He lunged and caught her under her arms.

She gripped his shoulders, got her footing, then looked up at him a bit sheepishly. They were so close he could feel her body heat.

"I guess my muscles weren't ready for use."

"Not after two days napping." He started to ease her onto the bed.

"No, no. Help me get upright."

So he did that instead, though he didn't think it was a very good idea. He held her as she straightened her legs, then gradually let her bear more of her own weight until she nodded, and said, "Okay, all good. Let go."

He let go, but kept his hands close.

Willow stepped from one foot to the other, bent her knees and straightened them. "Okay, I'm weak as hell but I'm good to go. I'm not even wasting the time to get dressed. Come on, Gringo, take me to your chariot."

There was a lot of objecting and scolding by staff as the two of them walked toward the elevator. He had her clothes in a plastic bag in one hand, and his arm around her, holding her to his side as they crossed in front of the nurses' desk. Someone shoved a clipboard into her face.

"At least sign this so we're not liable."

Willow took the pen and scrawled something illegible. The clipboard moved away, and the elevator doors opened.

A few minutes later, she was in the passenger side of his Jeep.

The top was down, and as soon as they hit the highway back toward Quinn, she peeled the band from her hair and shook it loose so it could blow freely. He could hardly keep his eyes off her to drive.

"Where to?" he asked.

"My place, but we're fixin' to take the back way in and park behind my cottage, so my parents don't lose their minds."

He didn't really want to get on the wrong side of her very huge family with its multitude of muscly, over-protective males, much less on the wrong side of his newfound half-brother. But he couldn't say no to her, so there was no point trying.

"You sure you're okay to be out of the hospital?" he asked.

"My head barely hurts." He thought that was a lie. "I feel fine. Weak, a little dizzy, but that'll pass."

"You probably ought to have some PT to get your strength and balance back," he said.

"What do you know about it?"

He shrugged. "Got the hell kicked outta me in prison. Had six weeks of PT after I healed up. On the outside, it would've been triple that, but that's the system."

She was looking at him, her head tilted, but he opted not to look back just then and kept his eyes on the road instead.

"How bad were you hurt?" she asked after a longer than normal stretch of quiet.

His gaze shifted her way without his permission. Her brown eyes were huge, round, and full of feeling. He focused on the road again. "Busted ribs, shin, nose, but the main thing was the pelvic bone. It was just a hairline fracture, but it was painful as hell to walk again after that. The PT forced me to do it anyway."

"What the *hell*, Gringo? What did they hit you with?"

He flashed back to seven men around him, pounding and kicking him while he curled around himself on the floor to protect his vital bits. Fighting back would've just prolonged his beating. He liked to think he was pretty tough, but seven-on-one was hopeless, even for him.

Her hand curled around his shoulder. He said, "I don't know. I prefer not to talk about it. You're the one injured now. Let's focus on that."

"Okay," she said. Then she yawned and settled more comfortably into her seat, leaning her head to one side, closing her eyes.

A little shiver went up his spine. "Willow?"

No reply.

"Hey, Willow." He clasped her shoulder, shook gently.

She opened her eyes, smiled slightly. "Just nappin'. Not passin' out."

"You sure?" But her eyes were already closed again.

Okay, so she was napping, not unconscious. But she'd left the hospital against medical advice, and he was terrified that her nap was taking her right back into trouble.

He needed help. It was the first time in his life he'd ever believed those three words to be true. He pulled the Jeep over, and she didn't wake. Her hair hung over her left cheek, and he got stuck on the shape of her face for a moment. God, she was beautiful.

Giving himself a mental snap-out-of-it slap, he took her phone from the console. She'd plugged it in as soon as she'd got into his Jeep, and it was still attached to power by its umbilical cord.

He tapped to unlock it, then said, "Hey, Willow? Open your eyes for me, will ya?"

She did, with a goofy smile. "Can't you let a gal sleep?"

He held the phone in front of her face. Her goofy smile became a frown. "What'cha doin'?"

"Letting your family know I'm taking you home. And asking Ethan to take my dog-sitter home."

"Why you need my phone for that?"

"I'm not on the family text chain," he said. "Though I've heard tell of its legendary power." He glanced at her, read her face, realized she didn't trust him as far as she could throw him.

Interesting.

"Here, you can watch me if you can keep your eyes open."

He opened her texts.

She snatched the phone from him, and tapped the screen herself, speaking her message aloud as she did. "Signed myself out. Gringo drivin' me to the cottage. Have someone take his dog-sitter home. I'm goin' to sleep so don't pester me 'til tomorrow." The phone whooshed. She locked the screen and tossed it back into the phone-shaped depression in the console between the front seats. "There." And she closed her eyes again.

The replies were pinging, but she was ignoring them, so he notched her volume down. She didn't notice. Seemed she was really sleepy. And he had no idea if that was normal or a sign of trouble.

When he pulled into the driveway of Skydancer Ranch and veered left past the main house toward her little cottage, he drove as slowly as possible, so she wouldn't bang her poor abused head on the window.

Her cottage door opened and her parents came through. Her

father headed for the passenger side of the Jeep, and Jeremiah unlocked the door. Wes opened it and scooped Willow into his arms.

She smacked his shoulders, though, and said, "Put me down, Dad, I'm fine. You're bein' a drama queen."

He ignored her, still holding her as he strode toward the house with Taylor keeping pace close beside her, searching her daughter's face, worried.

"My phone!" Willow called.

"I'll bring it." Jeremiah unplugged the phone from his dash and got out of the Jeep, closing his door, then moving around to close hers. Then he headed into the house. That door hadn't been left open.

He went in anyway. At least they hadn't locked it.

Wes Brand would have carried his daughter straight through to the bedroom, Jeremiah thought, but she demanded to be lowered to the sofa. "I'm good, I told you, I'm fine."

Headlights came through the windows as the troops arrived. Man, this family was a lot.

Willow closed her eyes, and muttered a cuss word under her breath.

CHAPTER NINE

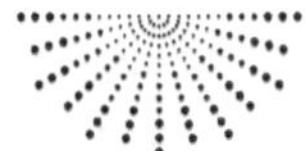

$\mathcal{H}$er family crowded the Gringo right out of her little place, but she never saw headlights through the front windows or heard his Jeep leave. Maybe he was hanging outside where it was less…Brand-y.

"You should stay down at the house where I can take care of you," her mom said. She laid a blanket over Willow where she sat on the sofa, even though it was still eighty degrees outside.

"No freakin' way, you guys aren't going to miss your big trip for me," Willow said. "Mom, that would make me feel terrible. I'm fine. And…Lily's an RN, and Gringo knows about PT, and…" She pressed a hand to her head. "Honest to goodness, I just need some rest and quiet."

Taylor sent a look toward Lily, her cousin Ethan's pretty wife. Ethan had gone outside, she realized.

"I thought you quit being a nurse," she said.

Lily did not take offense, though she probably should have. "One doesn't just quit being a nurse. Besides, I've been taking on per diem shifts at the ER when they're short-handed," she said. "Keeps me from gettin' rusty."

Willow knew Lily's confidence in her nursing skills had been restored after she'd saved Uncle Garrett's life last summer. She liked seeing it in her cousin-in-law.

"Honestly," Lily said, "all they'd be doing at this point is watching her and keeping track of her vitals. They've already run all the tests they could think of, and they all looked good. As long as there are no complications, she's probably right. All she needs is rest and, you know, *quiet.*"

Wes Brand took the hint. "Okay, I got you."

Garrett said, "Willow, anything you need—"

"You too, Taylor," Chelsea added. The others echoed their sentiments as the Elder Brands headed outside, no doubt to begin an emergency family meeting. Again, no headlights told her no one was leaving, so no doubt about it.

And the Gringo was out there, ripe for the questioning. The poor guy.

Her cousins didn't look like they were in any hurry to leave. Orrin, and Baxter were sitting on opposite sides of the edge of the hearthstone in front of the fireplace she hardly ever used, a pair of blue-eyed blonds. Between them, standing, was Trevor with his dark curls and swarthy skin. People often mistook him for her brother, but his coloring was from Spanish ancestry, not Comanche like hers. He had his hands in his pockets, and sent her a sorry smile when he caught her looking at him. Drew had dropped onto the sofa beside her. Maria and cousin-in-law-Lily took the easy chair and the rocker respectively, Maria's hubs, Harrison, stood behind her with his hands on her shoulders. Ethan was outside with the seniors, probably asking Jeremiah to explain what the hay he'd been doing at the hospital after visiting hours.

Willow glanced at Lily's belly, and said, "Dear Lord, your baby bump is bigger! Are you sure I was only out for two days?"

Lily ran a hand over her belly. "Our kid seems to be in a growth spurt."

Willow counted backwards, sighed and shook her head, realizing the window-smashing bandit was probably long gone.

She *sucked* at being a peace officer.

"Are you hungry? Can we fix you something?" Drew asked. And when Willow scowled, her youngest cousin beamed at her, "You might as well enjoy bein' waited on while you recover, right?"

She bit back her objection, relaxed deeper into the sofa, and said, "I could eat."

Drew headed to the kitchen, apparently happy to have a mission.

Lily got up. She had a little bag in one hand. "You care if I check your vitals, Will?"

"I do, yeah. I feel fine."

"Well, I can check them here, or they can check them back at the hospital where we'll be taking you."

"Yup," said Baxter from his fireplace seat. His dirty blond mane needed a trim. He wore khakis and loafers instead of jeans and boots like the others, and round, silver wire-rimmed glasses. "And there's too many of us to fight. Seven to one."

That made her think of Jeremiah, being so badly beaten in prison by other men. It made her stomach clench.

She shook the image away because Lily was taking out a blood pressure thingie.

"Fine," she said, and held out an arm.

While she pumped the device, Lily said, "Jeremiah drove you home, huh?"

"Yep."

Lily let the air out of the thing and said some numbers and nodded. "A little high, but probably because we're all up in your business. I know you don't like that."

"It comes with the family, though," Drew called from the kitchen. "Did you call him for a ride, or—"

"No! Why would I call him? He just happened to be there."

"At the hospital," Maria said. "After visiting hours."

"After we all went home," Drew added.

"*Guys.*" Lily popped a digital thermometer into Willow's mouth, preventing her from having to answer. But it didn't matter. The gang were quiet, waiting, every one of them trying to read her face.

She rolled her eyes. The device beeped and Lily removed it. "Perfect. You feelin' any dizziness?"

"No." Yes, she did.

"Pain?"

"Yes, you *all* are a pain." And so was her head.

Lily just arched her eyebrows a little higher, and she capitulated. "Mild headache and general ouchies."

"Where?"

"Kind of all over."

Lily said, "You can have ibuprofen."

"If I need it."

She nodded and put her things back into her bag.

"So?" Maria asked. "What do you think, Lil?"

"Someone should talk to her neurologist and provider. I think they'll say that as long as someone's watching over her for the next couple of days, who'll notice and bring her in if there's any change, she'll probably be fine at home."

"I'll talk to them myself. Or make my mother do it," Willow said. "And I don't need anyone watching me."

"Too bad," Lily said.

Willow started to panic. She didn't want cousins moving in, and racked her brain to think of how to prevent it. "Lily, you can't sleep on the sofa pregnant. It would be bad for the baby. Drew, you have those PI classes starting up, and Orrin has work. Ethan has to run the honky tonk, Maria has the vet clinic, and Harrison's got a project. Trevor, you can't let your ESL kids down. They count on those classes."

She swept her gaze over her cousins. "I, on the other hand, am fine."

Lily shook her head. "Maybe one of the elders, or—"

"No. No, I'm not havin' it. There's nobody in this family with the free time to babysit me."

The door opened and Jeremiah walked in.

Everyone looked at him. Willow shrugged and went for broke. "Fine. He can do it."

Jeremiah had gone outside to get away from the probing, curious looks being sent his way by every Brand crammed into Willow's tiny cottage. He had not expected them to follow him out.

Ethan came first. He'd been expecting that. And his brother didn't waste any time before launching the interrogation.

"So how did it happen that you were the one drivin' her home?"

"I was the only one there when she decided to leave."

Ethan waited for more. Jeremiah didn't offer it. Eventually, Ethan sighed, and said, "You shouldn't have let her do that. Sign herself out like that."

"And how, exactly, should I have stopped her?"

Ethan looked at him, shrugged, then narrowed his eyes. "I knew somethin' was brewin' between you two. Just how far have things gone?"

That was when the flood of elders came pouring out of the cottage. Jeremiah was not up to the third degree, but they were all discussing Willow, her accident, her health, her stubbornness, which her mother said she'd got from her dad, and most of all, whether she should be out of the hospital.

As if they had anything to say about it. How well did these folk know their niece, anyway? Jeremiah didn't think anybody could force Willow Stands Alone Brand to do anything she didn't want to do.

Ethan joined the family throng, and as soon as his attention was distracted, Jeremiah wandered into a shadowy part of the little yard, near a short, broad tree with plants growing under its sheltering limbs. The flowers that were usually there were all closed up for the night.

He lingered there for a minute, looking at the stars. Willow wouldn't be much help getting inside info on his old man, now that she was laid up. She wouldn't be back at work for a little while. No access to anything he needed.

He saw Ethan notice his absence and start looking for him, so he decided it was time to go home. Beans would be lonesome by now. But he ought to let Willow know he was leaving. He didn't want to just disappear. So he headed back inside, and as soon as he opened the door, Willow met his eyes and said, "He can do it!"

"I can do what?" he asked. And then he realized every set of eyes in the place was on him.

Behind him, Ethan stepped inside, looking around in a what's going on sort of way, and Willow said, "Will you do it, Jeremiah? Spend the next coupl'a days or so watchin' me in case I die?"

He grinned at her joke, "Yeah, sure, I'll even prop my eyes open with toothpicks and watch you sleep. He-heh…heh." Nobody was laughing.

Drew, Maria, and Lily exchanged laden looks, and then the redhead said, "I think it's the perfect solution. Will won't feel guilty for making one of us change our plans—which would be fine with any of us, by the way. And you don't really have anything goin' on, do you, Gringo?"

He sought an answer. He had a lot going on, hunting for his father's hidden treasure mostly, but it wasn't like he could tell them that.

And then he found a reason. Beans! Already pulling his weight. "I'd have to bring my dog—"

"Ohmygod, Beans? Yes, bring Beans," Willow said, and realized it was the first time she'd smiled since being carried through her own front door.

He looked around at all those sets of eyes, and everyone with different but similar thoughts going on behind them. What was up with him and their cousin? Was she safe with an ex-con, even if he was sort of related?

Did they trust him with their girl?

But it was Trevor who spoke, and said, "I didn't even know you had a dog."

"Puppy," Willow said. She leaned forward on the sofa. "Some kids threw it in the creek. Jeremiah went in after him."

"I'm really just fostering him for Frankie, his rightful owner," he said. "Sooner or later circumstances will change, and he can have his buddy back."

"He's so cute, Trev," Willow said. "He has giant feet and a giant head and a gangly body. He's about so high." She held out her hand.

Jeremiah reached out to take her wrist and raised her hand a couple inches higher, and he let his fingers brush her skin as he took them away.

She looked at him, then widened her eyes. "He's grown that much?"

"Vet says it's normal."

"Now I really want you to come."

"You didn't *really* want me to before?"

"I was just tryin' to set some boundaries with my family." She broke eye contact with him, and sent an innocent blink-blink their way.

For his part, Jeremiah had forgotten they were there.

She said, "Go pack up a few things for you and the pup and then come back." Then in a stage-whisper, "They aren't fixin' to leave me alone until you do."

He lowered his head. "Okay. Okay, sure. I'll go right now."

He turned to head out the door only to find his half-brother, Ethan, holding it open for him. "I'll come along. Help you pack," he said.

Willow woke to find Jeremiah sleeping beside the impossibly bigger dog in front of the fireplace on the dog bed on the floor, because she had fallen asleep on the sofa while he'd taken Beans for a midnight stroll. Lily had hung around until Jeremiah and Ethan's return, then she and Ethan had wished her well and headed home themselves around midnight.

She sat up slowly, one hand on her head like holding onto it would prevent it from spinning or throbbing. But neither of those things happened, so as she sat upright, she lowered the hand. Then she figured she'd try standing up.

Paws pounded and Beans jumped, hit her with his front paws, and set her right back down again.

"Hey, hey, down boy!" Jeremiah, probably roused by the floor vibrating beneath him when his pup galloped across it, grabbed the pup and set him down and told him no. The pup, she thought, had no idea what he was saying, but adored him all the same.

"How did he grow that much?"

"He's an English mastiff. Vet says he could hit two hundred pounds in his first year. Then the second year, he'll fill out."

"Maybe he should live in the stable," she said, "with his own kind."

"I never would've known when I pulled him out of the creek."

She smiled, reminded that he'd done that. "He's doubled since then," she said.

"So Lily's coming over later to show me how to use the blood pressure thingie," he said. "She left it. And the thermometer and a thing that clips on your fingertip to measure oxygen. Man, your family."

"I know." She tried standing upright again. The pup tensed, and Jeremiah said, "Wait," and held his hand out flat palmed over the dog.

Beans settled, but in jittery, wiggly, I-can-hardly-stand-to-sit-still way.

Willow made her way to the kitchen. "I don't know about you, but I'm starving."

"That's good, because I'm cooking," he said.

"Even better, because I need a shower." She changed direction mid-step. He had the dog by his side, petting him to keep him calm.

"Do you think you can manage that alone?" he asked.

"Yeah, I think so."

"Dang."

She rolled her eyes at him but blushed, too, as she left him.

She took the most careful morning shower ever. It turned out, every turn or twist or change of head position could incite dizziness, so she moved slowly, washed away the hospital smells and scrubbed at multiple patches of gooey adhesive residue. Her body was covered in bruises from where her poor horse had landed on her. Purple patches decorated her shoulder, hip bone, rib cage, both arms and one thigh, and she had to wash those tender areas with care.

At least nothing was broken.

When she finished, she could smell coffee, so she dressed quickly and exited the bathroom.

Jeremiah said. "Yeah, that looks good," he said when she came out in warm-up pants, a football jersey, and a damp ponytail.

She glanced down at herself, then up at him, raising one eyebrow. "It does?"

"I was pretty sure you'd come out in a uniform, determined to go in to work."

She lowered her head, shaking it on the way. "I'm stubborn, but not suicidal. I intend to take it extremely easy today. I mean, Come on."

"Exactly." He took two plates out of the oven using pot holders and set them on the table, each with mounds of French toast and fried potatoes. Then he went back for a bowl of fresh berries. Finally, he topped it off by placing a steaming cup of coffee in front of her plate and pulling out her chair with a flourish. "Your breakfast, milady."

She sat down. "It looks fantastic and…enough for four of me."

"Well, to be fair, I can pack away enough for three of you, so…" He took his seat across from her.

"Where did all this food come from? I mean, I know you made it, but the ingredients? Fresh berries?"

"Your mom brought them last night. I was still awake when she came sneaking in and scared the daylights outta me. It was too late for the stores to be open, so I'm guessing she raided her own supplies."

She sipped the coffee, then spooned berries and poured maple syrup over her French toast. Then she tried her first bite and closed her eyes in pleasure. "Oh, man, that's good." She had a second bite. "Where did you learn to cook like this?"

"Remember I told you we had a great chef for a while?"

She nodded, but was too busy eating to speak.

"He was an ex-con and a genius who was wasted on me. But my old man had to have the best of everything. I used to go down to the kitchen, bored as hell in that big empty house, to watch him cook. Then I started helping, when nobody else was around to see."

She lifted her head, watched his face. "Why couldn't anyone else see?"

"My father had very clear ideas about what he wanted his firstborn son to learn. Cooking wasn't part of the plan."

She lowered her eyes. "Criming was."

He nodded.

"Did the chef get in trouble for teaching you?"

"No. We kept it secret." A shadow passed over his eyes.

"Tell me," she said. "I'm not fixin' to judge."

He studied her face for a moment, then said, "My senior year of high school, I cajoled the chauffeur, Cal, into letting me take one of the cars. I had a date. Now my old man was all right with me driving the cars, but he wanted to know in advance when, and where I'd be going, and with whom, and he'd send one of his enforcers out to keep an eye on me, supposedly from a distance, but always obvious. Taking a car without advance consent was a big violation."

"And what happened?"

He sighed, shrugged. "I took the car, had a great time. The next day there was a new chauffeur. I never knew what happened to Cal, but I never saw him again."

"Holy… Do you think he's all right?"

He shrugged one shoulder. "I don't know. The more I find out about my old man, the more I think he might not be. Here, let me top that off." He got up to fetch the coffee pot, then refilled her still nearly full mug.

Jeremiah cleaned up the cottage while Willow napped on the sofa after breakfast. She hadn't intended to nap, and that she'd drifted off told him how much the accident must've taken out of her. That tightened the knot of worry that had been living in the pit of his stomach since he'd seen her lying on the pavement. He even made her bed and picked up her discarded clothes and damp towels from the bathroom.

By the time he finished, she was rousing, stretching, and then frowning. "I fell asleep. Jeez."

"Well, you're supposed to be resting, so that's probably a good thing."

"I want to go outside, check on Sundance."

"I kind of thought you'd laze around the house all day—"

"Not sure it's in me. Come on, we can discuss terms on the way."

"Terms."

"You should be getting something for this. A paycheck, some samolians, you know. Cold, hard cash." She went to the door and stepped into her tall brown boots. She took her hat from a peg by the door, plopped it on her head, then winced and took it right off again. When she replaced it, she did so more carefully.

Willow in a cowboy hat had an effect on him such as few things ever had. His heart skipped, he lost his words, and his train of thought jumped plumb off the track. Happened every time he saw her in one.

"You comin'?" she asked, opening the door.

"Can Beans come?"

She tilted her head, then pressed a hand to it, but didn't acknowledge anything wrong. "It's probably good to expose him to all sorts of other animals as a pup. Just bring a leash, I don't want him spookin' the horses."

"C'mon, boy." He put on his boots, and took his hat off the peg. Beans' leash was hanging underneath it.

"That's a big collar for a pup," she said. "Then again, he's a big pup."

"Vet says he'll need a calf collar when he's grown."

"A calf collar!"

He slid the collar over the pup's head. It hung a little loosely. "It's kind of fun watching him grow. Seems he's bigger every morning than he was the night before."

"I still think he's gonna need a saddle one day."

They walked away from Willow's little cottage and down the walkway to the drive. It forked right toward the road and her parents' house, and left toward the stable. They went left. Beans was practically dancing, stopping to sniff every few steps. Eventually, the stable came into sight, where they trained and boarded horses and raised thoroughbreds.

Stretching out from either side and rolling behind the stable were meadows where the animals grazed. As they drew closer, the pup noticed the horses, and the horses noticed the pup.

Sundance came toward them limping a little, his foreleg wrapped. "Hello Sundance. Are you okay, boy?"

He nickered and shook his mane.

"I got a friend you should meet. Come 'ere." She pulled a sugar cube from a pocket and held it out on her flat palm.

The horse came closer, but his eyes were mostly on the dog. Beans began to wiggle, wagging his tail, but staying where he was.

Sundance lowered his head over the fence. The dog took a step nearer, and their noses touched. Then Sundance leapt backward a little, and pawed the ground with a forefoot, and the puppy crouched, ready to spring in response.

"Is Sundance *playing* with him?" Jeremiah asked.

"Sure looks that way," Willow said. "Good boy, Sundance. That's a good boy." She again offered a sugar cube. Sundance nuzzled her flat palm to eat it, and Beans sniffed as high as he could reach without jumping to get a whiff of the treat. She dug in her pocket and fed the pup a sugar cube, too.

Beans took it into his mouth, then pushed it back out again. It hit the ground, and Sundance leaned all the way down to snatch it, then turned and walked away.

"Do you want to go for a ride, Gringo?"

He glanced at the pup.

"Beans can ride with you," she said.

"I don't think teaching him to jump on a horse's back is the best idea. He'll be too big soon." Besides, he didn't think she ought to even *try* riding yet. He'd been paying attention to her on their walk out there, and her stride wasn't as strong as before. She was moving oddly, extra slow, extra cautious, wobbling here and there, holding her head a lot.

"Next time," he said. "But let's introduce him around, though."

She was disappointed, he could tell, but they walked around the pasture with the dog, and most of the horses leaned down to sniff and nuzzle him. Beans was loving it.

Willow had a treat for every horse, carrots and sugar cubes in her pockets. "This is Butch," she said, feeding a carrot to Sundance's twin. "He's not as spirited as Sundance. A nice calm ride." She patted the horse's neck and it leaned into her as if returning the embrace. "Yes, you're a good boy, aren't you, Butchy?"

Butch blew noisily and stomped and Willow laughed. An inside joke between the two of them, apparently.

Another horse came plodding up, mottled white and rather shaggy. "Hello, Daisy."

This horse, too, replied to her with a shake of her mane.

"It's right here, don't get so bossy!" Willow produced an apple this time. "Just for you, old girl," she said, ruffling the mare's mane between her ears with one hand, holding the apple in the other.

Daisy took the apple in her teeth and trotted away as if she'd just won the lottery.

"Daisy's a rescue. Humane Society called the Sheriff's Department for help placing her after she was removed. She'd been half-starved, hooves were so long they were curlin' up." Her face turned angry. "Well, naturally, we took her."

"Naturally," he said, though he didn't see it as a given the way she obviously did. "It's a beautiful spread."

"Thanks. I love it here, and I love the ranch. But it's on Comanche land."

"But…you're Comanche, aren't you?"

She said, "Comanche don't believe in ownin' land. We're just its caregivers and in return the land sustains us." She nodded toward where the creek ran through the horse pasture. "Mom thinks there might've been a village down there."

"That's exciting." She seemed something other than excited though. A little sad, a little contemplative. "How do you feel about it?"

"I'm still tryin' to figure that out. One thing I do know, I'm their only child, so they'll be leavin' this place to me, and I don't want or need nine-hundred acres."

"You're thinking of selling it?"

"I'd never sell Skydancer Ranch."

"I didn't think so."

"I'm givin' it back."

He raised his eyebrows. "You're what now?"

"Givin' it back to the tribe. I'd like to carve just a little piece for myself. The house and a few acres. Just enough for me and a coupl'a horses."

He was stunned right to his toes. "Do you have any idea how much all that land is *worth*?"

"Yeah," she said, gazing out toward the horizon. You could see forever looking east, as the hills were only little rises. "It's priceless. And it's not really mine to give. It's Comanche land. It was stolen." She looked again past the barn toward the creek. "I intended to take you down there to show you my favorite spot, but...dang, Gringo, I'm tired out already."

"I had a feeling you would be." He turned his back to her and crouched lower. "Climb aboard. Unless you think it'll make Sundance jealous."

"Piggy back?"

He looked at her over his shoulder, and saw her skeptical brow. "You said you wanted to go riding."

He was surprised when she put her arms and legs around him. He'd expected her to argue a little more. Then he forgot everything, including how to breathe. But he managed to straighten up and started back along the trail toward the house, carrying her on his back. "If you happen to come to the bunkhouse, don't think badly of me for the fridge full of beer. It was for the bonfire, but—"

"Whaddya mean *was*?"

"Well, obviously we didn't hold the bonfire without you, and we're sure as heck not having it on your second night home from the hospital."

He felt her twisting around to reach behind her, and the next thing he knew she was holding her phone in front of his head with both hands, so she could text and hang on at the same time. "Bunkhouse bonfire is ON. Tonight. There'd better be pizza."

She returned the phone to her back pocket and kicked his thighs. "Giddyap!"

He took off at a lopsided gallop, and she laughed like a little kid. And then when she stopped laughing, and he stopped galloping, out of breath, she said, "You can put me down now."

"You sure?" He stopped moving and turned his head to look up at her. They were only a few yards from the front door of her cottage.

She bent lower and kissed him upside down. He raised his arms to thread his fingers into her hair, pulled her down a little closer, and kissed her back. It was long and slow, and she sucked at his lower lip and made his blood heat.

When the kiss ended, she slid to the ground.A throat cleared. Drew was standing in the driveway, just in front of the cottage.

CHAPTER TEN

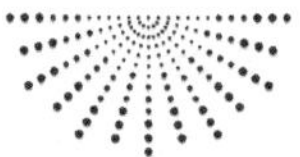

"Hey Drew," Willow said thrusting her thumbs into the waistband of her warmup pants and walking forward as if nothing untoward had happened.

"I'm done for the day," she said. "And Mom doesn't need me, so…I was gonna offer to take nursemaid duty and give Jeremiah a break. But uh, maybe you'd prefer I didn't." She wiggled her eyebrows toward Jeremiah.

He said, "Actually, I do have some things to tend to, if—"

"What sorts of things?" Drew asked.

"Beans has a play date with Frankie. Where is he, anyway? Beans!"

The dog came running from the cottage. Drew had left the door open.

"Sure, go ahead. It's fine," Willow said. "Thanks for stayin' with me. See you at the bonfire tonight."

"Yeah, see you there," he said. "C'mon, Beans. Let's go for a ride."

The pup cocked his head, then launched straight for the Jeep and stood beside it, barking. Willow was grinning at the dog when she met Jeremiah's eyes.

He'd been smiling, too. He touched the brim of his hat. "Ladies."

And then went to scoop up his dog, set him in the Jeep, and got in after him.

"*Well*, now," said Drew.

"Thank goodness you got here when you did," Willow said.

"Looked to me like the worst possible moment."

Jeremiah pulled out, moving past them slow and easy, giving them a wave, but not meeting Willow's eyes.

"He's hidin' somethin'," she whispered. "And I'm fallin' for him."

"Holy– Well, okay then. Maybe I did arrive at the right time." Drew's big blue eyes spoke full volume.

Sighing, Willow paced up the sidewalk to the cottage. "It's gotta be the bad boy thing, right? I mean, that must be it." She went inside and Drew came in behind her. Willow closed the door, went past the sofa and turned back to offer Drew a coffee, but her gaze fell on Jeremiah's big duffel bag on the floor, behind the sofa. Its zipper was wide open and its contents were strewn everywhere.

"Ohmygosh!" Drew moved further in. "The puppy—oh, this is on me. I left the door open."

"Well, we have to pick it up," Willow said. And then she knelt carefully, paused for her head to stop spinning, then began picking things up and putting them back into the duffel.

Drew went to the kitchen and poured them each a sweet tea from the pitcher in the fridge. When she came back, she handed one to Willow. "Well?"

"Dog toy. Dog toy. Dog treats. A blanket, no doubt for the dog." She was still gathering.

Drew laughed softly, and picked up some socks and boxer briefs, and tossed them into the bag. "Oh, yeah, he's a big tough loner, stranger in town, man incognito for the better part of a year. But he's apparently a puddle of goo over Beans."

"Apparently." But Willow said it absently as she picked up a stack of packets that unfolded in an accordion snake of condoms. "Confident, much?" she mused.

Drew snort-laughed, "At least he's bein' responsible," then slapped her leg and laughed some more.

"What's this?" Willow said, gathering up a folded paper square. "Wait, this is a map."

Drew stopped laughing and turned to remove three magazines, two remote controls and their sweet glasses from the coffee table. Then she wiped up the moisture rings with her shirt sleeve.

Willow leaned over and spread the map open. Drew ran to the front window, looked outside, then closed the curtains. She repeated with the window on the other side of the front door, and locked the door for good measure. Then she returned.

"He's got several locations marked here," Willow said, noting the little stars Jeremiah had drawn. "This one's the location of the former Bluebonnet Inn, and this one's the WTD."

"So they're probably all locations connected to his daddy, the dead crime boss."

"Probably," Willow agreed. Then she frowned. "A few of them have slashes through 'em," she said. "The spots he's already visited, I think."

"Will, I don't think this map is all that suspicious. He told you he wanted to retrace his father's steps. This is just a map of exactly what he said he was doin'."

"He said he hated deceiving me—to someone on the phone, I heard him."

"I still think you should just ask him."

"And expect him not to lie to me about whatever he's lying to me about? Drew, this is *huge*, this is my *life*. I want to be sheriff someday. And if I let myself fall for him—"

"Because he's an ex-con? Will, that's—"

"No. No, not that. But if he's an *unrepentant* ex-con who's still up to something nefarious, then—"

"Why do you think that?"

"Because why else deceive a deputy?" She shook her head, looking again at the map. "And then there was the camera turning off at the Bluebonnet at the same time I expected him to go back there."

"Are you sure he did that, though?"

She wasn't sure. She couldn't be sure. And when she thought of Jeremiah, all she saw in her head were those dimples when he smiled, those vivid blue eyes, and her stomach tied itself into knots.

"There are still a coupl'a stars without slashes through 'em," Drew observed, pointing them out on the map. "That one's Thompson Gorge, where the big showdown happened between his old man and the elder Brands."

"Well, he's bound to visit all of 'em," Willow said. "That's probably what he's doin' today, as we speak."

"Well...why don't we stake one of 'em out," Drew asked. "Spend the day and wait. Bring a book, plenty of water, some stakeout food."

"There's only wholesome, healthy stuff in the house," Willow said. "*Family*."

Drew rolled her eyes.

Will and her cousins often pretended to be irritated by their nurturing clan, when they were the farthest thing from it.

"Yeah, we'll stop on the way." Drew looked at the map, "The other three spots are in town. Easiest place to stay outta sight'll be the canyon."

"Let's get there."

"We might have to hike in. You up to it?"

"Nope," she admitted. "But I think I could ride."

Jeremiah had put his search on hold while Willow had been in the hospital. But she was okay—thank the powers that be, she was okay—and she was with her cousin. According to his journal, de Lorean had kept a safe deposit box at the bank. So that was the first place he went.

"Oh," said the teller, after clicking keys for a while. "It looks like that was an abandoned box. Note says the owner's information was fraudulent. Sorry."

"What would've happened to the contents?" he asked. As if, had someone found eight pounds of gold, they'd have turned it in.

Hell, he wasn't sure they wouldn't, here in Quinn.

"And was there anyone witnessing whoever opened it? Because I have reason to believe there could've been valuable property in that box."

The teller, a pretty Mexican-American, just blinked at him for a moment, and he realized she was waiting to see if his mini-rant had ended. He took a deep breath. "Sorry," he said. "Can you help me?"

"Have a seat," she said, and nodded toward chairs against one wall.

"I don't have a lot of time." As if she cared.

"Have a seat," she repeated.

So he had a seat. Eventually, the bank manager emerged from his office, through the swinging wooden gate that served no purpose and headed toward him. He was tall, white, bald, and Jeremiah didn't know him. But he rose, shook the man's hand when he introduced himself, and immediately forgot his name.

"Follow me," the man said, and walked him into a small conference type room. He gestured to a chair, and Jeremiah sat.

"So the belongings of any abandoned safe deposit box are put into storage. By bank policy, that can't be sold or given away, they must be kept. Every effort is made to contact the owners, and there's always hope they might one day return to the claim their things."

"I see."

"A three-person board supervises the opening of an abandoned box, and the items are catalogued in front of all of them." He crossed the room to a pitcher of water, poured some into a glass, held it his way.

Jeremiah shook his head, so the guy sipped it himself.

"I don't mean to be rude, but…who's on the committee?"

"Myself, the bank's attorney, and the sheriff."

"Sheriff Brand?"

"Yes, he was sheriff then, too, yes."

"Do you remember what was in the box?"

The man leaned forward and removed his glasses. "I'll never forget it. We had established by then that Daniel Carr, the name on the box, was an alias of Vincent de Lorean. He was a big-time criminal, you'll forgive me saying so."

"I'm aware." So the guy knew exactly who he was, Jeremiah realized. Everyone in Quinn knew he was de Lorean's son. It gave him an uneasy feeling to be reminded of that.

"So naturally, we expected, I don't know, cash or passports or weapons, something but the only things in the box were baby pictures. Newborn, in the hospital bassinet. Either you or your brother, we figured. There were no dates, nothing to identify the kid. Well, Sheriff Brand, he made color copies of 'em. Couldn't just snap 'em with your phone back then, you know. We put the originals into photo-safe sleeves and into storage they went. I can get them for you, though."

He didn't need baby pictures of himself or his brother. But he wanted to see everything all the same. "Yeah, could you get 'em for me?"

"I can have them in an hour."

Willow roped off a small area near a water hole for the horses. It was shaded by an overhang, and there was enough sweet grass to keep them happy for a couple of hours. Then she rejoined Drew on a high, flat rock formation that jutted out over the edge of the canyon the locals called Thompson Gorge. Their flat stone angled upward, so they wouldn't be seen from below.

They had binoculars, cell phones, soda, and potato chips.

They'd only been there two hours before the chips were gone, and about fifteen minutes after that, the sound of an ATV buzzed in the distance.

"Is that him?" Drew asked.

"Where would he get an ATV?" Willow asked, lifting her binoculars.

"Come on, all he'd have to do is ask. There are like six of 'em on the ranch."

"Where's he going?"

The ATV answered their question by stopping near a large rock formation. A man and a lanky pup got off it. "I remember that rock. It was in Uncle Garrett's notes about the big show-down with Ethan's birth father."

"See?" Drew asked. "He really *is* retracing his father's steps, just like he told you."

"Yeah," Willow said as her heart sank. "With a metal detector."

"What?" Drew pulled up her spyglasses and saw the same thing Willow had. Jeremiah, moving slowly back and forth, waving a metal detector over the ground as the pup ran a large figure-eight around him. "Son of a—"

"I knew it." Willow sank down low, turned around and leaned back against the jutting stone. "I knew I was fallin' too fast."

"Just because he's lookin' for somethin' doesn't mean it's somethin' illegal."

"Right. Just somethin' he wants to hide from his pal the deputy. Even while wheedlin' for information she hadn't ought to be getting."

"What information did you get that you shouldn't have?" Drew asked.

"None yet. But I called a friend and asked. It'll be waitin' for me when I go into the office."

Drew arched her brows.

"Background check on Juanita Lopez, the current owner of the Bluebonnet, 'til it sells, I guess. She was just a teenager when de Lorean was here."

"And we're interested in her because…?"

"Because Gringo is."

Willow looked at her watch. "He's fixin' to quit soon. Look, he's putting the pup on the ATV."

"Well, shoot, I need to go make brownies for the bonfire," Drew said. Then she wiggled her brows. "But everything I need's at your place. You want me to stay tonight? Or do you want the Gringo back?"

"You know damn well I want the Gringo back," Willow said.

Drew looked down at Jeremiah again and tipped her head to one side. "I'm not seein' it."

"Well, that's because he doesn't have dark brown curls and nerdy glasses," Willow said.

Drew grinned and punched her in the shoulder. They headed back to their horses and rode back to Willow's place. In the stable, they rubbed the horses down thoroughly, gave them oats with molasses, and turned them out into their cool meadow with plenty of time for grazing before they'd go in for the night.

Then they headed to the cottage

Willow was physically tired as hell. She was hurting more than she should've been, too. Already, she'd let the Gringo get under her skin.

"Take the first shower, Drew. I need to rest before the bonfire."

"You need anything?" Drew was already bringing her a glass of water and an apple.

"I'm good. Go on."

"Okay." Drew started for the bathroom. Then she paused, "I like him," she said. "And I don't think he's bad. I think maybe *he* thinks he's bad, but he isn't really. Not down deep."

"And you base this assessment on…"

"The whole saving the puppy thing, mainly," Drew admitted.

Her cousin had a solid point. It was hard to believe a guy who'd jump fully clothed into a creek to save a puppy could be beyond redemption. But she wasn't in the redemption business. She was in the law-enforcement business. When she fell for a guy, he had to come pre-redeemed.

No, she needed to leave Jeremiah alone. Period. She needed to end whatever was between them in no uncertain terms.

Either that or find out what he was really up to.

Tonight.

Country music played, the bonfire danced, and Jeremiah looked like her dream-man. Willow sat across the fire from him, watching him through the flames that danced in front of his face, striping it in yellow light and shadow. His hat was off, but nearby, and his golden hair was pulled behind his head in a band.

He was one of the gang around a central fire that included her six cousins and two cousins-in-law. Everyone had enjoyed a few beers—nearly everyone—so the mood was relaxed and easy.

Ethan, seated right beside his half-brother, gave him an affectionate slam on the shoulder as they both laughed at something. There was a serious bond shaping up between them.

Willow thought back to when she'd warned Ethan not to get involved with Lily, because if it went bad, it might put a rift in the family.

Even as she thought it, Lily, sitting on Ethan's other side with her lawn chair so close to his that their armrests overlapped, slid a hand over his knee.

She'd been wrong about that. It had worked out fine, they were married now and irritatingly blissful. Lily was one of the folks not imbibing in the beer, being pregnant and due right in the spring.

Jeremiah nodded at something Maria had said. Maria beamed back at him. She liked him. The whole family liked him. They'd wrapped their big Brand tentacles around him and made him part of the clan. They did that.

But he was up to something. He was looking for something. Something he must have reason to believe his father had buried there. Something metal, like coins, or jewelry, or gold. A little shiver raced down her spine.

He sat in a canvas lawn chair with his long legs stretched out in front of him, looking thoroughly relaxed, his dog lying beside him, snoring. The Gringo had a beer in his hand. It was the same one he'd been nursing all night. She'd been watching. He was pretending to drink it, but unless it was magically refilling itself, he wasn't actually drinking it.

He's even dishonest about that.

The flames shifted, lighting his cheek and casting that demon dimple in shadow. He must be smiling, she thought, her gaze shifting to his lips. Yes, he was smiling, but it was a slight smile, not meant to be widely seen, and it seemed mischievous. Her eyes shifted upward and found his already locked on her, beaming heat all the way through her, that mischievous hint of a grin for her alone. He shifted his gaze to the flames, took another fake gulp from his brown bottle, but midway through, he caught her eyes, and turned it into a real one.

Maybe deflection is his default, being raised in his old man's citadel of crooks.

"We really needed a good bonfire," Ethan said. "How you holdin' up, Willow?"

Beside him, Lily nodded. "We were so scared for you."

"I can imagine. I'm really sorry I put you all through that. I have the best family in the world."

"She's sorry she put us through it." Baxter was on Willow's left, his hair blond and shaggy, and the firelight made the lenses of his wire-rimmed glasses flash orange. He wore cargo pants and sneakers, and he reached across and gave her a shoulder-squeeze. "It wasn't your fault."

"It was a little bit my fault." She lowered her head. Her greatest fear was failing at her job as a deputy. And so far, that fear was proving prophetic.

Drew said, "Uncle Garrett's had the whole department on this. They found the motorcycle abandoned in a ditch a mile away from the accident. It had been stolen from a local who'd just bought it for his kid for his twenty-first birthday. Hadn't even given it to him or licensed it yet."

Drew glanced at her brother, Orrin.

Orrin nodded. "We have feelers out too, Willow. Mom, through her network and us through ours. So far nobody knows anything. The feelin' is that causing a cop to wind up in a coma likely scared 'em off."

"Then I let 'em get away," Willow said, lowering her eyes.

"Come on, Will," Trevor said. "You're alive. You came close to not being. That's worthy of celebration."

"Hear, hear," Harrison said, raising his beer. "Here's to Willow being alive and well."

"Hear, hear," said Maria, leaning closer to her husband and raising her bottle.

Everyone lifted their beverage of choice. Jeremiah hoisted his bottomless beer, Lily her sweet tea, and when they all shouted,

"To Willow." The dog raised his giant head and looked around, alarmed.

Jeremiah patted him. "All good, Beans. Settle down."

"He's so calm, for a puppy," Drew said.

"It's the breed," Jeremiah said. "I've been reading up."

"Ah," Baxter said. "That's what you were reading all those hours in the hospital waiting room where we all lived for a two nights and two days."

"Yep. Learned a lot. Beans'll have bursts of energy but he tires out fast. According to what I've been reading, right now it takes most of his energy to grow. And as he gets bigger, he'll just naturally be even more slow and easy. They're a calm breed."

"You hung out in the hospital waitin' room?" Willow asked. She didn't mean to, it just came out. And then she added, "All of you?"

"Well, where else would we have been?" Baxter asked

"Don't be dumb, Will," Drew said. "If any of us were in a trauma bed, you'd be in the same dang place."

Yeah, she thought, but if it were anyone else, would the Gringo be there?

"What did you do with the pup all that time?" she asked Jeremiah.

"Hired on Frankie as my official dog-sitter," he said. "I set things up with him right after your accident. Tell you the truth, I don't know how I'll get by without him, once school starts back up."

Willow tilted her head, watching the way Jeremiah's fingers were scratching on the back of the pup's head as he sat there. The pup was loving it.

"So what's up with your old man's will?" Orrin asked Jeremiah out of the blue. And Willow knew Drew had put him up to it.

"Somebody's challenging it," Jeremiah said, not even trying to lie. Okay, so he wasn't dishonest about *every*thing.

"Oh no," Maria said, sending a look at Ethan as if to ask if he knew about this, then refocusing on Jeremiah once again. "What are you gonna do?"

"Let it work itself out in court."

"Well, yeah but, don't you…" Maria bit her lip to stop the question.

"She wants to know what you'll live on if your old man's money goes to someone else," Willow said.

"Oh. Sure, no, the will doesn't cover everything my father left me. There was a trust fund set up when I was born. I got control of that right out of school, kept it invested, and it's still producing an income. And there are…other things. I'll be all right."

"Well, that's a relief."

"Still," Drew said, "A man needs something to do. How do you spend your time, Jeremiah? What is it you, you know, *do*?"

"Right now, most of my time is spent on Beans, here." He changed his stroke, and the dog sighed audibly.

A non-answer, and it had Willow curious. What *was* the handsome drifter good at, besides looking hot in a sombrero? Or out of one. And sex, he was really good at sex.

This was going to drive her crazy. Was he good or bad, and why was she having trouble keeping her mind as far from him as she'd placed her body? She'd sat on the opposite side of the fire. She should've realized that would put him right in her line of sight.

In the distance, dry thunder rumbled.

A quick frown bent Jeremiah's brows.

Drew leaned over from her seat on the right and whispered, "You still wanna get a look at his phone?"

"I don't know. I mean, it would be illegal."

"Wouldn't be admissible in court. Wouldn't be legally gained evidence in a case. But checkin' up on the guy you're sparkin'? Since when is that illegal?"

"We're not sparkin'!" Her whisper was on the loud side. A few heads glanced her way, so she faked a grin and chucked Drew's shoulder and spoke through a fake smile. "I don't know if I can cross that line, cuz. I want to be sheriff someday, I can't go breakin' the law just 'cause I feel like it."

"Fine, I will." Then she put an arm around Willow, tipping her chair dangerously in the process, and called, "Gringo, take our pic. The fire'll make a cool effect."

Jeremiah obligingly pulled out his phone, aimed it. Willow felt his gaze on hers through the lens and sent it right back as he tapped.

"That was way too easy," Drew said to Jeremiah, her tone teasing. "Do you always do what you're asked?"

"Spoken like a gal with another ask in mind," he replied.

Drew nodded. "We need more firewood, and our pile is decimated."

"We've had a lot of bonfires this year," her brother agreed.

"You want me to find firewood?" Jeremiah asked.

Drew blinked. "All you big, strong males, actually. So we damsels don't freeze."

Willow rolled her eyes. Drew was the most progressive of the bunch, so the guys should've all been suspicious at her playing the helpless female card, but the only ones who looked at her oddly were Maria and Lily.

Groaning, the guys all got up, though, Jeremiah included.

Drew cried, "Wait, Gringo, one more pic!"

He picked up his phone, snapped another shot, put it back in the cup holder on his chair, and fell into step with the guys. Drew lunged and yanked his phone out of the cup holder before the men were even out of sight.

"Jeez, Drew, all they have to do is look back!" Willow whisper-shouted, but Drew shot back to her chair before anyone did, tapping the phone the whole way.

"It didn't lock yet. Come on, what are we looking for?"

Maria and Lily were frowning at them.

Willow gave in to curiosity. "The seventeenth between one and two a.m."

"Lookin', lookin', lookin'…"

"What are you up to?" Maria asked. "Put that back!"

"No calls," Drew said. "There aren't any, incoming or outgoing."

"He must've deleted it."

"Tell us what's going on," Lily said as she and Maria came closer.

Drew ignored them both. "Maybe it wasn't a phone call you heard."

"Well, what the heck else could it—"

"Got it! Voice memo, right here." She turned the phone toward Willow.

Willow bit her lip. Maria and Lily were standing there, too. Maria shook her head left and right.

Willow looked at the phone and said, "Play it."

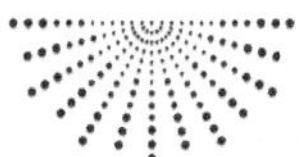

CHAPTER ELEVEN

Drew handed her the phone. "You play it."

"You're crossin' a line, Will," Maria said.

"I know." She looked at the highlighted recording in a list of them that was apparently several pages long. Rather than listening to what she'd already heard, she picked the one from the day when they'd first kissed and tapped Play.

Jeremiah's voice came, deep and soft. "Everything's goin' better than I could've hoped. How can I fail to find it when I have the help of a deputy who looks at me the way she does? I think Willow Brand'll do just about anything I ask."

Willow felt like she'd been gut-punched, and her breath gusted out of her as if she had.

Lily said, "Listen to the most recent one, Will. Or the first and the last, since there's no time to hear 'em all."

"They're comin'," Maria said.

Drew snatched the phone, tapping out of the app as she lurched toward Jeremiah's chair, dropped it into the cup holder, and kept going past it toward the beer cooler, as if that had been her goal all along.

But she hadn't clicked the phone off, so its screen was still lit up. And the guys were coming closer. Lily rubbed her baby bump and whispered, "You okay, Willow?"

And then Maria said, "That's not the whole story. It's out of context. You shouldn't have listened to any of it."

But Willow was still locked on that phone screen, willing it to go dark before Jeremiah noticed it. He was at the head of the gang, his arms full of deadfall from the scrub lot nearby. Ethan was beside him, Baxter on his other side, Orrin, Trevor, and Harrison brought up the rear.

Jeremiah got all the way to back of his chair, with the phone still lit, facing her, its back to him, and she was forcing her eyes to stay on his, and not shift downward, forcing her smile to not look like panic.

He frowned, though, dropping his armload of wood beside the fire pit, then turning back to reach for his phone, which was still lit up.

It went dark just before he made contact.

She sighed so heavily her back bent, and her cousins were exchanging looks of relief. And then, crisis averted, she let her smile die.

He was using her, had been the whole time, to find his father's treasure. And she'd given him everything Uncle Garrett had on his old man, and run a background check on Juanita Lopez to boot.

It hurt like a knife in the back. It pissed her off, too, but she couldn't find her anger just yet beyond the feeling of betrayal. She couldn't hope to hide it, either. There were some angry, ugly tears coming and she'd prefer to be alone when they spilled.

She got to her feet. "I'm more tired than I thought. I'm headin' home."

"Oh, hey, I got you," Jeremiah said, pocketing his phone, then pulling his keys from a pocket.

"No," she said, and she said it too fast. His eyes met hers, full of questions. She didn't have any answers.

Drew got to her feet. "I'm stayin' over at Will's tonight, so you're off the hook. She's helpin' me study."

"Oh." Jeremiah said. The word seemed heavy. He was still searching Willow's eyes and she was trying hard not to reveal a thing. But it probably showed.

"You guys can keep the party goin'," she told her cousins. "Love you." She headed around the bunkhouse and got into Drew's little car.

Jeremiah found himself alone with the Brand men shortly after that. Maria and Lily muttered to each other, and then to their spouses, and then waved goodbye and left together.

So he sat there with his half-brother Ethan, Ethan's cousins, Trevor and Baxter, and Ethan's brother-in-law Harrison. Orrin was missing as he'd gone inside to use the bathroom. Ethan kept clearing his throat and it finally hit Jeremiah that he was trying to get his attention.

"So about you and Willow," Ethan said, being the de facto leader of the gang.

Jeremiah looked around and realized this was going to be some sort of family talking-to. So he got to his feet, picked up his hat, and plunked it onto his head. "That would be between me and Willow," he said. "Night, fellas. I'm hittin' the rack. C'mon, Beans." He strode directly into the bunkhouse with his dog as close as his shadow. Orrin came out, dang near bumping into him in the doorway.

Jeremiah let him pass then went in and closed the door behind him. He had a feeling he'd been about to get the third degree about his relationship with Willow, and was glad to have avoided it.

Willow.

Something was up with her.

And he knew what, because she had a terrible poker face. The whole time he'd been walking back from the woods, she'd been shifting her eyes between him and his chair, or more specifically the phone in his chair, as had become apparent when he'd got closer.

And he'd seen the shift in the area immediately around the phone when its light had gone out, which told him it had been on. Someone had messed with his phone. They wouldn't know his password, of course, but then why was Willow acting so off?

He hit the bathroom and the shower, a deterrent, in case Ethan decided to come in for a one-on-one chat with him. He needed to find his father's gold and get the hell out of this town.

He took his time in the shower, and by the time he finished and came out, stepping over Beans who laid on the bathmat outside the shower door, it felt quiet. Everyone had gone.

He went to the back door wearing a towel. The firepit was black, beer bottles picked up, cooler gone, folding chairs folded and returned to the shed where they kept 'em. Someone had even piled up the scrub wood he and the guys had gathered.

Crossing the bunkhouse to the kitchen, he looked through the front window behind the kitchen sink, and saw all the vehicles had gone except his own.

His spine relaxed a little. Beans yipped. He was standing in front of his bowl.

"Shoot, you had dinner at six."

He barked again.

"Yeah, okay." Jeremiah obediently put some kibble in the bowl and watched the pup dive in. The vet said to feed him all he wanted for the first year. He had not found the "all he wanted" point yet.

Then he filled a glass with water and turned off lights on his way to the rearmost bottom bunk he'd been using since he'd moved in. Being flush with the rear wall gave him the fullest view of the place, both entrances.

He dropped his towel on the way, then slid between the fresh, clean sheets. He could barely turn his back without Miss Chelsea cleaning the place. She must've had a field day, him being out of the bunkhouse overnight.

The thought of Willow brought a sharp stab to his chest, and it surprised him. He missed her. He'd enjoyed being with her, regardless of his reasons. He sighed heavily, laid back on the pillows and reached for his phone. When he unlocked it, he frowned.

The journal app was open.

He hadn't journaled today.

He swore under his breath, reviewing what had happened before Will had turned on him. He'd taken photos with his phone. One, and then another just before he'd walked away. Why the hell had he left it behind? His brain had said he'd be apt to lose it in the woods, but she was the law. Had he even locked the dang thing?

He was getting sloppy, entirely too comfortable with this family. With Willow, especially. And now she'd probably seen something she thought was incriminating.

Hell.

He tapped the most recently opened files, one of which was his most recent entry, which should be there. What shouldn't be there was one several days old.

He thought back in his mind, realizing that was the day he and Willow had first kissed.

Son of a gun!

He played the recording, where he'd talked about using her to get the information he needed, and realized how it must look to her. An uncomfortably awful feeling unfurled from the pit of his stomach out into his body. He pushed it back with anger.

"How dare she go through my phone? No warrant, no nothing? She's s'posed to be the law. Ha!"

The dog had been about to climb onto the bunk, but instead he stood on hind legs to lick Jeremiah's face. He averted it. The pup sighed heavily and dropped to all fours, turned three times in a circle, then laid down on the floor beside the bed.

The law was the enemy. He'd been raised on that notion since the day his mom had abandoned him to a den of thieves. And yet he'd let his guard down. Had even fantasized that he had feelings for her. Him! An ex-con, going soft on a deputy. What a sad joke.

He went to the journal app and deleted every entry. Then he emptied the trash. He would make a new recording for every date he'd journaled, to overwrite the old files for good.

He tapped the button. "I trusted her, and she betrayed me, and I should'a known better." Then he saved it, and started the next. "The law is always the enemy. Dad always said so, and he wasn't lying." Funny how he'd pulled away from his criminal father, only to now realize how much he'd learned from him. Or should've learned. Apparently, he hadn't learned it well enough. Next recording, "Just keep the goal in mind. Forget about her."

Easier said than done. He was furious with her.

She was probably furious, too. And she had reason to be, based on what she'd heard. She ought to be mad. He tapped the phone. "She didn't even listen to my side of it."

His side of how he was using her to help him find his father's likely ill-gotten gold?

"I'm damn well gonna make her hear my side of it."

He put the phone down. The task wasn't done, but he'd spent all his rage. The awful feeling returned, and he was out of ammo to push it back.

Willow knew. She knew pretty much everything. And he was sick inside.

The pup climbed up onto the bed, his huge paws sinking into Jeremiah's belly, making him grunt. His hind paws followed as

Beans tromped over him, dug at the blankets, turned in a circle, trampling him again, and finally dropped like a sack of feed across Jeremiah's lower legs and feet.

He put his hand on Beans' head. "I shouldn't get so attached when I know you're not meant for me," he said. "In the end I have to let you go. Best we both keep that in mind from here on."

"I smell like wood smoke and beer. I'm fixin' to hit the shower," Willow said. She'd held it together this long, but something was clawing its way up out of her and she wasn't sure how it would emerge.

Drew just nodded. "Whatever you need. You feeling okay? Physically, I mean."

"I might throw up," she said. "Otherwise, all good."

It wasn't true. Her head was throbbing. She ducked into the bathroom, closed and locked the door, and then pressed her back against it and slid all the way down. Tears burned, but her mind raged. How dare he use her like that?

How dare I let him?

The voice in her head was sometimes cruelly accurate. She raised her head, then got up and went to crank on the shower knobs. But as she undressed, she kept her watery eyes fixed on her own mirrored gaze, and as she let herself feel the anger, the tears dried and left their burning salt behind.

"On the one hand, it's stupid to want vengeance. I knew who he was the whole time. I knew the risk. And I'm a shitty cop for ignorin' every warnin' sign. I got nobody to blame but myself."

She stepped into the shower. The flow was too hot. She didn't adjust it, but turned her whole body to feel the burn. "On the other hand," she whispered, "I'm fixin' to make that Gringo pay for breakin' my heart."

Her slow turn stopped. "I don't know why I said that. He sure as *hell* didn't break my heart."

A tap on the door. God, she just wanted to be alone and wallow in her emotions!

"Yeah?"

"Maria and Lily are here," Drew said through the door.

"Okay." Cause what was she supposed to say? Tell them to get out, and while she was at it, to get out herself?

She took a deep breath, "I'll be a minute."

"Take as long as you want, hon. We can clear out if—"

She didn't answer, because she was fully distracted by reaching out of the shower and feeling around the counter for her remote. She tapped its speaker icon, and said, "Play my Pissed-off list. Max volume."

The music came on. She sang along, even the swear words, not loud enough so anyone would hear her. Hell, she could sing as loud as she wanted and nobody would hear her over that female vocalist calling her man a liar and a cheat.

When Willow emerged some forty minutes later in stupid flannel pajamas and oversized socks, she was still good and pissed, but at least she had a plan.

"Hey, gals."

"Freakin' men, anyway," Drew said.

To which the happily married ladies replied with an unconvincing, "You said it!" and "Dang 'em all!"

Then came the obligatory group hug. She'd grown up with this. It was a ritual. She just wasn't used to being on the receiving end.

"I brought ice cream," Maria said.

"I stole booze from the bonfire," Lily added. "Nobody suspected me. I'm the pregnant one."

She nodded at the overstuffed beach bag she'd left by the front door. It was bulging with beer bottles.

"Why'd you stop the music?" Drew asked. Then, addressing the nearby speaker, "Resume the music. Volume down to medium."

The music resumed at a lower volume. Willow leaned over the speaker and tapped the volume down a little more. "I'm not going to be much fun, girls."

"No shit," Maria said, then clapped a hand over her mouth and widened her eyes. "I may still be buzzed from the bonfire," she said. "Let's keep it going!" She went to the bag of bottles and took three by their necks in one hand.

She returned, arm out. Willow took one, then Drew. "Hey, Lily, there's pop and sweet tea in the fridge. Put it in a fancy wine glass from the rack over there."

Lily rolled her eyes, but did exactly that.

They all drank, and then Maria said, "The question on everyone's mind is, what are we fixin' to do about this?" Her green eyes flashed. She was living proof of the hot-tempered redhead.

And then Lily said, "We don't know enough to do anything. We only heard a few linesof the journal. It's unfair to judge someone based on such a narrow sliver of information."

Drew nodded, "That's what I'm sayin'," though she hadn't been saying anything. "We need to know more. We need get our hands on that phone, listen to the rest. And in the meantime—"

"We can't do that," Lily said. "How would we react if he hacked into Willow's phone?"

"Well, how else do you figure we find out what he's up to?" Drew asked.

Willow held up one hand while drinking the beer with the other. She chugged the bottle, then smacked it onto the fireplace mantle. "I want to handle this myself. It's not…a family thing, it's a me and Jeremiah thing."

The other three looked at each other, curious, wounded, and irritated.

"I know you'll be there if I need you. You just have to step back until I do. Okay?"

"Yeah," Lily said, nodding. "Of course."

"I mean, I don't like it, but…" Maria shrugged. "Okay, I'll try to keep my nose out of it."

"Me, too," Drew said, but she didn't mean it. Willow knew it right to her bones.

She nodded, though, and said, "Thanks. Now, I'm goin' to be fine, and I really don't want an overnight nurse, so…if you all are still safe to drive home…"

"I can get 'em home," Lily said.

"Thanks. Night, gals. And thanks for bein' here. And uh… leaving that ice cream behind?"

They laughed. Maria said, "Go to bed, Will. We'll clear out, and lock up behind us."

So she did.

When she rose the next morning, her place was clean and empty, and the ice cream was still in her freezer. Excellent. She took a clean uniform out of her closet, and headed into the bathroom to get ready for work.

She hadn't even got there yet when Jeremiah blasted by her in his Jeep and pulled over up ahead of her.

Sighing, she signaled and pulled off to the side. She pulled her aviator glasses on before she got out and walked up to his car, reminding herself to be cautious. Jeremiah wasn't a good guy.

He leaned left and thrust both his open hands out the open window.

She rolled her eyes, and proceeded up beside it.

"May I get out?"

"No. What do you want?"

"I know you listened to my journal last night. Part of it. I'm kind of shocked, Willow. I trusted you, and you—"

"You trusted me?" She felt her eyes widen and wondered if they could pop from their sockets like in a cartoon. "You used me. You lied to me. You're lookin' for a buried treasure and usin' me to do it."

"That's all true," he said, his hands on the steering wheel. He was looking at her, but she couldn't meet his eyes. "Can I please get out of the car? C'mon, Will, I'm family. I'm Ethan's brother, I'm not gonna hurt you. Couldn't if I wanted to."

She thumbed the loop off her holster, and the one off her taser too, and took a step back. "Okay. Get out. Since you're family, I'll give you a chance to explain yourself."

"Good. Good." He got out of the car and stood facing her, only a footstep away. "See, it's true that I was using you, but that doesn't mean everything else was fake. Will, what was between the two of us, it was real. It was fire."

His gaze moved down her body, burning every spot it touched, then returned to her eyes again.

"Prove it," she said. It felt like some force was making her lean closer.

"How?" he whispered, and the way his lips formed the word made a chill race up her spine. "I'll do anything you want, I swear."

Some magnetic force drew their lips together. Their bodies entwined, while their mouths devoured.

"This is so stupid," she muttered when she scrambled for the Jeep's rear door, and when it opened, he fell in, across the cargo bay, pulling her on top of him.

She reached behind her to close them in. The space was tiny. All the better. "I'm an idiot," she said.

"I won't make you an idiot."

"You can't, I'm already there."

They were undressing as they spoke, kissing in between, and

eventually his skin was against hers, and she was in heaven. They were entwined, they were connected, and there was nothing else, just this. Just the two of them and this powerful thing between them. Passion.

Fire, the Gringo had said.

It was everything. She lost herself in him, forgot everything else in his arms. They didn't speak, they just kissed, and touched, and screwed as if they were the last two people on the planet.

After, as they fixed their clothes, and she watched for traffic before opening the hatch, she said, "You want to prove yourself? Let me listen to all of it." Then she jumped down from the Jeep.

Jeremiah came out behind her, but his back was toward her as he closed the hatch. "To all of what?"

"The recordings on your phone. Your journal. You said you'd do anything to prove yourself. Let me listen to all of them."

He took a deep breath, and closed his eyes. "I deleted 'em."

"What?"

"Sorry, it was instinct. As soon as I realized the app had been breached—it was automatic. It's what I was raised to do. First, wipe the evidence."

She watched his face and wondered if she'd be able to tell if he was lying. "They'll be in your trash—"

"I emptied it."

"They could still be restored with—"

"I overwrote the files," he said. "I'm just realizing that was probably a mistake, but it's done."

She put her hands on her hips. "Are you even kidding me right now?"

"I'm...sorry?"

She closed her eyes, disappointed right to her toes. People didn't delete files that proved their innocence.

"Then tell me what you're lookin' for." She already knew; she just wanted to hear him tell the truth.

"I…" He raised his hands, palms up in supplication. Then dropped them again. "…can't."

"Wow. Just…" She threw her hands up. "Wow."

"I have as much right to be angry here as you do, you know. You went in my phone—"

"I went in your phone. Did I lie my way into your bed, Gringo? Did I screw you for information? Oh, wait, no, that was you."

"Willow, I swear—"

"Nope." She held up a stop sign hand, then turned and strode back toward her pickup. "Next time I see you pass somebody on double solids, I'll do worse than ticket you. I'll take your license. You have a nice day."

She got into her truck and took off, not looking at him again as she passed him, then his Jeep, and headed toward downtown Quinn and the sheriff's department. Her hands were shaking on the steering wheel and her jaw was so clenched she was giving herself a headache.

"Why did I have sex with him again? Why?"

Willow had expected an argument with Uncle Garrett about coming back so soon. She'd have had one with her parents, but they'd left for the biggest horse show of the year for them. Two days and two nights. They'd be home in time for Lily's shower.

But she'd play the professionalism card if she had to, to keep Uncle Garrett from calling her dad. One did not rat one's deputy out to her parents. It would be unprofessional.

It never happened, though.

She ran the gauntlet of deputies who were surprised to see her back and all full of smiles and back pats and fist bumps.

Uncle Lash came out of Uncle Garrett's office and frowned at her as he gave her a hug. "Garrett know you're back so soon?"

"Where is he, anyway?" she asked without answering the question.

"Out."

"Obviously," she said. "Well, I won't be here long. I just want to check on a few open cases that are drivin' me nuts. You know how it is."

"Sure," he said.

So she went to her desk and checked what she'd missed in her absence. The recording of the anonymous tip IDing Jeremiah as the drugstore-window-breaker was there waiting for her.

She played it, rewound, and played it again. Male voice, apparently doing his best Batman impersonation. Maybe on purpose. Maybe trying to disguise his voice. Interesting.

"I knew I'd find you here," said Baxter. "Are you supposed to be back at work?"

Willow looked up fast, surprised to see her cousin's shaggy mane in the sheriff's office. "Accordin' to me, I am. Aren't you s'posed to be trying to grow soybeans in the desert?"

"I'm on a break," he lied.

She smiled. He worked a half hour away, so coming here on a "break" was unlikely. "What's up, Bax?"

"Orrin asked me to find you. Said he has info too sensitive to text and he wanted someone with you when you got it. Says to check your private email."

Baxter was the guy you wanted around if there was bad news. The strong shoulder of the family. Moreover, his brain was so sharp, he could often see solutions nobody else could.

Was she about to get bad news? She tilted her head sideways. "What's this about?"

Baxter looked around them, then said, "Can we talk in private?"

"Sure."

She got up and came around the desk, let him out through the front doors and onto the sidewalk. It was already pushing eighty. She walked to a bench further up the sidewalk, but she didn't sit down.

"After the accident," Baxter said, "Orrin caught wind that you thought Jeremiah was up to something with you."

She lowered her head. "Drew tells her brother everything."

"Yeah, well, nobody knew he was fixin' to do what he did, but…" He sighed, and pushed a hand through his hair, then paced past a black pole with twin streetlamps on top. "When he went into the bunkhouse durin' the bonfire, and—"

"Did he snoop through Jeremiah's things? Jeez, Bax—"

"No. He just…helped himself to a wadded up piece of paper on the floor next to the wastebasket."

"Bax!"

"I know."

"He's already furious that I went through his phone."

"You went through his phone?" Baxter asked. He looked horrified, too.

"Well, Drew did. Sort of."

He lowered his head with a heavy sigh. "Those two need a family intervention or something."

"Think they're freaking Holmes and Watson."

"Benson and Stabler," Baxter put in. And he sent her a grin.

"Mulder and Scully," she returned.

"Steele and Holt," he said, and when she frowned he added, "Remington Steele, Laura Holt."

"This game is no fun with you; you watch ancient television."

Her cousin winked at her, but it didn't ease the dread in her heart. She sighed and sank onto the bench feeling guilty as hell as she accessed her email on her phone and hovered over the one from Orrin.

"He said it looked like a page from Vincent de Lorean's journal."

"Illegal as hell," she muttered, shaking her head. "What would Ethan think?"

"You don't have to look at it," Baxter said.

"How can I not look at it?" She clicked Orrin's email attachment. It was a photo of a handwritten page crammed with text.

"Okay," she said. "I'll have to read this somewhere else. It's too busy here and I've got too much going on."

"Or you could decide not to and just delete it," Baxter said.

She met his eyes. "The Gringo's been lyin' to me," she said.

"The Gringo saved Uncle Garrett's life when he carried him outta that fire at Two Lilies. We owe him for that."

She squared her shoulders. "I have a right to be upset with him. You're gonna have to trust me on this."

"I do trust you," he said, pacing away. "And if he wronged you, cuz, I'll kick his ass myself. But if he didn't…this might not be the best way to…handle things."

He was quite possibly the most civilized of her cousins, so that passionate promise of ass-kicking surprised her. "I love you for offerin'." She chose to ignore the rest of his statement, though.

She got up off the bench and hugged his neck, the big handsome genius. "Now I need you to give me the respect and the autonomy to take care of this myself. Okay, Baxter?"

He took a deep breath, then nodded. "I'm fixin' to hang around up home today, in case you need me."

When any of them said *up home*, no matter where they currently lived, they generally meant the Texas Brand.

She sighed and shook her head. "I appreciate it. And do me a favor? Try not to let me and Jeremiah be the main topic on the soon-to-be-created Everybody-but-Willow text loop."

He averted his eyes so fast it made her suspect such a loop already existed. They'd probably created it right after her accident.

Yeah, see? I'm not such a bad cop.

CHAPTER TWELVE

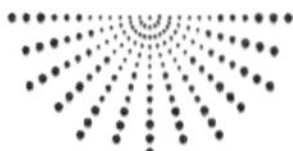

Her SUV had been waiting in her parking spot when she'd arrived at the station, just like always. She drove it to a secluded spot where teenagers liked to go parking. Or they had when she'd been in high school. She had a breakfast burrito, a cup of piping hot coffee, and her laptop, and she set to work on all three, perching the laptop on the console, safe from crumbs.

The background check she'd ordered on Juanita Lopez back when she was still dumb enough to think helping Jeremiah was a great idea, was awaiting her, and so was the image of the page from de Lorean's diary. Of the two, the diary interested her more, so that was what she looked at first.

She adjusted the image big enough to see but still small enough to prevent blur, and read while chewing a big bite of her burrito.

Everything bad happened to me in that godawful dustbowl of a town, at the hands of that phony-ass Brand clan. But one good thing, too. One good thing remains in Quinn, and nobody but me will ever know. A treasure, for sure. <u>Eight pounds and three ounces of solid gold</u>.

Willow choked on a bite, pounded her chest with a fist, and took a swig of coffee to wash it down. That last sentence was underlined in different ink and far less faded. Had Jeremiah underlined it?

This was it, then. This was why Jeremiah Thorne was walking through Quinn in his old man's footsteps with a metal detector. He thought he was fixing to find gold buried under the west Texas dirt.

The idiot.

She finished her burrito and shifted her attention to the background check. Now that she knew what she was looking for, it ought to be pretty easy to figure it out.

Jeremiah was sitting on the narrow wooden platform in front of the bunkhouse. It was more an apron than a deck. He'd pulled one of the kitchen chairs out and had it tipped back on two legs. "To hell with her, then," he said to himself for the tenth time, and he still didn't mean it. Why couldn't he brush Willow off the way he would anyone else who'd turned on him?

"She's the law." He'd reminded himself of that a hundred times, too. "The law is always the enemy."

Beans barked, and Jeremiah threw the tennis ball again. The dog loped after it, then came back, the entire ball concealed in his mouth, between those long, floppy jowls. He dropped it on the towel in Jeremiah's lap, along with a liberal slathering of drool, which was the reason for the towel.

A bicycle came down the dirt driveway, under the Texas Brand arch, then veered off toward the bunkhouse. He'd been expecting this visit.

Frankie jumped off the bike and let it roll on without him as he ran forward. "Beans!"

"Woof!" said Beans, as he ran to greet the kid, slamming his paws into Frankie's chest. Somehow staying upright, Frankie wrapped his arms around Beans and let him lick his face.

What the hell was happening? Jeremiah's throat was all tight and his eyes burned. That was... Man, what was happening to him?

He swallowed past a lump, wished he had something to drink, and said, "I'll get you a pop."

Frankie either didn't hear him or didn't care. He was on the ground, alternately hugging and playing with Beans. The pup was over the moon. It wasn't right those two had to live apart from each other.

He went inside, got a couple of Cokes from the fridge and took them back out. Frankie came to the stoop and took one, then he sat right on the floorboards with his feet on the ground. Beans turned in a circle, then laid right beside him, and settled his great big, oversized head onto the kid's lap. He sighed and closed his eyes.

"He missed you."

"I missed him, too," Frankie said, petting him. "I can't believe how big he's got! And it's only been a couple days."

"Almost big enough to handle two little sisters," he said.

Frankie lowered his eyes. "They went to the live with their dad. See we have the same mom, but different dads. And then our mom died."

"And your grandparents took you in. Your mom's parents?"

"Yeah."

"So it's just you and your grandparents now?"

"For now."

"So then...do you want to take Beans back?" His heart hurt when he said the words.

Frankie shook his head, and looked as if his heart was hurting, too. "Gram and Gramp are too old. Gram falls down a lot as it is, and he's so big and clumsy." He looked around at Jeremiah and his big brown eyes hit hard. "Do you mind keepin' him a little longer?"

"I don't mind a bit. I'll be sad when you do take him home. Listen, you rode your bike here, right? From where? Where do you guys live?"

"Not far, Oakley Road. Shitty house, though."

He didn't correct the kid for language. Screw that, he'd been through hell. If he wanted to swear, he could swear.

"There's a better one just around the corner from us right by the creek. I'm gonna live there someday. It's for sale, too!"

"Yeah?"

"Heck yeah. Gramp says we can't afford it and I shouldn't dream beyond my means."

He didn't want to contradict the kid's grandpa, but what a crappy outlook.

"So you really helped me out," Jeremiah said, "Taking care of Beans while Willow was in the hospital, so I could be there."

"It was great! I still have the money you paid me."

"Saving up to buy that house, I bet."

He smiled and nodded.

"Well, listen, kid, my brother wants me to help him out over at his honky tonk—"

"Two Lilies," Frankie said. "You going to make tacos? Or sling booze?"

The kid was a wise-ass beyond his years. "Bouncer," he said. "That doesn't get going 'til evening, and I need someone to stay with Beans."

His eyes lit up. "Every night?"

"Most nights. It's not like I can take him with me. Can you imagine Beans in a crowded honky tonk?"

"He'd go crazy!" Frankie said. "All those people, all that *food*!"

"He'd topple the tables," Jeremiah said.

"He'd tackle the dancers!" Frankie replied.

"He'd eat the tacos!"

"He'd drool in the beers!"

They both laughed so hard Frankie got tears.

"You're what, eleven, Frankie?" Jeremiah asked when they finally caught their breath. Frankie nodded. "So you want to start tonight?"

"Really?"

"Yeah. I'll be home by ten. Earlier once school starts. That's too late to bike home, so I'll drive you."

"Okay!"

"I'll call your grandma and make sure this is okay."

"She won't care."

"Well, still."

Frankie leaned forward over the dog, hugging him close. "I get to stay longer," he said. "We'll have so much fun!"

Willow found exactly what she was looking for in the background check, and then she drove to Juanita Lopez's place.

She found her in the vegetable garden beside her modest home. She wore a big straw sun hat and round sunglasses. Juanita got up, brushing off her garden gloves before removing them.

"Hello again," Willow said.

"Deputy," she replied with a nod that might've been resigned.

Willow said, "I want to ask you something, Juanita. Something you didn't mention the other day, when we talked about your time with Vincent de Lorean."

Juanita bit her lip, averted her eyes. Cleary she already knew what Willow would ask.

"I want to be clear, Juanita, I'm off duty right now, and this is unofficial. You do not have to answer me. But…I know you had a baby twenty-eight years ago."

She met Willow's eyes, and to her surprise, nodded. "I did."

"Was Vincent de Lorean the father?"

All her breath went out of her. She paced out of her garden, across her small back lawn, and sat down on the concrete steps at her back door. Then she peeled off her soil-stained gloves.

"Yes. I lied to you about that, I'm afraid. I fell hard for him when he stayed at the Inn. But then to find out he was a criminal, and I was a teenager. I was so ashamed."

"Juanita, you were a kid. You have nothing to be ashamed of. I'd arrest him for child rape if he was still alive."

She took a shuddering breath at the words. Then, "My mother told me he must never know about the baby, that she would never be safe from him if he did, nor would I, she said. So…I couldn't keep her."

Willow's hopes had been climbing with every word of the story right up until the end. "You…couldn't keep her?"

"My mother helped me arrange a private adoption."

"Oh." *Crash.* "And you haven't seen her since?"

The sad look left Juanita's eyes, and her smile then chased away the shadows that had briefly clouded them. "Oh, no, I see her all the time. I didn't for a while, but when she was thirteen, she asked and her parents helped her find me. I've been to very birthday party since, and a lot of the holidays, too."

Willow's roller coaster ride slowed to a halt. "It sounds like a happy endin'."

"It all worked out okay," Juanita said. "She's had a beautiful life."

She looked as if she meant it. Willow said, "Do you think she'd mind you givin' me her contact info? Even just an email—"

"I have one of her business cards inside. You want to come in while I get it?"

"I'll wait, out here." She'd intruded enough. Too much. But she was glad she knew more of the story now.

As Juanita headed inside, Willow thought about her decision to give her daughter up for adoption. It seemed all three women who'd given birth to children fathered by Vincent de Lorean had given them up. And two of them had died right after.

But something was niggling at her.

She emerged from her house with a business card, and handed it to Willow. Elena Montrose, M.D.

Elena Montrose? She was Juanita's daughter? Ethan and Jeremiah's sister?

"I've met her, your daughter," she said. "There was some vandalism at her house."

"She told me. Some local kid brought up badly, she thinks."

"So she's a doctor."

"*Sí*, and married to a lawyer, *gracias a Dios*."

"That's wonderful. You must be so proud."

"Oh, I am." She lowered her head. "Elena…she doesn't know who her father was. It's unfair of me not to tell her. Especially now that she's married."

Willow nodded. This was getting sensitive. She needed to let Jeremiah and Ethan know they had a sister.

"I agree with you that telling her the truth is the right thing to do. And…well, it's likely to come out. I'm surprised it hasn't already. You should be the one to tell her, Juanita, not the Quinn County grapevine. Besides, she has two half-brothers she knows nothing about."

Juanita blinked slowly. "Can you wait to tell them about her? Give me time to tell her?"

"I don't want to force anything on you that you're not ready to do."

"No, no, I've already waited too long. You've given me a reason to do what must be done. I…I'll tell her tonight. And I'll tell her you'd like to talk to her."

"Unofficially," Willow said. "She doesn't have to talk to me."

She nodded.

"Do you um…do you happen to remember how much Elena weighed at birth?"

"Of course I remember. A woman doesn't forget things like that. Eight pounds and three ounces."

"Eight pounds and three ounces of solid gold," Willow said. And she knew Juanita was wrong about one thing. De Lorean *had* known about his baby girl, somehow. Eight pounds and three ounces of solid gold, he'd written in his diary. He'd been referring to his daughter.

She'd suspected a baby as soon as she'd read the words. If it was gold, as Jeremiah apparently believed, he'd have just written eight pounds. But baby weights were always given, in pounds and ounces.

"Who all knew you were pregnant back then?" Willow asked.

"We kept it secret. I left town when I started showing. I still keep it to myself, though I imagine now that you know, and Elena will know, soon everyone will know." She sighed heavily. "I don't suppose anyone even cares. It's not a scandal anymore, having a baby without a husband, or giving her away."

"Not a scandal, ma'am. And I'm not fixin' to tell anyone except for her two half-brothers. But I won't do that until after I've talked to her and made sure she's okay with it. Is that all right?"

She nodded. "She'll want to know about her brothers. One of them's a music star, after all." Tilting her head, she asked, "What's the other one like? Jeremiah?"

"He's like…a chameleon. But I think I've glimpsed his true colors once or twice, and I can't shake the notion that they're good. They're just…repressed, I think." She realized she'd said way too much, letting her thoughts spill over.

Juanita was looking at her as if she'd lapsed into Armenian.

"He's a decent man," she said. "Thank you, Juanita. I appreciate you bein' straight with me."

"*De nada,*" she said. "It was time for it to be spoken."

Willow left Juanita and drove to Mad Bull's Bend, clocking in via the radio before pulling into Two Lilies, and around to the parking lot in back. The first vehicle she noticed was Jeremiah's russet Jeep. It was parked amid a dozen other vehicles, but the only one she saw. She had to remind herself to scan the lot for local troublemakers, Barker Boys included, or maybe that motorcycle thief who'd dang near got her killed.

None were present, so that was good.

She spent most of every shift at Two Lilies. After all, it was the reason there even was a constant police presence in Mad Bull's Bend. Frequently, but not regularly, she'd leave to take a drive around town, check in on all the other businesses. Sometimes she'd spend a little time at The Watering Hole, if the crowd seemed particularly large or rowdy.

She got out of her vehicle, pressed her lips and lowered her eyes. She didn't really want to see Jeremiah. It was too easy to fall into those vivid blue eyes of his, too easy to believe whatever kind of deceptive game he'd play with her next.

Well, now she was the one keeping secrets.

Secrets he has every right to know. So does Ethan.

Her inner voice was not wrong. But she'd given Juanita her word that she would wait until tomorrow. And that was only another eighteen hours at most. She planned to talk to Elena Montrose first thing in the morning.

She followed the new stepping stone path from the edge of the parking lot around to the main entrance on the side of the building—big glass double doors with the Two Lilies logo. Every so often one of the stones had an arrow pointing the way to the entrance, and they stretched the entire boundary of the parking lot, so you couldn't miss 'em. Ethan and Lily had also installed two bright lights at either end of the parking lot, and made the in and out signs reflective.

Willow went through the double doors into a blast of juke box country—the band wouldn't start until later. It was dim inside, the glass front walls in the large stage section with the stage and dance floor were still shuttered. A few people milled around, but the main action this early was through the archway in the original section, and as she crossed the dance floor, the din from there got louder.

In the original half of the place, what had once been Manny's Cantina, the bar was bordered by a stairway on the near side, and double doors to the kitchen on the far. Nearly every stool was occupied. Most of the tables were, too, and the glass doors in this section were open wide, with patrons already occupying a few of the outdoor tables.

She scanned the inside, and got stuck on his sombrero.

Yeah, he was wearing it, back at his favorite table, sipping something brown. Sighing, she decided to face this and get it over with. He was family, she couldn't let it fester and poison the clan.

She walked over. His eyes were on her all the way, had been on her, she realized, since the moment she'd come in. He had a line of sight clear to the door.

When she reached his table, he stretched out a leg underneath it and shoved the opposite chair out.

As invitations went, it was barely better than a grunt, but she sat down and nodded at his glass. "It's too early for tequila."

"Special circumstances." He didn't look up, so the brim of the hat hid his eyes.

"Yeah?"

"Girlfriend dumped me," he said. Then he poured the tequila down his throat in one gulp, pulled his lips away from his teeth, and sucked air.

"Is that what I was to you? Your girlfriend?"

"What did you think you were to me?"

"I'll tell you what I didn't think I was. I didn't think I was the most convenient source of information on your father."

"You were more than that," he said.

She shook her head hard.

He poured another shot. "What was I to you, then?" he asked.

"I don't know, Jeremiah. You didn't give me a chance to find out."

"I didn't end it, you did," he said.

"I didn't end it either," she snapped.

He didn't reply. The brim of his ridiculous hat rose a little bit. She could feel him frowning at her, and it pissed her off that she couldn't also *see* him frowning at her. She snatched the hat off his head, brought it around her and hung it by its string on the back of her chair.

He met her eyes, riffling his dark gold hair free of its sombrero-ring. No, she thought, it was more like tarnished bronze, his hair. And too long, so long she could bury her whole hand in it. And had.

"I'm sorry I went through your phone. In my defense, I wasn't the one who did it; it was just kind of grabbed and shoved in my face."

"And then you tapped 'play.'"

She nodded. "And then I tapped 'play.'" She shrugged. "I knew you were keeping things from me."

"I have a right to keep things from you," he said.

She lowered her head.

He said, "I'm sorry I used you. In my defense, it only started out that way. I was starting to really like you."

"I was starting to really like you back," she said.

He took a breath, watching her face with a kind of relaxed intensity she didn't think she'd ever felt in her life. Like he'd be okay with whatever he saw there. "So uh, neither of us ended it, then," he said, real deep and slow.

She could fall into his eyes, she could. The way they moved over her face was like a touch. The chatter and clatter of the patrons faded to a din. Right then all she wanted was to touch him. To just be close enough to touch him and—

No. She snatched the shot glass from under his chin and downed it in a single gulp, then slapped it down again.

"Shit," she said, wiping her chin. "I'm on duty."

"And you never cuss."

"Not before you."

A tap on her shoulder, and she turned to see her uncle and boss, the sheriff.

"I saw that," he said. "I was told you were returnin' to duty today."

"I am, I mean, I was, I just—"

"I'm glad to see you've decided against it," he said.

"I haven't—"

"Yeah, you did, niece, soon as you drank that Jose Cuervo. So you'd best get out of that uniform. I believe Lily keeps a few things upstairs."

Willow sighed. At least she wasn't in trouble with Uncle Garrett, at least she wouldn't be so long as she did as he said. "I'm needed here, you know," she said. "I don't see any other deputies around."

"You see me, don't you?" he replied. "Besides, Ethan's hired a bouncer to help out." He nodded at Jeremiah.

"Oh. I see."

A couple of discordant twangs from the adjoining room told her the band was getting ready to start.

"I'll uh…keep your date comp'ny," Uncle Garrett said, "while you go change." And when she got out of her chair, her Uncle Garrett slid into her place.

She sent Jeremiah a nervous look, but he seemed unruffled. Then she headed for Lily and a change of clothes.

Jeremiah waited for the set-down he knew was coming from the elder statesman of the clan. He probably deserved it, and was mentally rehearsing his response, his honest and heartfelt vow that he would leave Willow Brand alone.

Cat Shaw, full-time realtor and part-time bartender, brought a tall, foam-free, amber mug to Garrett and put it down.

The big guy took a gulp, wiped off his lip with the back of his hand, and said, "The way you look at her is like a neon sign. But she's a lot of woman. It'll take a lot of man to be worthy."

"I don't intend to—"

"Ah, hell, son, you don't think what you *intend* has anything to do with it, do you?" He took another sip from his glass.

Jeremiah was pretty sure it was iced tea. "I don't know what you mean," he said. "Sir."

"Suddenly I'm sir? Shoot, you got it bad." Garrett kept losing control of the grin he was trying to hide. "I feel compelled to look out for you, Jeremiah," he said. "You're my son's brother."

He'd had no idea the patriarch felt that way. "I don't mean any offense, sir. Garrett. But I've never needed anyone looking out for me."

"I sound like a knight. Sir Garrett." He laughed a little, easy, and completely unoffended as far as Jeremiah could tell. "You carried me outta the flames," he said. "That alone creates a bond."

He didn't agree or disagree. He hadn't thought about it, but there had been an odd ease, and a kind of familiarity settling in between him and Garrett Brand since that day.

"I uh…I died, you know."

The words startled him almost out of his chair. He tipped the tequila bottle to his bowl-like copita glass again. "I heard that. They said Lily did CPR, brought you back right before Ethan and I busted in."

Garrett nodded, and for a long moment his gaze turned inward. Jeremiah watched his face, curious what he was thinking, or remembering. What had Garrett Brand experienced?

Eventually, he went on. "I came back knowin' something. Just knowin' it. Nobody told me while I was…I just came back knowin'."

Jeremiah got the feeling there was a lot more to tell. "Knowing what?" he asked softly. He leaned forward without intending to.

"The only thing in this life that matters is love. Nothin' else even comes close. The rest is…it's made up, you know? Our governments, our businesses, our divisions—we make it all up. It's not real, none of it. Love's what's real."

His voice seemed to tighten.

"Don't you let it go, you hear? It's an insult to life itself to let it go. It's precious…more precious than gold."

Funny he should put it that particular way.

"That's…that's deep. Thank you, Garrett, for sharing that with me."

Suddenly the older man clasped his forearm firmly. "It's not an opinion, son. It's the truth, the only truth there is when it comes down to it. You take heed, you hear?"

His eyes were alight. He meant what he was saying. Jeremiah nodded. "Yes, sir."

Garrett smiled, relaxed his grip, then looked past him toward the bar. Jeremiah turned and saw Willow coming back down the stairs in a pair of jeans and a pretty white blouse with lacy insets at the shoulders. Her black hair hung loose, thank goodness. All he ever wanted to do when it was all pinned up for duty, was set it free.

"I got one more thing to share, Jeremiah," Garrett said.

Jeremiah nodded but didn't look at him. His eyes were on Willow's and hers were on him. "What's that, sir?"

"She looks at you the same way. Just like a neon sign." He chuckled softly. "It's like you two are the only ones who can't see it." He chuckled a little harder as he got up and walked back over to the bar.

Willow came to the table just as the band started playing. People were getting up and heading through the archway onto the dance floor, a river of them cutting off her approach.

So he got up and made his way toward her, and she toward him. When they came face-to-face, she clasped his shoulder to keep from being knocked back again and he held her waist, turning her in a circle until they were out of the current.

She looked up at him. He thought maybe she believed him. She said, "I'm of no use to you now. I'm not fixin' to give you access to stuff you ought not have access to."

"Are you fixin' to dance with me, though?"

She shrugged and her eyes dipped, but her lips smiled from below. "I mean, I could. Turns out I have the night off."

He pulled her into his arms and they joined the folks heading onto the dance floor. The band tonight was Dirt River, one of three local house bands who alternated nights whenever big acts weren't booked.

He led Willow Brand right into a two-step, and when she caught on, she smiled up at him in surprise. "You can dance."

"One of crime-dad's commandments. Know how to pass in society. I had to take lessons in dancing and etiquette and such."

"He made you do this from prison?"

"He was blind to the irony," he said.

She said, "I'm sorry your mamma was taken from you so young. It must've been awful, I can't even imagine."

"Don't try to," he said. "It hurt. You learn to live with it."

"What else *can* you do?" she asked.

He pulled her a little closer. "More cheerful topics?"

"Sure. You can tell me what you're lookin' for, out in the desert with a metal detector."

He wondered if she already knew. The answer was in his old man's diary, and Orrin had been alone in the bunkhouse with it. He'd realized just a shade too late how seriously little Nancy

Drew and her Hardy Boy Brother took their work as amateur private dicks.

Garrett Brand's voice played through his head, with a flash of his fiery eyes. *More precious than gold.*

"My father told me he left some gold here in Quinn. But he didn't say where."

She nodded. "What if you're wrong, and there's no gold? Have you thought about that?"

He shrugged, because he didn't want to think about that.

"You said someone is contesting the will. Have you looked into that at all?"

"The lawyer's handling all that." He frowned at her. "Why?" Did she know something?

"Look, on the way in here today, I got a message from dispatch. They sent me this." She pulled out her phone, and tapped it.

A hushed male voice said, "I saw who stole that motorcycle that caused the accident. It was that stray Brand that wears the sombrero."

Ice water filled Jeremiah's veins. He looked at Willow, searching her for the accusation.

"Now listen to this," she said, and held the phone out again.

"I saw the guy who threw the brick through the drug store window tonight. It was that blond-haired Brand, the country singer's brother."

He blinked. "But Willow, I didn't—"

"It's the same voice," she said. "The same person is IDing you for stuff you didn't do. We need to figure out why, and then we'll know who. So I got to thinking about the will and how you said someone's contesting it. I thought it might give us a possible motive."

He blinked at her. She said, "What?"

"You didn't ask if I did it."

"Well, duh. I knew that."

It took him a minute to process the words. "You didn't think, even for a minute, that I might've—"

"No! Jeez, Jeremiah. No."

"Well, why not?"

She gazed into his eyes so long it was uncomfortable, and then it wasn't. It was some kind of connection. "Because you're a good person. You're a good person, you saved the puppy, you're kind to orphaned children, you sprung me from the hospital, you saved my uncle's life." She put a hand to his cheek and said, "How the heck can you not realize that you are *good*?"

He couldn't answer. His mind was busy allowing the notion to settle in. What if she was right? What if he was actually one of the good guys?

"What if you didn't get a nickel from your old man?" She had stopped dancing. They stood in the middle of the dance floor. The glass front walls were open out to the patio, with its party lights and water feature. She was looking up at him, and everything in his body wanted to kiss her right there in front of the entire town.

Her cousins would have him lynched by morning, his own brother leading the pack.

"What would you be, if you could be anything you wanted, Gringo Sombrero?"

The words that floated to mind were, *I'd be your man, Willow Brand.* But he didn't say it out loud. So instead he said, "I'm writing, some." And he watched her face.

"Writing?"

"That's what the journal was for. I mean, I was raised by a drug lord from his prison cell with a cast of criminal caregivers. It feels like a novel."

She opened her mouth, closed it again. "A novel?"

He shrugged. "Although lately, I've been feeling a children's book coming on. Frank and Beans."

A smile took charge of her face. "Jeremiah, that's amazing. I had no idea."

He shrugged. "He's dog-sitting tonight, did I tell you?"

"Frankie is?"

He nodded. "The girls went to live with their father. But Frankie says his grandparents are too frail to manage such a big fella. 'Bout broke my heart. Poor kid."

He glanced down at her to see her eyes bigger and browner than he probably ever had, gazing up at him. Her mouth was open just a little. Then she whispered, "There you are," and she laid her head on his chest. "Oh my God, there you are Jeremiah Thorne."

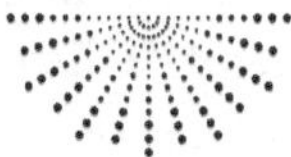

CHAPTER THIRTEEN

They danced twice more, and then they had tacos together. She wanted to tell him there was no gold, that the treasure was something even better. A sister!

But she'd promised Juanita and she couldn't break her word. She'd tell him tomorrow, after she'd spoken to Elena, just like she'd said she would.

After eating their fill, they danced again.

From behind the bar, Lily watched over her like a guardian angel, with the pale hair and blue eyes to prove it. Ethan was downstairs in the basement recording studio, playing with some tracks, thank goodness. Uncle Garrett had settled up and left the place, probably doing rounds about town like she usually did.

Jeremiah leaned down and whispered near her ear. "You want to get out of here?"

"I do," she said. "And while I'd prefer you throw me over your shoulder and carry me out to your Jeep, I think the better part of discretion is to leave separately."

He rasped his whiskers across her ear, and she melted and cussed under her breath. "Your place or mine?" he asked.

"Mine. My folks had to leave town, so it'll be private."

"I got a better idea." He slid his phone from his pocket and texted her an address. "Wait for me, there, okay?"

She lowered her chin as she read the message. "I'm sheriff. I can't be going on private property—"

"Now, Sheriff, you just told me I'm a good guy. Did you mean it?"

She blinked, and erased the doubt from her eyes, even though a tiny bit remained in her heart. "Okay, I'll wait for you there."

He smiled softly. Though her trust was real, she doubted that he believed that. She was still nervous as she punched the address into her GPS and drove back toward Quinn, and then through it. She took the opportunity to drop the SUV back at the sheriff's department and pick up her truck.

Her GPS took her through town, out toward the ranch, and up Oak Ridge Road, then off a private dirt road that didn't get much use, going by the grass growing up the middle.

Eventually the GPS told her she had reached her destination.

Willow looked around. It was dark outside, but her headlights picked out a driveway, and when she turned into it, the numbers on a log cabin lit up. Yes, this was the place.

She parked her truck, shut it off but left the headlights on and got out to the sound of rushing water. Hell, the creek ran right behind the house.

She lit up her phone and trudged around behind the modest cabin toward the creek. It wasn't far to its pebbly shore. The water bent inward, then out again, as if pointing toward the little cabin on its bank, and when she turned to look back, she saw tall windows, and deck facing her. It had two rocking chairs on it and seemed to be a visual invitation. The place was like a Kincaid painting.

She hiked back up to the cabin, walked onto the porch, and cupping her hands around the windows, peeked inside. No furniture. No curtains in the windows. The place was vacant.

Still, somebody must own it.

She tried the sliding door and found it locked, as expected. Around her, the woods were alive with the whir of bugs and the occasional cries of night birds. Whatever they were, they would call three times, like a mewling cat, then three more, and three more still, each time from a different source. Then they'd go quiet for a while.

The air smelled like sage and creek water, fresh and spicy-sweet. It felt ten degrees cooler than anywhere else tonight.

The right side had four windows. Through them she could see a big open space, a kitchen and a loft with two rooms. At the front, she crossed another open porch to the front door, and found herself standing on a welcome mat.

"You don't suppose..." She stepped off the mat, and crouched to lift it up.

A shiny key lay underneath.

She picked it up and slid it into the lock. Then she hesitated to turn it.

"Okay, Gringo. I'm trusting you. You cost me my badge, I swear to God..." She turned the key, then opened the door went inside, tried the light switch, but nothing happened beyond an ineffective *click click.*

The main room was wide, with a fireplace and large windows overlooking the creek in back and the woods on one side. The counter had stools, and the kitchen had white cabinets.

There was a vase on that counter with a white rose in it, and a card.

She went over to it, shamelessly opening it up, jumping to romantic conclusions.

Congratulations, Jeremiah. I think you and Beans will be very happy here.

Cat Shaw

He bought a freakin' house.

Willow wrapped her mind around that bit of new information slowly. That meant Jeremiah was staying in Quinn.

She went to the kitchen, opened cabinets, and found a bottle of whiskey with a ribbon around it, and a pair of glasses. That Cat sure did know how to treat a client.

She took the bottle down and poured, then checked out the simple white stove and fridge. No dishwasher, old fashioned porcelain sink and faucets.

She went through the doors to find a cute little bathroom done in pale green and white, with a big shower stall despite the small space, and a dual sink. The other door led into the master bedroom, which also had a door between it and the bathroom.

The bedroom was cozy, with a walk-in closet, big windows all the way around and a set of sliding doors out onto the deck, overlooking the stream.

She returned to the living room, and was about to go up to check out the loft, when headlights came bounding over the drive. Then the front door opened, and Beans preceded Jeremiah through and galloped toward her.

"Do this," Jeremiah called, holding his hands just so.

She did it, and the dog did not jump, but rather stopped in front of her and sat politely, thumping his tail like a jackrabbit's hind leg. She pet him, and he wiggled from end to end.

"Jeremiah, this place is amazing. You bought it?"

"I can afford it, even without the inheritance *or* the gold," he said. Then, under his breath, "Barely." Then he pointed behind him. "I have some essentials in the Jeep, you want to—?"

"Sure, I'll help out. So tell me when all this happened?"

"Today. It all happened today. Frankie told me about this place right near where he lives with his grandparents. Said he wanted to live in it someday, and said it was for sale. So I called Cat. She met me here tonight, and…it's perfect. In every way perfect. So…I told her I'd take it. We haven't done paperwork, of course."

"Of course."

"I figured I needed a place, and I like it a lot."

"I do, too."

"And it's so close to Frankie. I figured dog-sitting here would be almost as good as living here, you know? I dropped him off at his place on the way back here with Beans and the supplies."

He opened the back of the Jeep. The light came on inside, and the thing was packed full, but atop it all were grocery bags, containing toothbrushes, toilet paper, coffee and paper cups. He even had a coffee pot, brand new in the box.

"I figure I'll know what I need as I go along. I ordered and paid on line, and it was all ready to pick up. For tonight, just essentials."

He pulled out a box of cookies from the local bakery.

"Essentials huh?"

"I'm trying to woo you. I figured sweets—"

"You figured right. Com 'ere." She pulled him close by the collar of his shirt, cause she couldn't wait any longer, and then she kissed him.

He kissed her back, and his lips were smiling through most of it. And then they unloaded the Jeep a little faster, including a cooler full of perishables, his clothes and shower supplies, and two bundles of bedding from the bunkhouse.

"I didn't think Chelsea would mind," he said.

"I don't think she would either," she replied, and they tumbled together into the bedroom without even unbundling the bedding, undressing on the way.

He rolled onto his back, pulling her on top of him, though she thought he was probably harder than the floor. She ran her hands over his body, appreciating every bulge and ripple with her fingers, and then with her lips.

"You are one beautiful piece of manhood, you are," she told him. "Inside and out, it seems."

"Not good enough for a woman like you," he replied, his eyes holding hers like he wanted to show her he meant it. Then he pulled her down against him, chest to chest, and kissed her again. They melded into each other, clung to each other.

It was different than it had been with him before—different from anything she'd ever felt before. It felt like *more*. In every dimension, more; wider, taller, deeper than it had been.

They climbed to the highest peaks together, and crashed again still wrapped in each other's arms. He held her tight while her pieces melded themselves together once more, and being in his arms felt like the safest place in the universe.

It felt, Willow realized, like love.

An hour later, Willow's phone buzzed. They were still basking in each other, tangled in blankets they'd finally unbundled, snuggling as if they'd never untangle. Beans was snuggled up beside them as close as he could get.

Willow looked at her phone screen. It was Juanita. Guilt stabbed at her for not having told Jeremiah yet about his half-sister.

She said, "I have to take this," and got up, dragging a blanket with her, and going out the sliding doors onto the back porch. She saw the way he frowned at her as she closed those doors behind her.

"Juanita?" she asked, moving as far to the other end of the porch as possible.

"There's been an accident," Juanita cried.

Alarm trilled down Willow's spine. "*What?* Where? Are you okay?"

"It's Elena! She's in the hospital."

"Oh my God."

"You should come. You should…her brothers…they should come, in case…"

"I understand."

"Good."

"Had you told her, Juanita? Did she know?"

"*Sí*. We had dinner together. She was angry at first, but quickly forgave me for keeping such secrets. And she's excited to meet her brothers. I told her you'd be calling tomorrow, and she was happy." Juanita sniffled. "She was happy. Two hours ago, she was excited and happy and now…"

"We'll be there," she said. "I'm so sorry, Juanita. Please hold on, we're coming."

Willow disconnected and turned to see Jeremiah standing on the porch behind her. "Juanita?" he asked. "Would that be Juanita Lopez of the former Bluebonnet Inn?"

She nodded. "Yeah. She made me promise not to tell you until tomorrow but now—"

"Tell me what, Willow?"

Willow sighed heavily. "The eight pounds and three ounces of solid gold, that wasn't literal," she said. "It's a baby weight. I knew it as soon as I read it—"

"Read it how?"

"It doesn't matter how."

"Orrin was in my father's diary. I thought you weren't gonna invade my privacy again, Willow."

"First, I never said that, and second, this was before I never said that, and third, it was a wadded up page on the floor near the trash—right in the open, he wasn't snooping, really, and fourth, it doesn't matter right now. You're losing the storyline, Gringo. It was a *baby*. You have a sister. You and Ethan have a sister."

He blinked, stunned, so she rushed on. "Juanita gave her up for adoption to protect her from de Lorean. She thought he never knew, but he must have, to have mentioned her in the diary."

"There were newborn pictures in his safe deposit box," he

said, his voice hoarse with emotion. "I thought it was one of us, Ethan or I. Expected the dang box to have the gold, but—"

"She's the gold," Willow said. "Elena Montrose. But she's hurt. There was an accident tonight, and she—"

"Wait, how long have you known this?" he asked. "Why didn't you tell me? And now…how badly is she hurt?"

She flinched under his scrutiny. "I don't know, but it sounded bad. Juanita said you and Ethan should come to the hospital."

He swore and it hurt her physically. "I can't believe you kept this from me."

"I gave Juanita my word. She wanted time to tell Elena who her father was herself. It was only for a day."

"Maybe her last day," he said. "How could you do that to me, Willow?"

Her tears were streaming. "It wasn't my intent. I couldn't have known—"

"You should've told me." There was stark, bleeding hurt behind the anger in his eyes. "You should've trusted me."

He picked up his clothes and slammed into the bathroom. When he came out again, dressed, he said, "Please stay with Beans, or if you have to leave, just—"

"I got it. Go on."

He left without saying goodbye, or looking her in the eye, or forgiving her. She sat there, her heart, soul, and body naked on the floor.

Jeremiah was wounded deep, but the urgency of the situation kept him distracted enough to wade through. He had to drive to El Paso, find a parking spot at the hospital, find the right entrance, and then look around for Juanita Lopez.

She wasn't hard to spot, and she was there with a couple, tall and lean, nicely dressed, both Hispanic, and a thirty-something blond male who was sitting in a chair biting his nails.

"Jeremiah, thank goodness." Juanita came to him, standing on tiptoe to hug him as if they were family now. She was four foot eleven at best.

He hugged her gently and asked, "How is she?"

"We've heard nothing yet," she said, and she looked around him. "Where is Ethan? And Willow, she promised she would come." Then, "Wait, wait, Sophia and Miguel Rodriguez, this is Jeremiah Thorne, our daughter Elena's half-brother."

Miguel came and shook his hand, but his wife only sent a wan smile. She was seated, and looked rather limp and shaky.

"We're Elena's adoptive parents," Miguel said, then he turned to the other man, the blond one, who'd finally risen to his feet. He looked like he must be an actor. "This is her husband, Richie," Miguel went on.

"Richard Montrose," he said, giving a firm handshake.

Jeremiah nodded, then turned to Juanita. "Does anyone know what happened?"

"It was a hit and run," Juanita said, a cry in her voice. "She jogs every evening, out past the county line." She choked out the final word with a fresh flood of tears.

He swore under his breath and Ethan came around a corner with bed hair and his shirt buttoned crookedly. Something powerful moved through Jeremiah when his brother came up beside him and clapped a hand to his shoulder. "Willow called. What do we know? I heard that last bit, about the hit and run."

Juanita said to the others, "This is the other brother, Ethan. Ethan, we haven't heard…"

A pair of white-coated individuals arrived, a man and a woman, each with MD after the names on their badges, which were Gray and Cantrell.

"You're Elena Montrose's family? Asked the male, Dr. Gray, who was the color of his name.

They all said yes or *Si* and he spoke while the female, Dr. Cantrell, wore a look of weary patience.

"Well, she has some broken ribs, and a bruised spleen, which is our chief concern." Dr. Gray paused there, and every eye in the place shifted to Dr. Cantrell.

She said. "We think she's going to be okay. But we'll keep her here tonight, watch her closely, and reassess tomorrow."

Juanita started giving thanks in Spanish, and the couple hugged. Elena's husband lowered his forehead into his hand.

"You can see her," Dr. Cantrell went on. "Just two at a time, though, and since there are so many, let's say ten minutes each. She needs rest."

"We'll go last," Jeremiah said. "You folks, you go on in, see your daughter."

Sophia, the adoptive mother, took Juanita's hand. "Mothers first," she said firmly. "And if we take more than ten minutes, you can deduct it from the others."

Juanita clasped her hand and they exchanged a determined look, pasted smiles on their faces, and marched down the hall to their daughter's room.

Ethan and Jeremiah went over by the vending machines, away from Elena's husband and father. "Willow called me," Ethan said. "Can you even believe this? We had a sister nearby, all this time? And we didn't even know?"

"Apparently Elena didn't know either. Not until last night when her mother told her. Willow's known for I don't know how long."

"She only got confirmation yesterday," Ethan said.

"And didn't tell us."

Ethan tipped his head to one side. "She gave Juanita a day to tell her daughter the truth about her parentage. That doesn't seem unreasonable to me."

"Would it have been reasonable if Elena had died tonight?"

Ethan frowned hard. "You're really angry about this."

"I am." He took a breath, paced away, took another. "I really am."

"You think maybe it's about more than Willow keepin' a secret for a day?" Ethan asked. "I'm not the therapist in the family, but—"

"I trusted her. She broke into my phone. I forgave her. She had Orrin take pics of my father's diary. I'd forgive that, too. But then she kept my sister from me."

A soft gasp made him turn to see Willow standing there in the hallway, only two feet away, having heard everything he'd said.

He lowered his eyes, shaking his head and walking away.

Ethan went to his cousin, hugged her, and started filling her in on the details while Jeremiah walked further down the hall to a coffee machine.

As he did, two Texas Rangers approached him, and he knew as soon as he met their eyes that they were there for him.

"Jeremiah Thorne?"

Feet tapped closer. Willow said, "Wait a minute, wait a minute, I'm Quinn County Deputy Brand, what's goin' on here? What do you want with him?"

"We just have a few questions, Deputy. This happened outside your jurisdiction on a state highway. That puts it in ours. We can question him here or–"

"We'll do it here," she said quickly.

Jeremiah sent her a look that was meant to convey, "Oh, no, we won't."

"Here," Willow repeated, letting him know this was happening. Avoiding it would make him look guilty. "There are some chairs by the window at the end of the hall, out of the way."

The mothers returned, looking at them curiously as they went back to the waiting room. Then Elena's adoptive father and husband went to take their turn at her bedside.

Ethan was right beside Willow, and he looked worried. The five of them, Ethan, Jeremiah, Willow, and the two rangers went to the alcove at the end of the hall with a padded window seat, but nobody sat down.

"Mr. Thorne, we need to know where you were tonight, about ninety minutes ago."

"I don't recall and I want an attorney," Jeremiah said in a monotone.

"He was with me," Willow told the rangers with an impatient look his way. "We were celebrating at the log cabin he just bought in Quinn. All night. Until the phone rang to tell us Elena was in the hospital."

They looked at each other, looked at Jeremiah. "That right?"

He nodded but didn't speak.

Elena's two mothers had wandered closer, pretending to look at flyers stuck by thumbtacks into a corkboard wall.

"What made you suspect him, anyway?" Willow demanded. "Wait, don't tell me. Anonymous tip?" She knew by the quick look they exchanged that she was right. "Male, disguising his voice resulting in a Batman-like raspy whisper?"

"How did you—?"

"Because he's implicated Jeremiah in two other crimes we know for sure he didn't commit. Jeremiah didn't even know Elena existed until I told him tonight."

At that, the cops reacted in blatant disbelief. One even rolled his eyes. "Oh, he knew, all right," he said. "We aren't here based on the tip alone, Deputy. Elena Montrose was contesting her birth father's will, and Thorne was fighting it. How could he not know about her?"

"It was *her*?" Jeremiah asked, too shocked to maintain silence.

"That's ridiculous." The two mothers stopped pretending not to listen in and came closer. Sophia said, "We'd certainly know if our daughter was suing anyone."

Juanita added, "She didn't even know de Lorean was her birth father until I told her last night. She was shocked and shaken by the news, even angry that I'd kept it from her. She could not fake those things, not and fool me."

Jeremiah decided maybe silence wasn't the best option all the time after all. He said, "My lawyer did tell me someone was contesting the will. They were anonymous and I just let him handle it. He'll verify that."

"The lawsuit is filed in her name," cop number two said. "Elena Montrose."

"Well, who else could sue on behalf of Elena?" Sophia asked.

And just then, Elena's dad and her husband came from her room and looked around at them as everyone stopped speaking.

Willow gripped the first officer's arm and spoke low, and close to his ear. "The Montroses had a brick thrown through their window. The husband, the only one on the scene, identified Jeremiah's Jeep in the area when I know for a fact he was with me. I'd love to compare his voice with those anonymous tips."

She said, turning to look at Richard Montrose as he stood in the hospital corridor. The cops looked at him, too, and he shifted his feet, and rubbed his forearm like it itched. His wife's room was behind him.

"If he did this," she said, for the rangers' ears alone, "he nearly killed his wife, and he nearly killed me." She reached for her handcuffs, and realized she wasn't in uniform, so she yanked a pair from the nearest officer and strode toward Montrose. "Turn around and put your hands behind your back."

He turned around, all right, took off running. The two rangers looked at her, and she said, "Well? Go get him! Notify us when you do. Here." She handed back the handcuffs, and the Rangers took off after the son of a gun.

"What in the world is going on?" Juanita asked. "What did Richard do?"

Everyone was lookin' at Willow, like she had all he answers. She said, "I haven't worked it all out yet—but I'm afraid he tried to kill Elena."

Sophia pressed a hand to her chest, and her husband put his arm around her.

Juanita looked instantly furious, but she turned to Jeremiah and Ethan. "You should go see her now. I told her you were coming, and they gave her a shot for sleep, so hurry. But tell her none of this. Not yet."

"No, she's right," Sophia said. "Let her have a night to heal. None of this makes sense now."

Jeremiah and Ethan exchanged a look. Willow could see clearly that Jeremiah didn't believe for a second that his half-sister hadn't been involved in contesting the will. But they both nodded in agreement, then walked down the hall with Juanita, two feet shorter, walking in between them to the correct closed door.

CHAPTER FOURTEEN

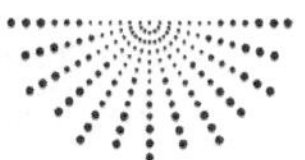

Jeremiah stepped through the door first. Ethan came in right behind. He was struck by the big brown eyes of the woman in the hospital bed. She gazed at him from within a mass of wavy brown hair and skin the color of almonds. She looked past him, and he remembered Ethan and moved in further to make room for his brother to enter.

She wasn't smiling, exactly. She looked nervous and sleepy. Even in the state she was in, injured and traumatized, she was pretty. Her brown eyes reminded him of Ethan's.

She said, "They tell me you two big Texans are my brothers."

"Seems like," Ethan said.

Jeremiah couldn't find words, and when he did, they were dumb. "Are you okay?" Of course she wasn't okay, she was laying there in a hospital bed.

But not near death. Not even close, from what he could tell, though she might have inside damage, he supposed.

"I think I'm gonna be fine. They can't keep anything from me, I'm a doctor."

Ethan elbowed Jeremiah. "Our sister's a doctor."

"We get no credit for that, brother." Jeremiah went closer to the bed, and Ethan came with him, standing beside him. "I'm Ethan," he said.

"Jeremiah."

"I'm Elena. I want to get to know you. I want you to sit down and tell me everything about yourselves. But I'm afraid I can't keep my eyes open much longer. If I drift off, it's not because you're boring me."

"My wife Lily says gettin' hurt bad like this takes the vigor right outta you," Ethan said. "She's an R.N."

Jeremiah hitched his chin at him. "This guy just likes saying the words 'my wife, Lily.'"

"Yeah, I do," Ethan drawled with a grin.

"Yeah, you do," Jeremiah said.

"Newlywed?" Elena asked.

"This summer. She's expecting a baby in early spring."

"You work fast." She smiled, but her voice was getting softer, her eyes less wide. "I already know you're a country singer. My parents have been fillin' me in. You met them, right?"

"All three of 'em." Ethan said.

"And what do you do, Jeremiah?" she asked, shifting her gaze to his. The way her eyes moved over it made him feel exposed.

"For the moment, I'm a bouncer at Ethan's honky tonk."

"He's been busy romancin' my cousin, Willow, and tryin'a keep it secret," Ethan said.

Jeremiah sent Ethan a quick look that must've shown the knife in his heart that statement had just twisted. Ethan's smile froze and faded, while his eyes asked what was wrong.

"I know Willow. You have good taste," Elena said. "Gosh, I never imagined...my birth father was a criminal. I don't know how you deal with it." Her eyelids fell closed but popped open again. "And I never imagined I had brothers. I'm so happy...about that." Her eyes fell closed again.

The brothers exchanged a soft smile, then walked quietly back into the hallway, where Jeremiah let his smile die. He kept on walking, but Ethan stopped, grabbed his shoulder and turned him around.

"You don't believe her mothers, do you?" he asked. "You think she really was the one fighting you for the inheritance."

Jeremiah shrugged. "I'm ready to breathe some air that's not antiseptic-scented."

Ethan gripped his forearm and dragged him down the hall. Elena's three parents were still in the waiting room. Jeremiah pasted a smile on his face, and waved as they passed. Willow was nowhere around, and maybe she'd left already. He wondered what she'd done with Beans.

Ethan didn't slow down until they were outside on the sidewalk, then a few yards down it, where a wood-and-metal bench sat under a light on a pole with a halo of bugs.

Ethan let go of his arm and faced him. "Why would she pretend not to have known we existed? Why would she even think of deception on the worst day of her life?"

"I don't know."

"And Willow? You're not giving her the benefit of the doubt, either."

"You want me to give *her* the benefit of the doubt? After all her snooping and withholding information?"

"Yes, that's exactly what I want you to do."

"Why? Why the hell would I do that, Ethan?"

"Because she's done the same for you. You've been sneakin' around and keeping secrets, don't tell me you haven't."

"I had cause."

"Too freakin' bad. Forgive her anyway. You love her, you idiot."

He could have punched him in the face and stunned him less. Jeremiah rocked back on his heels as if he had.

"And she loves you back."

"She does not—"

"And I know for a fact she loves *me,* and she had a damn good reason for keeping quiet about Elena. She thought she was doin' the right thing, or she wouldn't've done it."

Jeremiah didn't know if he could argue with that line of logic.

"I know she snooped. She's a cop, it's in her nature, and she's in love with an ex-con who's actin' suspicious A F, to put it crudely. What's she supposed to do?"

Jeremiah shrugged.

"You've got a real problem trustin' folks, brother."

"Yeah, doin' time for another man's crime'll do that to ya."

"On the order of your own father."

"Our own father."

"Not mine. I traded up."

Jeremiah nodded. "That you did, Ethan. That you did."

"So have you. You're here now; you're with us now. A part of this clan. You can relax your defenses, brother. When part our family has a problem, every Brand and Brand-adjacent human from here to Big Falls, Oklahoma closes ranks around 'em. We take care of our own. And I don't know how you don't know it yet, but you're one of our own." Ethan clapped him on the shoulder.

Jeremiah's phone chirped. He didn't pick it up right away, because he was too choked up by Ethan's declaration to speak. Then Ethan lowered his hand, nodded at the phone.

Jeremiah and he picked it up. "My lawyer," he said. He'd ignored several calls from the guy. Now there was a voice message. He tapped play.

"The judge ruled earlier today. I've been trying to reach you. The plaintiff is your half-sister, Elena Montrose. She was granted half."

Jeremiah lowered his head shaking it slowly.

"As you know, everything's been liquidated at this point, and the judge ordered the money deposited to your respective accounts immediately. It's probably already there. Call me if you have questions."

He sighed heavily as he put the phone back into his pocket. "You know what's ironic? If Elena had just come to me and asked, I'd've split it with her happily. She didn't need a lawyer to get her share."

But Ethan was shaking his head. "This doesn't make a lot of sense, Jeremiah. Her mothers both said they'd've known if she was contesting de Lorean's will. Juanita claims she only told her who her father was last night. And she told us herself she was surprised to find out about us."

"She was medicated," he said.

"Makes her more likely to tell the truth, not more apt to come up with elaborate deceptions. Besides, Willow says she didn't know, and Willow wouldn't lie." Ethan poked him right in the center of his chest with a forefinger. "Not about somethin' like this. Not to me, she wouldn't. Not to you, either. And if you'd been payin' attention, you'd know that."

He looked up. "*Somebody's* lyin', brother."

"Maybe. But it ain't Willow."

Willow hadn't wanted to be there when Jeremiah got home. She'd taken Beans with her to the hospital, and then back to the cabin. She knew when Ethan and Jeremiah left the hospital, because she'd asked her cousin to text her an alert. That gave her a half hour, so she walked around picking up the boxes and bags they'd unloaded from the Jeep earlier. Anything left within the puppy's reach might wind up becoming a chew toy.

In the bedroom she bent to gather up the blankets and sheets, but she could smell their lovemaking in the bedding. She brought the covers to her face and wet it with her tears. It seemed like a lifetime ago they'd been entangled in these blankets and each other.

Flinging the bedding to the floor, she left it there and settled for closing the bedroom door to keep the pup out of mischief. She made sure the bathroom door was closed too, triple checked the living room and kitchen for items Beans could reach and chew, gave him food and water, and kissed him goodbye. Then she drove home and cried herself to sleep.

At seven a.m. She had a text on her phone from dispatch, forwarded from one of the Texas Rangers.

Ranger Stevens: Montrose's alibi checked out. Couldn't hold him.

She pulled her head out of her heartache long enough for her cop-brain to kick in, rolled onto her back, and realized she needed to get back to that hospital to talk to Elena Montrose in an official capacity, and to hell with the Texas Rangers claiming jurisdiction.

She got up fast, hit the shower, and put on her uniform. She didn't even turn on the kitchen light, just grabbed her keys on the way out her front door.

An hour later, she was leaning into a hospital room, smiling at Elena Montrose.

"Hello, Elena."

"Deputy Brand. How nice to see you again."

"I wish it was under better circumstances. Are you up to answering a few questions about the hit and run?"

"Sure." Elena raised her bed so she was more upright. Willow went into the room and sat down in a blue-padded chair beside the bed. There were flower arrangements on the windowsill, and get-well cards thumbtacked to a cork board opposite the bed. She didn't have an IV or anything.

"You were contesting your birth father, Vincent de Lorean's will, correct?"

Her dark brows came together. "What?"

"Um, yes, Vincent de Lorean, your birth father? The records show you contested his will."

"No, no, that's a mistake. I didn't know who my father was until night before last." She shook her head rapidly. "I was so in my head about it, I think that's why I didn't see the truck that hit me."

"So you blame yourself for the accident?"

She nodded. Then she stopped nodding and frowned, and then said, "Well, it did seem like they were way too far to the right, you know? Almost like it veered toward me."

"It veered toward you."

"Yeah. I figured there was something in the road, a squirrel or something."

"So you got a look at the vehicle?"

She nodded. "Rusty yellow pickup truck. Three guys in it, two in the front and one in the back."

"Son of a—"

"What?" Elena looked alarmed.

"Nothing. No, all good."

"Good."

"But about the will—"

"I'm telling you, I don't know what you're talking about. Please, explain it to me."

Willow nodded slowly. "Ethan was the sole heir to de Lorean's fortune—or what the government left of it, which is significant. Ethan refused it so it all went to Jeremiah. However, it's been held up because an unnamed person contested the will, a person we found out yesterday was another of de Lorean's offspring, one Elena Montrose. You were awarded several million dollars yesterday."

She blinked as if Willow were speaking gibberish. "I promise you, I wasn't. And none of this makes any sense."

"No, it doesn't," Willow said. "But it will. I have a call in to the lawyer representing you. Several calls actually. In the meantime, I'm gonna talk to the fellas who ran you down."

"You mean you know who it is?"

"I have a pretty good idea. I'm fixin to have El Paso PD put an officer on your door, just as a precaution. Don't let it scare you."

"Too late," she said. Her face had changed. Her eyes were wider, her full lips parted. "Do you think somebody ran me down on purpose?"

"I just think it's a heckuva a coincidence that you were awarded a huge sum and hit by a truck in the same day, is all. I mean, it could be a coincidence, but it can't hurt to take precautions, can it?"

Her eyes shifted lower, to Willow's badge, and then she frowned. "The other cop didn't mention any of that."

She shrugged. "Let me get on this. I'll keep you posted, okay? Here's my number. If you need anything call me. I mean it." She fished a card from her pocket, scribbled her personal cell number on the back, and set it on the tray table.

"Thanks, Willow." She looked at the door. "Am I...safe? There's no officer out there yet."

"Yeah, there is. He's at the nurses' desk pleading for coffee. You're safe. Besides, it's just precaution. Okay?"

"Yeah, okay."

"We're gonna be friends, I think," Willow said. Now that she was looking, she could see Ethan's eyes in Elena Montrose, and Jeremiah's dimples when she smiled.

Jeremiah called the El Paso lawyer he'd hired to handle the inheritance. The conversation was short. There was cussing, followed by, "I've been trying to reach you for two days. I learned the name of the person contesting the will. Not that it matters now, the judge has ruled in her favor."

He kept the Jeep rolling through flatlands speckled with scrub brush and tumbleweed. The desert was creeping in around the edges a little more every year.

"I've been busy. Mainly finding out I had a sister."

"If you'd returned my calls—"

"Next time text me. Now, here's the thing, I'd have given her half of the old man's loot if she'd asked."

"What'd she say when you told her that?"

"I didn't. She was lying' in a hospital bed at the time, doped on morphine."

"What happened to her?" the lawyer asked.

"Hit and run," he said.

"When?"

"Last night," he replied. "I met her for the first time in the hospital. She said she knew nothing about contesting the will, claims she didn't even know who her father was until yesterday."

"That's not possible. I've spoken with her about the case multiple times, her and her husband both."

He lowered his head. "Yeah, I figured." He pulled into the driveway, then took the left fork out to Willow's cottage, but her truck wasn't in the driveway. He sighed, turned around throwing up a cloud of dust, and headed back toward town. He didn't think she was anywhere near ready to return to work, but knowing Willow...

He'd best check the sheriff's office.

What Ethan had said to him at the hospital was still echoing off the rafters of his brain. *You love her, you idiot. And she loves you.*

Was it true, was that what this thing was?

How the hell did you know?

He had every right to be angry, but being angry at Willow felt bad right to his bones. Her eyes, brown and swimming with tears, kept re-appearing in his mind. He'd hurt her. It felt wrong.

And wondering if it was over between them—that felt like wondering if his life was over.

Hell, maybe he did love her.

He drove a little faster.

Willow was pounding on the door of Matty Barker's place by nine a.m. The old woman came to the door, a cigarette in her lips. She wore an unsnapped denim shirt, pajama shorts, and a pair of men's moccasin-style bedroom slippers. She was braless, so the unsnapped shirt was dangerous. Willow kept her eyes up, on Matty's red ones and her short gray curls. "Need to talk to your boys, Matty."

"Ain't here." She puffed without removing the cig from her lips.

"No? Then who's playin' video games back there?"

"I said they ain't here. You callin' me a liar?"

"Pretty much. Hey boys," she called. "I know you ran down Elena Montrose this morning. I got witnesses. I got a piece of your truck that fell off at the scene, and I can the see the blood on your bumper from here."

She didn't have a piece of the truck, nor could she see blood on their bumper. She was a bluffing. But she wasn't dealing with geniuses here.

The firstborn and designated team leader, Stu, came to the door. Matty cuffed him right upside the head. "What fresh trouble you brought home to me now?" She gave him a withering look, and scuffed back into her home somewhere. Willow heard footsteps on stairs.

The other two appeared as soon as their ma had cleared out.

"She dead?" Tank asked. He was the biggest, hence the name.

Stu elbowed him in the solar plexus. "Shut up!"

"You shut up."

Tuck said, "Tank didn't want to do it."

"Shut the hell up!" Stu said.

"I didn't want to do it either," Tuck went on, "but I didn't argue as much. It *was* a lot of money."

"We don't get it if she didn't die, though," Tank said.

"Somebody paid you run that woman down?"

Tank opened his mouth and Stu punched him in the face. Willow snapped a cuff around Stu's wrist just as he drew back for a second blow. She put her foot right behind him as she pulled him out of the house, so he tripped, and as he landed on his knees, she got the other wrist cuffed.

His brothers had come out but hadn't decided what to do fast enough. She pulled Stu to his feet by one arm, and kept her other hand near her gun. "You two stand right there. You move, I'll shoot you." She wouldn't.

She put Stu into the back of her car and closed the back door, then she opened the driver's door and reached in for her radio mic. "I'm bringing in the Barkers on that hit and run."

"All three?" Came the reply and it wasn't the dispatcher—it was Uncle Garrett. "Wait for backup, Will."

She put the mic back, fished her extra cuffs out of the glove box, and turned around just as the rusty yellow pickup roared to life with Tank and Tuck inside.

She swore and dove behind the wheel, pulling right out behind them as they took off spitting dust and gravel at her windshield.

She backed off a little, having learned that lesson the hard way on her poor horse, and got on the horn. "In pursuit of a rusty yellow 1985 Chevy Pickup. Hit and run suspects. Heading north on Abbott. Requesting backup."

In the back, Stu was laughing. "You really thought one little lady deputy was gonna be enough to get all three of us."

She glanced at him in the mirror. "It was enough to get you."

He stopped laughing.

She rounded a sharp curve in the road, and that's when she saw the rusty yellow truck was lying on its side in the brush. It wasn't a bad wreck, it looked like they just ran off onto a soft shoulder and lost it. Hadn't hit anything or rolled all the way over.

But there was smoke coming from somewhere.

She grabbed the radio mic while skidding to a stop and throwing on her lights. "Suspect vehicle is off the road at Piker's Bend. I see smoke. Get me fire and EMTs."

"Uncuff me, goddamn it!" Stu was shouting. "Lemme out of this car!"

"I got this." Willow got out and ran to the wreckage.

The engine was smoking. The truck had tipped driver's side up, and Tank was behind the wheel, held there only by his seatbelt. If it gave, he'd fall atop his much smaller brother in the passenger seat.

She pulled out a pocket knife and climbed up top, reached down a hand. Tank gripped it. "You're a big guy, Tank. Brace your feet on somethin', so you don't fall on your brother when I cut you loose."

A little tongue of flame appeared in her peripheral.

"Do it now," she said. She kept her tone calm and hoped Tank hadn't noticed the dancing lick of fire.

He pressed one foot against the headrest of the passenger seat, carefully avoiding his brother's head. Tuck wasn't moving at all.

"Okay," he said. His eyes were wide as he gazed up at her. Gray blue, not vivid like Jeremiah's. Terrified, too. Okay so he'd noticed the flame.

Willow sawed through the seatbelt, gripping Tank one-handed. She hoped he had most of his weight, because she couldn't handle more than half. The belt gave and Tank dropped but caught himself. Willow caught him too, by his other arm, and pulled for all she was worth as he found toe holds anywhere he could and painstakingly made his way up through the window. Halfway out, he fell forward and took her with him all the way to the ground. Every bit of air gusted from her lungs under his weight, and the places her horse had crushed got battered all over again.

"Get off!" She shoved at him when she could get her breath again.

He moved, rolling onto his back.

Willow sprang upright and climbed back up onto the vehicle, hurting all over. The flame from the engine was bigger now. She heard sirens, but she didn't think they were close enough to make it. There was no time to make a decision, no time to think it over. She slid headfirst through the open window, hooking one leg over truck roof to keep from falling.

Tuck was unconscious. He had a cut on his head that was bleeding. His seatbelt was not fastened. There was a loud *pop*, and she looked left, to see the flames in the engine burning frighteningly high. She grabbed Tuck's shirt, and pulled him toward her enough get a grip on him, then pulled him further until she could hook both her arms under his, and then she pulled some more. She barely moved him at all. The flames burned higher, and she could feel their heat now.

"Hang onto him! I've got you!"

That was Jeremiah's voice!

Then his arms were closing around her legs and pulling her out. She linked her fingers behind Tuck's back, under his arms, and he came with her. Jeremiah got hold of her waist and pulled even faster, as she in turn, pulled Tuck.

The three of them tumbled to the ground together and she looked up to see Uncle Garrett putting handcuffs on Tank farther away, and EMTs running toward them with a stretcher.

She scrambled to her feet and said, "Come on, get him, get him, hurry."

Jeremiah already had Tuck over his shoulder. He put an arm around her, and they ran back across the meadow toward the road. When the truck exploded, the blast knocked them both face-first to the ground.

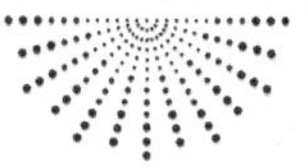

CHAPTER FIFTEEN

Everyone came running toward them after debris stopped raining down from the explosion. EMTs loaded Tuck onto a stretcher and double-timed it back to the road, while Willow was still pushing herself up off the ground.

Jeremiah, already upright, reached down a hand. She looked up at him and ignored it, getting up on her own, brushing off her jeans.

"Thanks. I'd have got him out, though." She started for the road and the others, who'd slowed their approach now that they saw them both upright and walking toward them.

"Willow—"

"I'm workin'."

"You're two days out of the hospital yourself."

"And one day out of bein' called a liar and dumped. I think I'm doin' pretty well, all things considered."

"I didn't call you a liar."

"You didn't believe me, either. Which means you don't trust me."

"And you trust me? You can't see past my time served."

"That's not true!" She whirled as she said it, then stood there facing him. She was out of breath and her heart was pounding. Their backdrop was the Barker boys' burning yellow truck.

He said, "I'm sorry."

And she said, "I'm workin'." Then pivoted and stomped the rest of the way to the road.

Now, Willow was sitting beside Tuck Barker's hospital bed waiting for him to come to. They'd crashed in Quinn County, so she didn't need to worry about stepping on some other department's sensitive boots. The docs told her there was no reason Tuck shouldn't come around soon.

Uncle Garrett was questioning his brothers, of course, but he wasn't getting anywhere. She hadn't read them their rights before they'd blurted their confessions, so the department was gonna need fresh ones.

As she sat there beside the bed, she wondered how the hell Jeremiah had shown up when he had, and why he'd risked his life just because she was risking hers. She was the law. It was her job. It wasn't his.

Tuck had leads taped to his head and his chest. They'd shaved parts of both. There were monitors showing his brainwaves, heart rate, temperature and a bunch of stuff she didn't know about. The beeps were overlapping and incessant.

There was a tap on the door. She turned to see Jeremiah standing there. He said, "He talking yet?"

"Still unconscious. So I'm still workin'."

"Yeah, I got that. I'm not here about…that. I um…I got you this." He held out a large yellow envelope.

She frowned and took it. "What is it?"

"A photo of Elena, walking into an attorney's office with her husband the day they filed to contest the will. It's grainy, from a surveillance video."

"And how did you get it?" she asked as she slid the print from the envelope.

"I know people. Some still owe me favors."

She looked down at the photo, then frowned. "That's not Elena."

"Nope."

"That *is* her husband, though."

"Yep."

She lifted her head slowly. "She never contested the will. She was tellin' the truth when she said she knew nothin' about it."

He nodded. "I think her husband and his accomplice..."

"Lover," she said. "Look at the way she's lookin' at him."

He looked at the photo again. Something came and went in his eyes.

She saw it, wondered about it even as she fit the pieces together. "As soon as he got word that they'd won their case, and the money was deposited, he tried to have Elena killed, so he'd get all of it. Problem is, he hired the most incompetent trio of criminals Quinn County has to offer."

"I wonder how much he paid 'em."

"A hundred thousand," came a weak and hoarse voice from the bed.

Willow returned to her spot beside it. "Hey, Tuck. I gotta tell you your rights, okay?"

He nodded, and she recited the Mirandas, then explained what they meant and asked if he understood. He said he did.

"So I need you to tell me, if you still want to," Willow said. "who offered you money to hurt Elena Montrose?"

"Mr. Montrose. Elena's husband. He said he wanted her dead fast, and we'd get paid soon as it was done." He shook his head. "We done a lot of shit for him, my brothers and me. Bustin' out windows and stuff. The pharmacy, and even Montrose's own house one day."

"And the WTD," Willow said, "on a stolen motorcycle."

"No ma'am," Tuck replied. No hesitation, no forethought. "That wasn't us. That one he done himself. Then he asked us to take the motorbike and hide it somewhere near the bunkhouse over on the Texas Brand." He shrugged. "But we know better'n that."

They'd better, she thought.

"We never kilt anybody before. I said no way. So did Tank, but you know, just with his eyes."

"With his eyes."

Tuck nodded.

Jeremiah was riveted, wondered if Willow was getting it all down, and saw her phone in her hand. She was recording.

"Tell me how it happened," she said.

"We was in the truck, the three of us. Stu wanted to go for a ride, maybe get some beers. But he drove past the Bend, way the heck out past the county line, and there she was, out jogging on the street. I saw the look in Stu's eyes. He knew she'd be there, I'll tell you what. And he just…he just stomped it, turned the wheel and he hit her." He closed his eyes and shuddered. "She flew, man, I never saw nothin' like it. Landed like a rag doll. I was sure she was dead." He lowered his head, shaking it hard. "I was some relieved when you told us she wasn't."

"Then what happened?" Willow asked.

"We went home. Later on, Tank and me, we talked about it some. Tank said Stu took it too far this time and he was fixin' to land us all in prison." He sighed heavily. "And he was right, wasn't he?"

"Maybe not if you tell the truth. Maybe Tank won't either, if he cooperates. Right now, all you've confessed to is vandalism. But Stu's gonna do some time, I gotta be honest with you about that."

Tuck nodded slowly, sniffled twice, and then knuckled tears away from his pooling eyes.

"You've followed your big brother all this time," Willow said. "This is gonna be a chance for you to see what kind of a man you are without him leading you by the nose. This can be a fresh start for you and Tank both. Stop bringin' your poor ma heartache and make her proud for a change, huh?"

He nodded at her. She got up out of the chair and her knees went a little weak, but she caught herself. Jeremiah came nearer, took her arm to support her. His touch burned her straight to her toes, just like it always did.

He felt it, too, she knew it when his eyes shot to hers and held on.

Jeremiah said. "I want to be with you when you tell Elena it was her husband who tried to kill her, okay?"

"Yeah," she said. She sent the recording to Garrett, so he could send someone out to arrest Richard Montrose, then left the room. She and Jeremiah headed down the hall to the elevator and up a floor to where Elena's room was. It was only one floor up, a very short ride in very close proximity. It was stupid that she wanted to lean into him and feel his arms come around her, and turn her face up toward him, and then he'd kiss her, and then—

The doors opened with a ping. They stepped out. He was looking at her every few seconds, but she was trying not to look back. She just kept walking to the end of the hall where Elena's room was, to find its door open. They stepped inside.

There was a blonde woman in Elena's bed, with a nurse nearby holding a tiny cup with pills in it.

"Excuse me," Willow said, "where is the patient who was in this bed? Elena Montrose?"

"Oh, Elena was released this morning," the nurse said. "She was so relieved when her husband arrived to pick her up."

Jeremiah's brain went dark and his heart sank to his stomach.

Willow said, "Where's the cop who was on the door?"

"His captain called him off when Dr. Montrose was released." She looked suddenly worried. "What's wrong, Deputy?"

"Who walked her to the exit?" Willow asked.

"Helen did. Her shift just ended, you want me to—?"

"I need Helen," Willow said loudly. She was wearing her uniform and striding to the nurses' desk. "Is Helen still here? Helen?"

A door opened and Helen came out shushing, then stopped mid-shush when she saw Willow in uniform.

"You walked Elena Montrose to the exit. Did you see the vehicle?"

"Sure did. Corvette," she said. "Red with the sparkles, you know?"

"Metalflake," Jeremiah muttered, his brain coming back on line one function at a time.

Willow pulled out her cell phone and started tapping while walking. It was all he could do to keep up with her. "I'm having Garrett look up the 'Vette registered to Richard Montrose and put out the call. We'll head to their house in case he took her home."

She was tapping her phone again. His own phone chimed in his pocket. Frowning, he pulled it out, and saw the Brand clan text loop. He'd been added. The freaking thing had way too many people on it.

There was a new message from Willow.

> Willow: Jeremiah and Ethan's sister Elena in danger from hubs who just picked her up from hospital. Metalflake red Corvette, Garrett has plate and home address.

The Montrose's home address followed.

Jeremiah frowned at his phone, and then at Willow, but she was focused dead ahead, walking as fast as she could've run. He just looked at her while keeping pace, and avoiding collisions with carts and trays and goosenecked devices and people in scrubs until they were crossing a lobby into the hospital parking lot.

She jumped into her truck and he jumped in beside her. She turned and looked at him sitting there and opened her mouth to tell him to get out.

"What are you waiting for?" he asked before she could speak. "Let's go!"

So she went.

She didn't need the address. She'd been to the Montroses' before, when the Barker boys had thrown a brick through one of the tall, gorgeous windows. The Corvette was in the driveway.

"At least we know they went home." She drove by slowly, still not in her police SUV, and maybe that was a good thing. She didn't want to do anything to set Montrose off. "Did you get Elena's number when you met?"

"Yeah," Jeremiah replied.

"You think you should give her a call?"

"Maybe I should give *him* a call," he suggested. "He can't get mad at her for that." Then he pulled out his phone and tapped his newfound brother-in-law and possible sister-killer's number as Willow watched.

He put the phone on speaker and set it on the console.

Montrose picked up on the first ring. "Jeremiah?"

"Yeah, it's me, bro. I went to see Elena but they said she was so much better they sprung her." He tried to make his voice upbeat, happy even.

"Yeah, they did."

"That's great news! You care if I talk to her?"

"Yeah, thing is, I don't know if she was really ready to come home. She passed out soon as I got her into her bed."

Willow swore in a whisper.

"Yeah, I thought maybe. That's why I called you and not her, I didn't want to wake her. Anyway, you can pass this on for me, then. Tell her, no hard feelings."

He was silent.

"About her contesting the will. Shoot, I told my lawyer this morning, he didn't have to go to the trouble. I'd have split it with her if she'd asked."

"That's…generous of you."

Willow was typing madly on her phone, and he knew why when a text from her popped up on his.

> Willow: Make up some paperwork he has to sign. Get inside.

"Anyway, uh, things aren't quite final yet. The deposits have been made, but uh, they won't clear the bank without one more signature. I have the paperwork on me. I could bring it by."

Another long pause, then, "Sure. If you can give me an hour—"

"I'm actually in neighborhood."

Silence.

"Dude, I don't know about you, but I been waiting a long time for this money to come through. I'm on the brink, you know? I need funds like, *today*."

"Frankly, same," Montrose replied. "Okay, you can stop by, but listen, we'll talk on the back porch. I don't want you goin' inside and disturbing Elena."

"For sure. See you soon, dude." He hung up. "Why did I keep calling him dude?"

"Doesn't matter. He bought it." She pulled over, and when he sent her a questioning look, she said, "Let's wait a couple of minutes. We don't want him to know we were right outside."

"I don't like her in there alone with him."

Willow looked at her watch, tapping the steering wheel. "I don't, either. So listen, you keep him distracted on the back porch. I'll get in the front, and find your sister. All right?"

"Okay, good. You be careful, though."

"I will."

She put the car in gear, but he shifted it back, then pressed a hand to her cheek to turn her face. Then he leaned in and kissed her.

Damned if a tear didn't roll all the way to her lips before they parted. "Gringo, you got me turned upside down and inside out, you know that? Am I comin' or goin'?" She shook her head, pulled the car into gear and drove. She parked two houses away, putting a bushy tree between her pickup and the line of sight from the Montrose house. The sister killer wouldn't see Jeremiah getting out the passenger side that way.

"Turn off the sound on your phone," she said. "Haptics too. But keep an eye on it, and don't let him see it. Now, how are you gonna let me know when the coast is clear?"

"I'll send an emoji. I can do that quick and easy."

"Okay," she said.

"Okay." But he didn't get out. Instead he leaned her way.

She swayed out of his path. "Oh, no. No, uh-uh. Go."

He sighed, and then he opened the door and got out. She watched him walk along the sidewalk to the Montrose home and then toward the house, but instead of going to the front door, he vanished around the side, headed, she knew, for the aforementioned back porch.

She waited, drumming her fingers until her phone pinged, which reminded her to turn off the sound. Then she looked at Jeremiah's text.

Hot Gringo: 🤍

She got out of the truck and walked casually up the sidewalk, but before she even made it to the front door, somebody came up behind her, and slid a hand over her shoulder.

She looked up fast, startled. "Ethan! Sheesh, you got here fast."

"Whole fam's here. You just can't see 'em. What's the situation?"

"We think she's inside. Husband says she's sleeping. Jeremiah's distracting him with some made-up inheritance paperwork he doesn't have on the back porch. I was plannin' to slide in the front."

"You don't have a warrant."

"I have probable cause to believe Elena is in danger."

Ethan nodded. "And the rest of us just went in out of concern for our cousin the deputy."

She looked ahead and saw Baxter already at the door, playing around with the lock, swingin' it open with ease. He went inside.

"Keep the others out here in case we need backup," she said. "We don't want to make a racket."

Ethan was texting before she took off for the front door and followed Baxter inside.

Baxter was tiptoeing around the living room, peering around corners, so she headed for the stairway, and walked softly up. It was hard to place each foot with care when she was so impatient to reach the top. But then she did and started checking bedrooms.

Elena was in the first one she checked, splayed on the bed, atop the covers. Her mouth was slightly open, her eyes were closed. Willow leaned closer, feeling her neck for a pulse, and turning her cheek toward Elena's nose and mouth to feel her breaths.

And she did.

"Thank God." She shook her. "Elena. Hey, come on, you were not hurt that bad that you should be this out of it."

Elena had no response.

Willow heard footsteps on the stairs, so she went to stand behind the door, which put her right over a small wastebasket with a syringe lying on top, and a vial of something in the bottom. She took the plastic liner right out of the can, knotting it to her belt as the person reached the top and stage-whispered, "Will?"

She came out from behind the door and poked her head out. It was Baxter. "She's in here. Alive, but unconscious."

Baxter crossed the room to the bed as she said, "We have to get her out of here."

"Well, now," said a man who should not have been there. Richard Montrose was in the bedroom doorway. "What have we got going on here? A little breaking and entering, a little kidnapping?"

"A little attempted murder," Willow said. "What did you do with Jeremiah?"

He shrugged and started to raise the gun that had, up to then, been hidden by his sweater. But Jeremiah appeared behind him, his head all bloody on one side. He poked Montrose in the back of the head with something and said, "Put. It. Down."

Montrose lowered the gun to his side and Jeremiah took it from his hand. Other booted feet came up the stairs, then, Uncle Garrett and Lash leading the way.

Jeremiah turned Richard Montrose around toward Garrett, and Willow saw what he'd been poking him in the head with. The metal handle of a kitchen spatula.

Behind her, Baxter was gathering Elena Montrose up from the bed, speaking softly to her.

Willow looked from the spatula to Jeremiah's eyes and he smiled with one side of his mouth, then dropped to the floor like his bones had all dissolved.

—

CHAPTER SIXTEEN

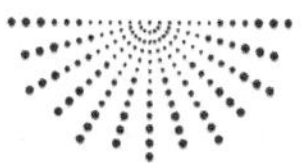

Jeremiah was beside his sister's hospital bed for the second time in as many days. His own head was bandaged up, thanks to Richard Montrose hitting it with the jagged end of a meat hammer.

Willow and her relatives from the Quinn County Sheriff's Department were taking care of logistics on one end of things, and he figured he had to take care of them on the other. But not until things settled down.

Elena opened her eyes to gaze at him sleepily, then, frowning, she looked around the room. "Why am I back in the hospital?"

A throat cleared. Ethan had come in, and he walked over to the chair on the opposite side of her bed.

"There's no easy way to tell you this," Jeremiah began.

And she said, "It was Richard, wasn't it? He did something to me."

"Injected you with insulin," Ethan said, real softly. "But we got to you in time."

"Willow did, really," Jeremiah added. "And Baxter, and then the whole dang clan." He shook his head in wonder yet again. Yes, he'd heard about this sort of thing but he'd never seen it.

"Why did he do it?" she asked, her throat tight. "Why did he want me dead? Wait, the hit and run, was that him, too?"

"He hired some local troublemakers," Ethan said. "The Barker boys. One of 'em's in jail, awaitin' trial, and he'll do serious time. The other two will testify against him. They claim they objected to what he did to you, but they were in the truck when it happened."

She swallowed hard and looked at Jeremiah. "What else?"

"It was about the will," Jeremiah said. "My fa—*our* father's will. Your husband had some woman pose as you, go to a lawyer with him, and contest it. The court awarded you half." Jeremiah said, "And I'd have given it to you anyway, I want you to know that. And I want you to have half. You were his daughter, too."

"What about you?" she asked, looking at Ethan.

"I signed off on it," he said. "He killed my mother."

"And drove mine to suicide," Jeremiah said.

"And drove mine to give me up," Elena added.

"The judge made the decision the same day as the hit and run," Ethan told her.

She lowered her head, closed her eyes.

"Listen, Elena," Ethan said, putting a hand on her shoulder. "You have family now. A lot of family, most of whom were traipsin' through your house to save your life earlier today."

"They're not my family—"

"Yeah, they are," Jeremiah said, like Eeyore would have said it. "I'm not related to 'em by blood, either, but I'm Ethan's brother, so they've done claimed me. They'll do the same to you. It's not optional."

"Listen to this guy, pretendin' to hate it." Ethan clapped his brother's shoulder.

Jeremiah shrugged. "It kind of grows on you, actually." He leaned in close and gave his sister a hug. "I'll be back in the morning, little sister." He grinned because it felt absurdly good to say those words. "Right now, I have a mission."

Willow stayed until the last bit of paperwork was done. Stu Barker was in a cell in the back. He was the only prisoner in the place. The judge had released his brothers on their own recognizance. They could be charged for leaving the scene of an accident with injury. They should've called it in. And of course, for the smashed windows around town. But with their testimony against their brother, they could plead down to a misdemeanor, maybe serve a few months and move on.

Stu was bein' charged for attempted murder.

Richard Montrose had escaped the custody of the Texas Rangers and was currently on the lam. When they caught him, he would be charged with attempted murder, soliciting a murder, conspiracy, filing false police reports, and an ever-growing stack of fraud counts. His lover would be happy to testify against him to save her own backside. And they had him dead to rights on every bit of it. Turned out he'd lost his job with a high paying law firm when they caught him over-billing and stealing from clients. His law license was suspended while the Texas Bar reviewed his case, and he had no income. That was when he'd decided to investigate his wife's parentage, in case her unnamed father was someone with money. And he thought he'd hit the jackpot.

Montrose had figured if Jeremiah were sent back to prison, the judge would award the entire inheritance to Elena. And if he killed Elena, he'd get it all. That part of the plan still applied, even though she'd only been awarded half.

Nobody thought Elena was in danger. Richard would have nothing to gain by her death now, but the poor woman was scared all the same.

Willow logged out of the computer and got up. Her muscles begged for mercy.

"I thought I told you to get home," Uncle Garrett said.

"It was my bust. Mostly."

Her uncle smiled, but there was something else in his eyes. She said, "What's goin' on with you, Uncle Garrett? I know there's somethin'."

"Well, I died and then I came back. And that's…kind of big."

"It kind of is. Are you okay?"

He actually considered his answer. "I think so."

"You talkin' to Aunt Chelsea about it?"

"Wouldn't know what to say just yet. I'm…ponderin' I guess." He shook off the distant expression in his eyes and said, "You need to go home and go to bed, and stay there for at least three days. You hear?"

"I hear."

"I do need a favor from you, but later, when you're up to it."

"Yeah?"

"Your mom was fixin' to get out your baby cradle as a gift for Ethan and Lily's baby. She never got it out for me before they left, and I was supposed to do some work on it before the shower. You think you could find it for me? I got no idea where, and that house is—"

"I'm sure it's in the attic," she said. "No worries, I'll take a peek."

"When you've rested," he said. He opened his arms, then, and she went in for the hug. "You did great, Willow. Your instincts are dead on. I'd just like you to take a little more care from now on. Wait for backup—it's not a one-woman department. All right?"

"All right."

"Now get on home."

She got on home, leaning back against the door and closing her eyes once inside.

Poor Elena, to be so betrayed by someone she loved. It kind of put things into perspective. Still, Jeremiah had been furious, and even if he'd seemed rather over it, she wasn't.

She lowered her head. There was no point thinking about it

now. She was exhausted. Uncle Garrett was right. She needed to rest and recover. She hadn't had time. She dragged herself into the shower, and fell into bed, and she didn't wake until the scratching sounds interfered with her dreams.

She opened her eyes.

The scratching sounds came again, from the front door.

Okay, fine. She rolled and got out of bed, shocked when she saw the clock. She'd slept twelve straight hours.

Sitting up, she pulled on a bathrobe, walked barefoot to the front door, and pulled it open.

Beans stood in the doorway, smiling up at her. She bent to pet him—she didn't have to bend far. He gave a happy woof and wiggled in joy. He had an envelope dangling from his collar. It had her name on it.

Without removing it from the collar, she flipped the envelope open and slid out a single piece of card stock with yellow roses in the corners.

"Don't give up on us yet. Please come to dinner. My place. 7:00. Circle yes or no."

She rolled her eyes, but went to the kitchen for a pen, and then hesitated over the card. Beans had followed her in and was wandering around smelling things. The two of them had become a unit, hadn't they? And Frankie, too. There was a kindness to Jeremiah, a goodness that ran deeper than his childhood, deeper than his bloodline.

She nodded then and circled yes. Then she called the dog, slid the card back into its envelope, and opened the front door.

A loud whistle came from a few yards down the drive, where she saw Jeremiah's Jeep. Beans raced that way, and when he opened the door, the pup leaped right into his arms and Jeremiah laughed as the dog licked his face. Then he set him on the passenger seat, and got in himself. She saw him pull the card out and look at it. He sent back a wave and then off he went.

Willow dressed casually, so he wouldn't think she was expecting anything. She still took pains, though. Her blouse was pretty, her jeans were flattering and her undergarments sexy and matching, just in case.

She arrived at his new home to find the door wide open and Beans lying on the front porch. There was furniture, a cute little table and four chairs in the kitchen, and an entire suite in the living room. A vase of red and white roses and champagne in a bucket of ice sat on a coffee table, with two fancy glasses nearby. The dinner table was set.

"You furnished your house," she said.

"I was not wise with my money today, I admit it. This dinner? Catered."

"Out here?"

"Yeah. Aunt Chelsea even delivers." He opened the oven and used a potholder to bring homemade pot pies with golden crust in earthenware bowls to the table. Then salad from the fridge, and homemade bread, already sliced, from the counter.

"This is…wow."

"And I have a gift," he said, and he held out his hand.

A thumb drive rested in his palm. She picked it up, turned it over, then lifted her questioning eyes to his.

He said, "It's my novel."

She lost her breath, she was so surprised. Her hand went to her chest. "You said you were *thinking* about writing…"

"I…didn't trust you then." He cleared his throat. "I trust you now, Willow Brand, with something I wouldn't trust to anybody else."

She held his gaze, looking deep into his vivid blue eyes. "I trust you, too, Gringo. I will never snoop on you again."

"You'll never need to. From now on, I'm an open book where you're concerned."

Tears burned in her eyes. "Holy God, I love you, Jeremiah Thorne."

"You do?"

She nodded, leaned in closer to kiss him, but he held her away, just a little. "It's looking rough for Frankie's grandparents, medically," he said. "He's gonna need a place to live, before long."

She stared at him for a long moment. Then she said, "Didn't Frankie tell you he was gonna live in this house someday?"

"Yeah. And I'm hoping to make that happen. I thought you should know that first."

"First?"

"Yeah. Before I…" His hands were resting on her hips, but he took them away as he dropped onto one knee and pulled out a ring. No box, just the ring.

"You really *did* go on a spendin' spree today, didn't you?" she breathed.

"Willow Stands Alone Brand, I am your man. I can't ever belong to anybody else the way I belong to you. I…you're it, you're just…something I never thought…" He stopped, took a breath, swallowed hard. "I love you, Deputy. You want to get married?"

She looked from his suddenly uncertain blue eyes to the ring sparkling in his fingertips, back to his eyes again. "Yeah, Gringo. Yeah, I do."

She offered her hand, palm-down, and he slipped the ring on, then kissed her finger, rose up and gathered her close. They kissed like the end of a Hallmark movie and then he picked her right up off her feet.

"Where we goin'?" she asked. "Dinner's waitin'."

"We can reheat," he said. "I want to show you the bed I picked out." He kissed her again as he carried her to the bedroom. She opened her eyes once, looking over his shoulder and holding up her hand to admire her ring. Then she buried her fingers in his hair, and focused on the sweet, loving taste of his kisses.

Mmm-mmm-mmm!

EPILOGUE

Do not skip this part.
I mean it.

"Now that you're my fiancé, you have to help me move heavy things," Willow said.

She had hold of Jeremiah's hand and was leading him through her parents' large home. She hadn't given him the tour but instead had dragged him straight up the stairs to the back hall, and up a steeper, narrower flight to the attic.

"I'll carry anything you want, long as we're together."

"You learn that line from my sappy newlywed cousin Ethan? Guy's so in love it's sickening." She turned, smiling as she said it, and he leaned up and kissed her thoroughly. Even before their lips parted, Willow was pulling an overhead chain to turn on a dangling lightbulb. "It's the only part of the house they haven't made nice." She waved some cobwebs aside as she reached the top of the stairs and opened the rickety red door there.

Then she stepped into the attic and turned a switch. Two attic lights came on, while the third flickered and died.

"It has a floor," Jeremiah observed. "We won't fall through the ceiling like Chevy Chase in *Christmas Vacation*."

The attic was filled with discarded joys of the past, discarded furniture too worn out to pass on, broken toys too bound up with precious memories to throw away. Sheets were over some items, and she said, "Look for one shaped like a cradle. You take the left; I'll take the right."

They used their phone's flashlights. After only a few steps, Willow spotted a cradle shape beneath an old quilt. She pulled the quilt away, and yes, there was her wooden cradle, handmade by an old shaman friend of her parents. Her name was carved on the headboard. She ran her hand over the letters.

W I L L O W

"Found it," called Jeremiah.

"What?" Willow asked. "No, you didn't. It's over here."

"Um, beg to differ. I am definitely looking at a cradle."

Willow crossed the attic to where Jeremiah was. He had pulled the old sheet halfway off, revealing what looked just like her cradle's headboard. Frowning, she yanked the cover the rest of the way off and gasped at what she saw. "What is this?" she whispered.

Reaching out a hand, she ran her fingers over the name carved into the cradle's headboard.

W O L F

ALSO BY MAGGIE SHAYNE

SMALL-TOWN CONTEMPORARY SERIES

The Texas Brand

The Oklahoma Brands

The McIntyre Men

The Texas Brand: Generations

THRILLERS & ROMANTIC SUSPENSE SERIES

Brown and de Luca Return

The Fatal series

Shattered Sisters

Danger After Dawn

PARANORMAL ROMANCE

The Portal

Wings in the Night

The Immortals

By Magic

ABOUT THE AUTHOR

New York Times and *USA Today* bestselling novelist Maggie Shayne has published 112 novels and novellas for numerous major publishers. She also spent a year writing for American daytime TV dramas *The Guiding Light* and *As the World Turns*. But her heart was in her books, and she'd found it impossible to do both.

Now, she is excited to be publishing with dream-publisher, Oliver Heber Books and she's having more fun than ever.

Maggie lives in a century-and-a-half old farmhouse with two waterfalls outside, in the rural hills of Cortland County NY with her husband Lance, who builds waterfalls for a living, and their dogs. There are always, always dogs.

Sign up for Maggie's NEWSLETTER!
Early looks at covers, new and upcoming releases, behind the
scenes trivia, dog pictures, and sometimes a recipe!

MaggieShayne.com
Sign up at the top of the page.

facebook.com/MaggieShayneAuthor
instagram.com/MaggieShayne
bsky.app/profile/maggieshayne.bsky.social
bookbub.com/authors/maggie-shayne
amazon.com/author/maggieshayne
goodreads.com/maggieshayne

A small press bound by the belief that every voice matters.

Sign up for our newsletter to learn about new releases and more.
https://oliver-heberbooks.com/subscribe/

Follow us on social media:

facebook.com/oliverheberbooks
instagram.com/oliverheberbooks
amazon.com/oliverheberbooks
youtube.com/@OliverHeberBooksPublisher